Sorcha

The Beginning

By

S D Cardea & C L Beck

Steven Douglas Cardea
Visit my website at www.ravensglenntrilogy.com

Printed in the United States of America
First Printing: August 2014
Published by Sojourn Publishing, LLC

ISBN: 978-1-62747-135-0
Ebook ISBN: 978-1-62747-136-7
LCN: Pending

Dedication

This book is dedicated to our families, friends, and all the fantasy readers who dare to dream.

Acknowledgements

For their advice, and expertise on various issues with this book, a special thank you to Tom Bird, and RamaJon. And, a deserving thank you to Jessica Osorio Ortiz, Pam Gisi, and Terry Langford, for their helpful comments and suggestions.

From the beginning, a coven of witches skilled in the art of warfare have ruled the place they named Raven's Glenn, and, from the beginning, messengers of darkness have tried to destroy them as well as the prophesy that one day, a witch will be born of the dark and light and rule the realms of evil and good.

Chapter One

From a distance, Greythorn appeared as a small, humble, peaceful village. Openly exposed on the east and west sides, the early rising eastern sun warmed, and the fading light of the western sunsets cooled the small village. Protected on the north and south sides by a dense mature forest, Greythorn hid from the closest road. Approaching travelers or visitors strained their eyes to see the few dozen small humble huts located throughout the cleared meadow.

In one of the huts closest to the forest and furthest away from the center of the village lived Celeste and her child Talia. Celeste had eyes the color of storm clouds, appearing tall and graceful, her every movement commanded attention. Past childbearing age, her long, silky, black hair appeared marbled with grey, yet she still looked young. Gentle and yet stern, the villagers liked and respected Celeste. Once the village held an archery contest, Celeste appeared with a long bow and when it was her time to shoot, she quickly released three arrows, one after the other. The arrows, as if guided by some mysterious force, floated through the air, before the first arrow hit the target the second arrow was on its way, three perfect scores ... dead center. The men of the village envied Celeste's skill with the bow and arrow, and the wisdom she often displayed at village meetings amazed even the elders of the village who often consulted with her in private.

No one knew where Celeste came from; she never talked about her past, and even Talia never asked her about such things. One day, Celeste and a large, tall, burly man arrived at the village. At that time, Celeste was with child, and soon after they arrived, Talia was born. The villagers, mesmerized by Celeste and her seemingly endless abilities, convinced her to join them in Greythorn. Twelve years later and now somewhat aged, Celeste's memories of the outside world had faded, and as those twelve years passed, the simple, calm village life suited her and Greythorn became her home.

At twelve years of age, quick witted and outspoken, Talia stood apart from the other children. She was the tallest child in the village; her radiant long black hair covered her back, reaching her waistline. She was the only child in the village with green eyes, deep bright-green eyes that often appeared to glow, causing many who made eye contact with her to walk away with an unsettled eerie feeling. Her eyes highlighted her high cheekbones and distracted others from seeing the innocent expressions found only on a child's face. Thin and yet strong for a child, Talia loved to compete—the challenges excited her. Talia was smarter, stronger, and faster than the other children were. Often found alone and bored, she would lie down in the open meadow and watch the clouds and birds fly above, and in her mind imagine she was a bird, soaring on the winds. Celeste would often find Talia in the meadow, lost in thought, staring at the sky.

Talia liked to talk with the elders of the village and listen as they told tales of witches and dragons. The suspense and mystery that colored their stories amused Talia; whenever a story had a dark or evil twist to it, Talia would stare in disbelief and question the elders, sometimes finding fault with the story. Celeste often retold the same story if Talia questioned her about it, and included just enough facts to make it believable; somehow, Celeste was always able to satisfy Talia's curiosity.

Talia's father was a hunter and farmer; he sometimes worked from sunrise to sunset in the fields, planting or harvesting crops. Unlike the other men of the village, he also spent a lot of time in the forest hunting, and when planting or harvest season was over, he would take long trips away from the village. Talia did not know her father very well; she lived with the memories from his past visits, endlessly waiting for his return, never knowing when he would leave again.

Although the weather was mostly mild yearlong, the days were starting to cool; the nights arrived sooner and the crops had grown. Swaying in the breezes, the tall, mature crops signaled harvest season had arrived. Talia knew that when harvest season came, her father would soon be home. Early the next morning while Talia and Celeste slept, a tall man entered their hut. Inside the hut, a smoldering fire inside the fire pit gave off just enough light to cast his shadow over the inside walls. Next to the fire pit, neatly stacked, laid several pieces of firewood; the man reached for a small log and tossed it on the fire. The wood crackled and tiny illuminated cinders shot into the air. As cinders floated downward back to the fire, he quietly walked over to where Celeste slept. A noise from within the hut caused Celeste to stir and her eyelids started to flutter; a large firm hand cupped her shoulder; she opened her eyes—Talia's father was home.

"Shhh.... Do not wake Talia." Celeste nodded in agreement.

The early morning darkness surrounded Talia while she slept on top of a straw-filled mattress. Snuggled under a wool blanket safe and warm, she dreamed of colorful places far away, and of strange-looking people with inhuman powers. Talia's father approached the window and opened the wood shutters. The rising sun's light crept through the open window and crawled across the floor, slowly parting the darkness in its path. The radiant light slowly moved closer and closer to where Talia slept. Talia's father stood between Talia and the approaching sunlight, blocking the light before it reached her. He called her name, and Talia stirred. The large man called her name again; Talia opened her eyes and looked up. A tall shadow outlined in a bright light appeared to stand before her; she rubbed her eyes as if trying to wash away the darkness, and stared at the dark image, straining to see who it was. The man leaned forward and, away from the approaching sunlight, he pushed down on the straw mattress, and his face appeared out of the darkness. Talia screamed with joy.... "Father!" and leaped into his outstretched waiting arms.

"I knew you would return when it was time to harvest the crops," Talia whispered as she hugged her father.

"Yes, child. Have you missed me?"

"Oh, yes, Father, and so has Mother."

The room soon filled with sunlight, and the waking noises from the village flowed through the open window. Preparing the morning meal, Celeste glanced up and ordered them to sit at the table and eat.

"The crops will not wait forever," Celeste commented. "Our share of the crops depend on you."

"I will join them in the fields and help with the crops," Talia's father replied. "After the harvest, we may have to leave Greythorn."

The comment took Celeste by surprise. For twelve years, she and Talia have lived in Greythorn. Greythorn was their home. Worried that her past may have caught up with her, she asked, "Do they know where we live? Were you followed?"

"I do not think I was followed back here. Many villages have fallen to the darkness that is spreading throughout the lands. We are safe for now, but soon they will find us. I fear we cannot hide forever."

After their meal was finished, Talia said good-bye to her father. He and several men from the village gathered their farming tools and left to work in the fields. Around midday, the clear blue sky slowly darkened over the men. A thick, black, eerie fog formed above them and slowly settled over the field, blocking out the suns light and concealing the men as they worked. From within the dark fog, sounds of animal hoofs stomping the ground and snarls from a beast no one could see pierced the darkness. Overcome with fear, their hearts beating rapidly, the village men dived to the ground and covered their heads. Slowly, the fog dispersed, the blue sky returned, and with the sun's rays beating on their backs, the men stood and looked at each other ... Talia's father had vanished. Quickly, the men searched the nearby forest and lands just outside Greythorn; after several hours, they gave up searching, and the days passed by. Talia's father never returned to Greythorn and no one knew what became of him.

Early one morning while Celeste and Talia prepared their morning meal, Talia, eager to greet the new day, opened the wood shutters that covered one of the two windows in their hut. The sun's light forced its way into the room, bringing with it the beginning of a new day. Talia looked out the window; the village was still, quiet, and sleeping. A calm and peacefulness had settled over the village and made Talia feel safe and secure. The sky was deep blue and filled with white puffy clouds; a large raven circled above, soaring, floating on the winds. The raven cried out and Talia looked up. The flight of the raven mesmerized Talia, but soon her thoughts shifted, and a great sadness filled her heart. Talia turned away from the window and looked at her mother. *I miss Father*, Talia thought to herself. Celeste glanced up at her child and was about to speak when Talia asked, "What evil took Father from us? Who will hunt our meat and harvest our crops? How will we survive?"

"We will survive," replied Talia's mother.

Humming a tune she learned as a child, Talia's mother handed Talia a cup of fresh goat's milk. Outside, the village was quiet and peaceful; only the chirping of a nearby bird broke the silence. Talia and her mother finished eating their morning meal when suddenly, a horn from within the village started to blow—three short burst from the horn ... signaling trouble. A look of fear appeared in Celeste's eyes; the sounds of distant horns became clearer and louder as approaching hordes of heavily armed, devilish, evil beasts and human warriors moved closer. The ground around Talia started to tremble and Talia cried out ...

"Mother, what is it?"

"Run, child, hide thyself ... quickly now!"

Talia stood and ran towards the door, glancing back at her mother. Talia stopped and yelled, "Mother ... I do not want to leave you."

"Run, child, they have come to kill us."

Talia could hear the pounding of men's feet as the attacking army ran into the village. Well-armed with swords and spears ... men and hideous looking creatures attacked Greythorn. Soon, smoke from the burning huts filled the air, and the horrid screams of men fighting blended with the sounds of swords striking each other. Fire and smoke quickly engulfed the small village and meadow. Brightly lit cinders floated above the flames and rained down on the doomed villagers. Death had arrived and hid within the flames. Swallowing all life, the warm morning breezes spread the fire in all directions.

Again, Celeste pleaded, "Run, child ... hide!"

Talia ran and just as she reached the door, she heard a loud, "CRACK!" Her mother crumpled to the floor—their home was on fire. Afraid and, overwhelmed with fear, Talia screamed. She ran out through the door and into a cloud of smoke. Men entered her hut, and then she heard her mother's cries for mercy. Hidden within the smoke, Talia ran as fast as she could. When she reached the outskirts of the forest, she tripped and fell, her mind blackened as she landed head first in a ditch.

Blackened and smoldering, the cries of its inhabitants silenced, Greythorn was no more. Talia awakened to the smell of burning huts and human flesh. The smell of the burning dead was awful. Her home was gone, burnt to the ground. The lifeless body of her mother smoldered in the ashes. Overpowered by the sights and smells, Talia fainted.

Night arrived and out of its smoke-filled darkness, the sound of a woman's voice called to Talia,

"Wake up, child!"

Talia opened her eyes and looked up. A tall woman stood over her, her arms folded within the cloth of her long black hooded robe. Her long dark hair glittered in the moon's light. Her eyes appeared to glow a reddish yellow in color. She smiled, a warm pleasing smile, as she looked down at Talia.

"Who are you?" Talia asked.

"That's not important right now," replied the tall woman. "Come with me, child, I will care for you."

Talia tried to stand, but her legs were weak and she fell. The tall woman reached down and grabbed her hand. The touch of her hand sent a strange, unsettling feeling through Talia and she quickly jerked her hand away.

"Come, my child," said the tall woman. "We haven't much time and a long ways to travel."

Talia looked into the woman's eyes and a sudden unexplainable fear came over her.

"Why do you want me?" Talia asked.

"Want you!" laughed the tall woman. "Come with me and you will learn our ways."

The tall woman again reached out and took Talia's hand into hers. This time, Talia felt a caring warmth and belonging, and the tall woman smiled.

"My mother is dead," Talia, cried out. "My village and home are gone, I am alone."

"I know this, child. I was too late. Come with me, the path to Raven's Glenn waits for you."

Greythorn, burnt to the ground, destroyed, was no more. The burning village was soon far behind them, the smell of smoke and burning flesh fading with each step. The cries for mercy from Talia's mother haunted Talia and a great sadness filled her heart while tears filled her eyes.

"What was ... is gone," said the tall woman. "Be brave, Talia."

"How do you know my name?" Talia asked.

"You are the chosen one," replied the tall woman. "We from Raven's Glenn have always known your name, for the Ancients of Raven's Glenn speak of you. There is a small village up ahead. We will rest there."

They entered the village from the east side, their shadows in front of them as if guiding their movements. The village reminded Talia of Greythorn. The huts were similar in size, shape, and spread across an open meadow. Unlike Greythorn, this village had an eerie feeling to it. The village did not feel calm and peaceful. Where were the villagers? Looking around, the tall woman suddenly stopped.

"Wait! A great evil is here.... Stay close, child. It is not safe here."

"Where is everybody?" asked Talia.

"We will find food and leave this place," responded the tall woman.

They entered a large round hut with two open doors and no windows. The smell of cooked meat heightened their senses. In the center of the room hung over a fire pit was a large metal pot full of gravy, cooked vegetables, and goat's meat. On a nearby table, Talia spotted several chunks of bread ripped from a fresh loaf. Talia quickly grabbed a chunk of bread then dipped it in the pot.

"Eat, my child," said the tall woman, "We must leave this place soon."

"I hear voices," Talia whispered.

"Quiet, child. Hold me tight."

The tall woman slowly raised her hands and arms towards the sky and chanted,

"Goddess of darkness, shadow of light, I call for thee let no one see."

Suddenly, the room turned from light to dark, their shadows disappearing as the room darkened. Talia looked up at the tall woman and asked, "How can you do this?"

"Quiet, child, we must not be seen or heard."

Talia heard footsteps outside and, through cracks in the wall, saw the sun's reflection glimmer off armors and swords as the men passed. None entered the hut. Soon, the darkness faded and the room filled with light.

"We leave now," said the tall woman. She grabbed Talia by the hand and moved towards the door.

"What are you, and where are you taking me?" asked Talia.

"We go to Raven's Glenn, you will be safe there. Come now, we have no time to discuss this."

"Raven's Glenn? My father spoke of a place called Raven's Glenn, he said only witches live there. Are you a witch?" asked Talia.

The tall woman laughed and replied, "We must go child you will learn soon enough."

After walking a few miles, they stopped to rest and the tall woman asked Talia, "What do you dream of, child?"

"Birds," replied Talia. "Sometimes in my dreams I can fly like a bird. I would fly over strange places where people would raise their arms up to me. The earth and air would smell like fields of flowers after a new rain."

"Could you see through the bird's eyes?" the tall woman asked.

"See through the bird's eyes? How can you see through the birds eyes?"

They continued walking and the tall woman looked down at Talia and said,

"Your dreams from night, your restless soul, will give birth to a future ... a story not yet told."

Talia did not understand and she looked up at the tall woman who glanced down at her and smiled. Their journey continued towards Raven's Glenn. The tall woman kept Talia close and watched her constantly as they walked. Often, she gave warning of obstacles on the path, and yet Talia still managed to stumble over the smallest ruts and rocks. The day was long; since early morning they walked, and Talia's was tired. Sunset was approaching; the tall woman quickened her step, reached down, and, with a soft but firm grip, grabbed Talia's hand. Talia looked up and whimpered, "I'm tired."

"Child, before darkness falls, we must make it to the forest that surrounds the Land of the Dead," said the tall woman.

"The Land of the Dead?" asked Talia.

"Yes," the tall woman replied. "A Dark Lord created a place now called the Land of the Dead. It is full of evil creatures that he controls, a place void of sunlight where no plants or animals live. The Dark Lord is evil and very powerful. He lusts for more power and wishes to rule over all the lands. We must hurry, Talia, the Guardian of the Forest waits for me."

A slight chill went through Talia and yet she felt safe with the tall woman. *Land of the Dead, Guardian of the Forest, what is she talking about*, Talia's thoughts drifted to her mother and father and she whispered, "What will become of me?"

The tall woman and Talia continued onward with their journey, both sun and moon filling the sky above them. Nightfall would soon remove the sun's light and replace it with the glow of the moon. The tall woman looked up at the sky and smiled. *Soon, Talia*, she thought to herself, *soon, you shall know me*.

"Do you know of the forest?" asked the tall woman.

"What do you mean, 'of the forest'? The forest is all around us."

"The secrets of the oak tree and wildwood, of the Ancients," explained the tall woman.

"My father spoke of the goddesses of the forest and of a great witch named Kali, the protector of our lands. Are those the Ancients you speak of?"

"Kali—your father spoke of Kali?"

"Yes," Talia replied. "He said she was a high priestess of long ago."

"Long ago?" replied the tall woman.

"My father said Kali was defeated in a great battle with dark evil creatures."

"Enough!" said the tall woman. "We must enter the forest up ahead and find the Sacred Grove of the Ancients."

The forest was dark and the path tricky to follow. The whiteness of the birch trees would mark their path and guide them through the darkness of the forest, keeping them on the correct path to the Sacred Grove of the Ancients. As they approached, the forest appeared to come alive. There was no breeze, yet the top of the trees swayed back and forth, and the lower branches and leaves fluttered softly, their movements appearing as a haze, tricking the eye. Talia blinked and stared at the trees; she became dizzy, stumbled, and turned her eyes away.

"Listen, Talia, do you hear the rustling of the tree leaves?" asked the tall woman.

"Yes," replied Talia.

The tall woman smiled and said, "The forest speaks to me."

The tall woman then raised her arms and hands towards the sky. She tilted her head slightly back, the palms of her hands faced upwards, and she closed her eyes and chanted,

"Here now, upon the earth, beneath the sky, remove the spell that tricks the eye."

Talia could hear the sounds of the trees and bushes as they parted in front of her. There, floating among the trees, dressed in a long flowing robe, was the transparent image of an old woman. Her robe was the color of the trees, as if her robe was a tree itself. Her long white hair floated above her shoulders ... covering all but her eyes. Her image appeared attached to the forest as she floated above the ground and Talia could see right through her. Behind the old woman appeared a narrow path, the path darkening as it led deep into the forest. The old woman raised her arms and birch trees appeared on each side of the path. When she lowered her arms, the whiteness of the birch trees illuminated and the path through the forest was lit, now easy to follow.

"Who is she?" asked Talia.

"Be quiet, Talia, the Guardian of the Forest welcomes us."

"I can see through her, who is she?" whispered Talia

"The Guardian of the Forest is a spirit that protects the forest and those from Raven's Glenn who pass through the forest."

"She moves towards us!" Talia cried out.

"Quiet, Talia ... be still." The tall woman grabbed Talia by the shoulder before she could run off.

The old woman approached, her robe flowing over the trees and ground, taking the darkness of the forest with her. She floated through them, circled back, and disappeared into the shadows of the forest. The tall woman and Talia entered the forest, following the path where the whiteness of the birch trees appeared to glow ... guiding their way. Deeper into the forest they walked; soon, the darkness within the forest around them began to fade, replaced by an increasing glow of light.

"I'm scared," said Talia, reaching for the tall woman's hand.

The darkness that surrounded them was gone; the moon's light had replaced the day's sun, and the moon's light filled the spot where they stood. The light rapidly became intense and the glow awakened the forest. Talia buried her face in the robe of the tall woman and started to cry.

"Talia, behold! See what is around you."

Talia opened her eyes and circled around. A large clearing in the forest appeared before her, with a four-foot high wall made of stone that circled around the clearing. Brighter, yet different from sunlight, the yellow-orange glow of the moonlight increased and the area within the circle of stone glowed with a vivid yellowish orange color. Located in the center of the circle was a large stone altar.

"What is this place?" Talia asked.

"The Sacred Grove of the Ancients," replied the tall woman. "We have work to do and little time to finish ... we must hurry."

The tall woman entered the Sacred Grove of the Ancients and walked to the center of the circle where the large stone altar was located. Placing both hands on the stone altar, she chanted.

"From life is death, from death is life, protect our blood we leave this night."

From beneath her robe, the tall woman pulled out a small vial filled with blood. The large stone altar shook; pieces of dirt and very tiny stones, blanketed in dust, fell to the ground. The stone altar then slowly moved backwards, uncovering a shallow hole in the ground. The tall woman placed the vial in the hole and stepped back. The altar shook again and moved forward, once again covering the hole.

"Remember this place, Talia. The blood I leave here tonight will save your life from the darkness that awaits you. Join me and help gather leaves for a fire. We must honor the Ancients—it is their blood we leave here tonight."

Talia and the tall woman made a pile out of the dead fallen oak leaves. When the pile of leaves was large enough, the tall woman started a fire and soon smoke engulfed the grove. Talia could barely see as the tall woman moved in and out of the smoke, as if dancing on air. Talia could hear the tall woman speak, but the language was from another time and she could not understand what she was saying. Soon the smoke cleared and the moonlight began to fade.

The night became once again dark and Talia was afraid. "You will learn to follow the ways of the Ancients," said the tall woman. "Never fear the forest or what hides within it. Trees and animals give us life and wisdom; we must honor and respect them, never fear them."

"Why do you not fear what is in the forest?" asked Talia.

"I know the secrets of the oak tree."

Talia did not understand and drifted off to sleep. The night air chilled around her while memories of her village filled her mind. Awakened by the screams of her mother, Talia sat up and covered her mouth with her hand ... her screams fell silent. The tall woman was gone and fear came over her. The Sacred Grove of the Ancients had disappeared, the sun's rays now flickered through the treetops, and the sounds of the forest had returned. Talia started to follow the path out of the forest when she saw the tall woman with a raven perched on her arm. *How can this be?* thought Talia. *She talks with birds*. Sensing Talia's presence, the tall woman looked away from the raven and stared at Talia. She then raised her arm, and the raven spread its wings and took flight.

"Come, Talia, we must continue to Raven's Glenn."

"I saw you talking to that bird."

"The raven can see what we cannot see; he brings sight from above for our journey through the Land of the Dead."

"How can you speak to birds?"

"There is you Talia, you and the land, you and the sky, now and here ... you, and you are separated from all these things. I am of the land, forest, and sky. I am the Spirit for the Five Points of the Star, and protector of these lands. I am Kali, high priestess and ruler of Raven's Glenn."

"Kali? But my father said you.... "

"I am here!" Kali interrupted. "We go to Raven's Glenn where you will learn our ways and those of the Ancients. Come ... Raven's Glenn waits."

The path out of the forest led to an open meadow full of colorful, fragrant flowers and tall green grasses. The smell was that of new rain and fresh flowers. Talia looked out over the meadow and remembered her dream of seeing this place. Kali and Talia looked across the open meadow before them. Flowers covered the meadow and gave off a rainbow glow across the tops of the grasses. The smell of fresh rain greeted their senses. Kali closed her eyes and slowly raised her arms from her sides, palms facing towards the sky. She took several deep breaths, opened her eyes, and lowered her arms,

"The Summerlands," Kali whispered.

"What are the Summerlands?" asked Talia.

"It's a place in the other world that waits for us when our light dims. Here and now, Talia, the Summerlands tease us. We have not passed over to the other world; what you see in this meadow is a vision of the Summerlands. Come, Talia, we must cross the meadow."

"Will I enter the Summerlands?" asked Talia.

"It is written that you will cheat death when it comes for you. You will never enter the Summerlands," explained Kali.

A narrow well-worn path of soft soil and fallen green grasses would guide them through the meadow. Full of sweet smells, rich, clean air, and vivid in bright colors—the flowering meadow offered inner peace and comfort to those who passed through. Many a witch from Raven's Glenn had walked this path, the meadow often supplying them with plants for healing and spell making.

"You will learn from the plants and animals that live here," Kali whispered. "You will join the witches of Raven's Glenn and learn our ways, for it is prophesized by the Ancients that your powers will be the greatest of all. Come, we must now cross the river up ahead."

A long winding river flowed throughout the lands of Raven's Glenn and beyond. Through the open meadows and fields, and into the western mountains, the river flowed. Shallow and easy to walk across, the river widened and narrowed at different places. The clear cool water was calm and quenched the thirst of many travelers. Water witches protected the river and drew most of their magic powers from the water; with magic spells, and hard work, they kept the river clean and alive. Kali and Talia approached the river and, from a distance, they could see a coven of witches eager at work.

"Who are those people by the river?" asked Talia.

"Water witches. I see Queen Isle is with them."

Dressed in long green hooded robes, locked arm in arm ... shoulder to shoulder, the water witches stood in a large circle. First, they circled to the left ... stopped, then they circled to the right. Kali and Talia could hear the witches chant as they approached.

"Wait ... Talia, they are preparing the barley straw. We must not interfere."

"Straw…? Why do they prepare straw?"

"The river feeds the streams and ponds; the witches use the barley straw to purify the water."

"Look!" cried out Talia. "The woman in the dark-green cloak approaches."

"Welcome, High Priestess Kali, your visit honors our land. What brings you to the river?"

Selected by Kali to rule over the one hundred or so water witches and their several covens, Queen Isle was a wise and a powerful force. Tall, fair-haired, and light in color, her deep blue eyes spoke of water. Born on the river's edge and raised by water witches, she quickly mastered their craft and became the most powerful witch among them. Strong, fair, independent, and fierce in battle, the other water witches admired her skills and loved her deeply.

"I take the chosen one to Raven's Glenn where she will be my maiden until grown," replied Kali.

"I have heard the Ancients speak of this child," said Queen Isle. "Teach her well, I fear darkness awaits her. It is two days past the witch's moon ... our ritual tonight will honor your visit, High Priestess Kali."

"We are days from Raven's Glenn and must leave," replied Kali. "Come, Talia, we must find the centaurs, they will hasten our journey."

"Wait! High Priestess, I know of a centaur family not far from here."

"Where do they live?" asked Kali.

"They live east of the meadows, behind the three hills of stone."

Half horse, half man and an uncouth... rude lot, centaurs stood much taller than the average person did. Fierce fighters and swift on their feet, they often caused Kali grief with their independent ways and stubbornness, endlessly breaking the rules of the land that Kali set forth to keep peace among the different life forms that lived throughout the Lands of Raven's Glenn. Independent and free, the centaurs enjoyed a simple family life. They lived in small groups and raised their families independent of each other but banding together in times of trouble or war. They were famous for their skill with the spear and sword, and not easily defeated in battle.

Kali and Talia headed east, the three large hills of stone were just on the other side of the meadow. Soon, they were within sight of the centaur's home, a simple structure built into the side of a hill. The tall outside walls consisted of layers of large rocks mixed with wet clay. A roof covered with dried grasses and straw extended out of the hillside and past the tops of the walls. The home was larger than it appeared; carved deep into the hill, the centaur's home had plenty of room for the centaurs to move around in. Talia and Kali walked up to the centaur's home and peeked inside the opening. The room was empty—there was no trace of the centaurs.

"Where are they?" asked Talia.

"I do not know, but it seems there was trouble here," replied Kali. "Look, you can see blood stains on the ground, and what's this ... feathers from a birdman!"

Kali, surprised to find the feather, spoke aloud, "We must be careful, Talia, the Glarton—birdmen from the Land of the Dead—are close by."

"They are gone!" a voice from behind them bellowed.

Talia turned and saw a young centaur as tall as Kali; he stood there with a large smile across his boyish human face. Light tan in color with long brown hair, his playful bluish eyes focused on Talia. Talia blinked with surprise; she had never seen a half horse half human before, and his appearance puzzled her. Stomper moved closer; Talia took a step back and stared at Stomper. *What are you?* Talia thought to herself and then asked aloud, "What are you, horse or human?"

Stomper laughed and replied, "My mother and father fought with the birdmen and chased them away. My name is Stomper ... son of Lamehoof, and this is my home. Look! My father and mother return."

Kali and Talia looked out over the open field where they saw two small clouds of dust moving towards them. In a fit of glee, Stomper raised his front legs and shouted as he galloped out to meet his parents.

"I will let my father know you are here and mean us no harm."

Stomper and his father Lamehoof galloped up to Kali and Talia. Stomper's mother ignored the visitors, galloped past them, and entered her home. Lamehoof, a self-proclaimed ruler of his kind, was a large centaur—taller than Kali—with wide shoulders and large muscular arms. The reddish brown fur on his body and legs matched the color of his shoulder-length hair, and his deep set, dark black eyes glittered in the sunlight. Wise and fearless, he stopped, looked at Kali, and snarled, "What business do you have here?"

"I am High Priestess Kali of Raven's Glenn, ruler and keeper of these lands. You will show me the respect I deserve or I will turn your crops to dust."

Lamehoof, surprised by the sudden and forceful response, replied, "I honor your visit, High Priestess Kali. I thought you were one of those witches from the water witch coven and have come to take my straw."

Her attention claimed by the passing clouds, Talia pointed towards the sky and cried out, "Look, the birdmen return!"

"Hurry, we must hide or fight!" Lamehoof shouted. "The birdmen have been flying around here for days. Something is afoot."

"Wait!" Kali replied. "I will help you if you will help us on our journey to Raven's Glenn."

"What? I will help you.... Hurry, the birdmen are attacking!"

Kali reached into her robe and pulled out a witch's wand. Forged from the tree of wisdom, made powerful by the life forces within the forest, a gift from the Guardian of the Forest, the wand was several inches long, thin, and had a slight bend to it. With the wand, Kali made a large circle on the ground and entered the circle.

"Quickly, everyone come inside the circle."

Kali pointed the wand towards the birdmen as they approach from the sky, her wand lit up and glowed yellow within a whitish blue haze that surrounded it. She shouted,

"Thou demon of flight from within the sky, feel no wind of flight, for it shall fail thee."

Half human and half bird ... the screams from the sky echoed across the meadow as the Glarton ... the demon birdmen from the Land of the Dead, fell from the sky and crashed into the earth.

Kali in a stern voice yelled out, "Now hurry before they come to! We must leave quickly! They are not dead."

"Not dead?" shouted Talia,

"No, Talia, my spell took away their flight, but they will soon recover and come after us."

With the tip of her wand still glowing, Kali placed the witch's wand securely back under her robe.

"Now then, Lamehoof," Kali caught his eye and stared at him, "you are to help us as agreed."

"You must first protect our land as you promised," Lamehoof replied.

"Very well ... form a circle around me, and be quick."

Kali stood in the center of the circle and picked up a handful of dry dirt. A slight whitish glow came over her eyes and, with shallow breaths, she called on the Ancients of Raven's Glenn,

"From east to west, north to south, I summon thee, protect the lands that belong to thee, for as far as the Ancients' eye can see, Raven Glenn and all these lands belong to thee."

Kali tossed the dirt into a passing breeze and watched. A brief image of one of the Ancients appeared within the dust and vanished. "It is finished," Kali whispered.

"Lamehoof, we must go now," Kali ordered.

"Come, Kali ... jump on," said Lamehoof. "The little one can ride on Stomper. Who is she? Why do you travel with this girl?"

"This is Talia, the chosen one," replied Kali. "I must get her to Raven's Glenn where she will be protected and learn our ways."

Surprised, Lamehoof briefly stumbled and said, "I have heard stories of what she is and will do ... I never really believed. The Ancients tell of a story of a ruler in our time, one who will battle the dark evil of our land and fall victim to the dark evil, only to be reborn immortal and ruler of the dark and light."

"Is she ... Talia, the chosen one?" asked Stomper.

"The Ancients had me search for her and while her village was under attack, the Ancients protected her by having her fall into a ditch and hit her head. Talia lay hidden in the ditch until the attack was over. I knew just where to find her. The Ancients protected her and led me to her. Now, Raven's Glenn waits for this child and we from Raven's Glenn believe Talia is the chosen one."

"Stomper, can you gallop faster, this is fun," asked Talia.

"Hold on tight," replied Stomper

As Talia tightened her hold around Stomper, she closed her eyes, and a cool breeze passed across her face. Stomper's stride was swift and smooth, his hoofs barely touching the ground. Talia held on tight, her hands clenching Stomper's sides.

"Talia, are you afraid?"

"No, Stomper, just worried about what will become of me, and maybe a little scared."

Stomper slowed down and said, "The Land of the Dead approaches—hang on tight!" Beating on his chest, he bragged, "I will protect you."

As they got closer to the Land of the Dead, uneasiness started to consume everyone.

"Remember, this place will make you think the worst things possible," said Kali. "You must not let those thoughts control you. The faster we travel through the Land of the Dead, the better."

"I agree," said Lamehoof. "Stomper, you must stay close—and Talia, you must hold on to Stomper ... hold on tight."

After a short swift ride, they reached the edge of the meadow and approached the Land of the Dead. Greeted by a dark fog filled with swirling winds, they halted. The Land of the Dead lay before them, a dark, cold place devoid of life and color. The darkened sky above the Land of the Dead never allowed the sun's light to enter and, over time, the leafless trees and plants blackened and became colorless. A dark fog swirled low to the ground and covered the surface. The dark air had a bitter taste to it, and faint disturbing cries—sound of agony and despair—traveled from far way ... someplace off in the darkness.

"Can't we find another way to Raven's Glenn?" asked Talia.

"This is the only way," explained Kali. "Once we enter, you will be able to see little, for the fog is thick. You must keep your eyes open and your ears alert, there are creatures in there no one has ever seen outside of this land. Is everyone ready? We have to reach the other side before nightfall."

The force of the swirling winds increased as Stomper and Talia galloped out in front.

"Wait!" Kali shouted. "Before you are three paths; only one is true, for the other two are paths of no return."

"How do we know which path to take?" asked Lamehoof.

"The Ancients of Raven's Glenn have marked the path well if you can truly see. Look for the blackened chicory plants. The Ancients planted the chicory plants to mark the path and give those who understand and know the power of the chicory the strength to continue, for the journey is dangerous. We must not leave the path."

The path marked by the chicory plant would lead to three Circles of Stone, sacred places made by the Ancients for the witches of Raven's Glenn to rest and restore their powers as they passed through the Land of the Dead. The passage between these sacred places was long and dangerous, and evil waited at every turn. Kali had walked this path many times but never with the chosen one. Few had ever seen the evil force that ruled over the Land of the Dead; even his name was a secret, and yet, he and all the creatures that lived within the Land of the Dead were aware of the chosen one and that which the Ancients had foretold. *This journey would be different*, Kali thought ... *very different*. The sunlight began to dim and a chill fell upon them as they moved forward into the Land of the Dead.

Dark fog concealed them as they galloped into the darkness. Talia could feel a strange power come over her. She was not scared; she felt different, somehow needed. From somewhere deep inside her, a power was starting to emerge. Stomper could feel her energy as she rode on his back and was about to speak when he came to a sudden stop and shouted, "Look!"

Before them, blocking the path, a large black dragon waited. Stomper's sharp vision spotted the large dragon that blended so well with the darkness. Lamehoof reached behind for his spear that hung by a leather strap tied around his midsection; the spear, within easy reach, was swiftly in his hands.

The dragon spoke, "Hello, Kali. I am Dragmier. I have been waiting a long time for you."

"I do not understand—what do you mean you have been waiting? I come this way when need be, why have I not seen you before?" Kali replied.

"You have not needed my help," replied Dragmier, "therefore, you could not see me. The Ancients knew this day would come and placed me here so I could protect you when the time came. The time is here, and the chosen one is with you. You must hurry through the Land of the Dead. Talia is not safe here."

"Talia, what is it?" Stomper asked.

"You do not hear that?" Talia asked.

"What are you hearing, Talia?" asked Kali.

"I can hear voices speak to me," Talia replied. "They say we can trust the dragon and what he says is true."

"The voices also speak to me," said Kali. "I did not know that you could hear them. The Ancients talk to both of us."

"There are other dragons around here," interrupted Dragmier. "They serve their master, the Lord of Darkness, who can be very deceiving."

"I am the high priestess, why would the Ancients put a dragon here? I can just cast a spell."

"Not all the creatures in this land can be stopped with a spell," replied Dragmier. "The Lord of Darkness has spent many years creating creatures to destroy you. He knows that Talia could be the chosen one, and that she must not reach Raven's Glenn."

"Does the Lord of Darkness know we are here?" asked Kali.

"Evil in many forms has been following you since you left Raven's Glenn for Talia's village, and evil is sure to find you soon."

"Why do you help us?" asked Lamehoof.

"Many years ago in a battle with the witches of Raven's Glenn, the high priestess before Kali spared my life.... I had to take an oath to protect the chosen one when the day came. I leave you now—you need only call out my name and I will return."

Lamehoof spoke. "My spear is ready. We must go, the day grows darker."

A few hours later, Stomper and Lamehoof stopped. Strange sounds filled the darkness around them. Sounds of agony—the cries of the dead—surrounded them, and the creatures hiding within the darkness watched them. A large shadow darker than the darkness appeared and passed over Stomper. Blood appeared in Stomper's eyes and he fell to his knees. Talia cried out as she fell off Stomper's back and hit the ground.

Kali rushed to Stomper's aid. She knelt in front of him and, with both hands, reached out and held his head up. Her powers weakened by being in the Land of the Dead, she could do nothing to help Stomper. She called on Talia,

"Talia! You must act quickly—only you can save Stomper."

"How can I?"

"The power is within you," said Kali, "deep within you. Think, Talia ... feel, feel within."

Talia wrapped her arms around Stomper's neck and Stomper looked into Talia's eyes. Her heart began to beat faster. A slightly deep amber glow appeared in her eyes and, from somewhere deep inside her, a strange, unknown power began to emerge. Stomper began to fall forward, and Talia tightened her hold. An eerie chill swept through Talia and she gasped for air. From deep within her midsection, a strange feeling—a warmth—started to slowly grow outward and spread throughout her body, finally reaching her fingertips and Stomper. Talia placed her lips close to Stomper's ear,

'Stomper," whispered Talia, 'I feel the evil has left you and passed through me. Get up, Stomper, the evil is gone, get up I say!"

A little weak in the legs, Stomper slowly stood and smiled at Talia. Lamehoof circled the two, spear in hand and aimed at Talia; his eyes watched Talia's every movement, his hoofs stomping the ground as he circled, not sure about what he just witnessed. He was protective of his son and suspicious of Talia. Kali pushed the spear aside and glared at Lamehoof. The look in Kali's eyes and fear of what Kali could do brought Lamehoof to his senses; he lowered his spear and pointed the spear away from Talia. Kali reached out and put both hands on Talia's shoulders; she whispered so only Talia could hear, "You are indeed the chosen one."

Thump ... thump ... thump! The ground around them shook.

"What is it?" asked Stomper.

"Dragons!" replied Kali. "There is a dragon crossing up ahead. Be still and quiet; when the dragons have passed, we will continue."

They stayed far enough away from the crossing for the darkness to hide them and waited as the ground trembled around them. Several dragons passed by, smelling the air and snorting as they passed; once passed, the dragons spread their large mighty wings and took flight. Lamehoof, eager to continue, galloped out in front,

"They're gone, let's go!" Lamehoof cried out.

An image in the form of a shadow in humanlike shape appeared in front of Lamehoof, blocking the path and moving closer. Lamehoof, taken by surprise, sidestepped the dark shadow as it approached and raised his spear; he then thrust his spear into the shadow.

"Stop!" yelled Kali. "You cannot harm a messenger from the Lord of Darkness with a spear."

"What do you want?" Kali asked the shadow man.

"I come for the chosen one. My Lord wishes to meet with her."

"It's a trick!" interrupted Stomper. "They come to take Talia."

Stomper charged the shadow man but Kali was quicker and jumped between the two.

"Wait, Stomper," said Kali, "this messenger can do us no harm. This shadow man is an image sent by the Lord of Darkness."

Kali pointed at the shadow man. "Be gone with you or I will expose you to the light you hide from ... be gone!"

The shadow man hissed as his image faded.

"We must hurry," said Kali, "the first Circle of Stone is close by."

They continued down the path and soon saw a flicker of bright light in the distance. A bright haze of light melted away and pushed back the darkness that surrounded the first Circle of Stone. The stones on the path began to glow, guiding them into the circle of glowing stones. All around them, and placed on the ground in the shape of a circle were stones that glowed. The light brightened as Kali moved around within the circle.

"No harm will come to us here," explained Kali. "The darkness around us cannot be with the light before us, so we are safe."

"Is there no way to keep this light with us?" Talia asked. "If we can use the light, it will make the journey easier, and we will be able to see better in the black fog."

Kali chuckled and replied, "That is not how it works. The Circle of Stone offers a safe place for the witches of Raven's Glenn. Within these sacred places, we can perform magic and cast spells; however, our powers in the Land of the Dead are limited."

Talia mumbled, "It would just be easier to take one of the glowing stones with us. This makes no sense. If this is the only way to Raven's Glenn, you would think they would have come up with an easier way to get through this awful place."

Stomper heard Talia and nodded his head in agreement.

"What would happen if we took one of the glowing stones with us?" asked Stomper.

Kali whirled around and said, "The stones are sacred; they must not be removed, or the whole system will be destroyed. The stones' glow protects us while we are in the Circle of Stone. The stones will not glow if removed."

Kali walked to the center of the circle where a large stone of strange color lay half buried in the ground. Around Kali's neck hung a pendant with the image of Raven's Glenn engraved on its surface. Forged by the Ancients and high priestesses before her, the pendant held the secrets to the powers of Raven's Glenn. Kali removed the pendant and placed it on the stone. A reddish blue light appeared around the stone, and then Kali reached within the light and chanted,

"Messenger of light, messenger of flight I summon thee."

From out of the stones' light, a large raven appeared. Perched on the stone, the raven stared at Kali, and the two communicated with thoughts, never speaking.

"What does the raven say?" asked Talia.

"The raven comes for you," replied Kali. "You must try and talk with the raven."

"I cannot talk to birds," Talia replied.

"Come here, Talia, and stand in front of the Raven. Close your eyes. Try to see the Raven. Can you see the raven?" Kali asked.

"Yes! I can see the raven!"

"Reach out and touch the raven," Kali instructed.

As soon as Talia touched the raven, she could see, but not as she would have seen if her eyes were open ... it was different.

"What do you see?" Kali asked.

"I ... I see me!"

"Then you can see from within the raven through the raven's eyes," Kali replied.

"Stay focused, Talia. When the raven takes flight, you will be able to see through the raven's eyes."

As the raven flew above, Talia could see the lands below. The raven circled the sky and Talia saw many men, beast, and shadows moving across the land.

"Kali, they come!"

"Talia, come back. I see what you see, and they do not come for us."

Talia refocused her thoughts and the connection between her and the raven was broken. Standing within the stones' light, Talia looked up and asked Kali, "Are you sure those men and creatures will not attack us?"

"No! They go to attack another village outside the Land of the Dead. Soon, they will pass and we will leave for the second Circle of Stone. Lamehoof, you and Stomper prepare, we leave shortly."

Kali placed the pendant back around her neck and Talia climbed on Stomper's back. Talia saw that the trail before them had a slight glow radiating from the stones placed on the path.

"The stones glow," commented Talia. "Kali, you said only in the Circle of Stone is there such light."

Kali smiled.

"The powers of Raven's Glenn are great," laughed Kali. "The stones along the path will only glow for a short time. We must hurry to the next Circle of Stone."

Kali mounted Lamehoof and they galloped out towards the second Circle of Stone. As the glow from the first Circle of Stone faded behind them, a dim light from the second Circle of Stone pierced the darkness before them. Soon they arrived at the second Circle of Stone and as before, Kali placed her pendant on the center stone and chanted,

"Messenger of light, messenger of truth, I summon you."

A bright white light radiated from the stone and the transparent image of the eyes of a woman appeared.

"Who is she?" asked Talia.

"She is the Keeper of Knowledge, counsel to the Ancients. She is a spirit that has been with Raven's Glenn since the beginning. Throughout the lands of Raven's Glenn, she holds the knowledge of all things past, present, and sometimes she can predict the future," Kali replied.

A voice from within the image asked, "High priestess of Raven's Glenn, how may I serve you."

"What other dangers wait for us on our journey to Raven's Glenn?" Kali asked.

"You must prepare yourself," she answered. "In the dark around the second curve just past the third Circle of Stone waits a trap."

Kali picked up her pendant and placed it back around her neck; she then thanked the Keeper of Knowledge and watched the image of her eyes fade back into the stones' light. Kali then warned the others of the trap that waited for them just past the third Circle of Stone. Soon, the glow from the second Circle of Stone disappeared behind them. At a fast gallop, they approached the third Circle of Stone and passed through. Just outside the circle and around the second curve, the dark sky opened, exposing a sky of blackish grey clouds. From out of the clouds, several birdmen appeared.

"Dragmier! Dragmier!" Kali shouted.

A large dragon appeared in the sky and darted downward towards them. SWOOSH ... the dragon swept low just under the birdmen ... stealing the air from under their wings. Circling back around, Dragmier attacked from a different direction then clipped a birdman with his wing, knocking him out of the sky.

"Follow me!" yelled Lamehoof.

Spear in hand, Lamehoof galloped down the path and right into three hooded men. The closest man removed his hood and the reddish glow from his eyes revealed the pointed fangs between his lips. Kali was quick to respond and shouted,

"Stay away, Lamehoof, stay away from the vampires and do not let them grab you!"

Kali reached into her robe, pulling out her witch's wand then pointed it at the vampires, shouting,

"Evil of the night, lost souls of the day, fall to the light, this path make bright!"

A bright beam of light emerged from the wand and covered the path. The vampires started to burn and dived off the path in agony, smoldering in the dark. Kali looked towards the sky and two dragons appeared. From above and behind them, Dragmier reappeared and swooped downward on a collision course with the other dragons. The impact was deadly. Three dragons fell from the sky, spiraling downward. His wings tangled beneath him, Dragmier lay on the ground ... mortally wounded. Talia ran up to Dragmier and touched his giant head—but nothing stirred within her. She then placed both hands on his head and tried to reach deep within herself for the power to save him. There was no light, just darkness.

"Dragmier," whispered Talia. Tears filled her eyes.

"The Summerlands call Dragmier," said Kali. "He will be rewarded by the Ancients. The path is now clear to Raven's Glenn. Come, child, we must go."

Saddened, Lamehoof commented, "He was a great dragon, the last of his kind."

A light breeze circled around Dragmier, as if protecting him. Kali stood there and looked at Dragmier.

"The light defeated the dark today," explained Kali "Remember Dragmier. He gave his life for us, for the Ancients, for Raven's Glenn. Dragmier will be remembered."

The foothills of Raven's Glenn were close by and Kali offered Lamehoof and Stomper a chance to stay and visit Raven's Glenn.

"I've never been to Raven's Glenn" Stomper commented. "Can we visit, Father?"

"For a couple of days, I can use a rest," Lamehoof replied.

"The path through the mountains still waits for us," explained Kali. "The journey is not over yet, we must still travel to where the ravens sleep. Soon we will feast at the tables of Raven's Glenn."

The black fog faded as they made their way out of the Land of the Dead. Once again, the colors of life flourished before them. After walking a short distance, they came to the base of a large mountain range where a new path would lead them to Raven's Glenn.

The path up the mountainside was made of exposed stone and rock, formed over the years by the witches of Raven's Glenn. The walk up the mountainside felt effortless, and the path before them appeared to call out their names as they approached Raven's Glenn.

"The other four high priestesses of Raven's Glenn know we are here and prepare for us," commented Kali.

"How much farther?" asked Talia.

"Within the hour we will arrive," Kali replied.

As they continued up the path, they came to a spot where the path split into two separate directions, left or right.

"Which way do we go?" Kali asked Talia.

"I do not know," replied Talia.

Kali smiled and she asked Talia, "Do we go left, right, or do we go straight ahead? Come, Talia ... think, you must know." Kali pointed straight ahead and said, "Why not straight ahead?"

"There is no path," Talia replied. "How do we go forward with no path?"

"You cannot see, child? Watch!" Kali looked straight ahead and then pointed at the ground. She then chanted:

"Stones in hiding by the gate appear, reveal the path that is so near, and open the gates that blind our path, show us the way and allow us to pass."

The path before them blurred and tricked the eyes; a moment later, the path came back into focus, and a new path leading straight ahead appeared.

"See—we go straight," said Kali. "You will learn to see and learn our ways. Raven's Glenn waits for us at the end of this path, just beyond the second hill."

The mountain path climbed upwards and curved around the first hill. Behind the second hill, the path headed downwards. Off in the distance, surrounded by the mountains in a large valley, a glen appeared.

"Is that Raven's Glenn?" Talia asked. "It looks so beautiful."

Below ... colorful bushes, flowers, trees, and plants intertwined with a clean, well-maintained path made of carefully cut and shaped stones. The path formed a large circle and led to six large round buildings. Each building was made of mountain rock and held together by mud and straw. The pitched roofs were made of carefully trimmed logs tightly tied together, which formed a point high above the center of the buildings. When looking down from the mountains, Raven's Glenn took the shape of a large star with a house located on each point of the star. A large round stone path connected each point of the star and formed a large circle. A large house was located inside of the circle, and a smaller circle made of stone lay near the center of Raven's Glenn. Witches dressed in dark green, brown, black, or white hooded robes, moved freely from house to house and throughout Raven's Glenn. Above in the sky, ravens and hawks circled.

"Looks like a giant star," said Stomper.

Kali quickly turned, exposing the pendant that hung from her neck. The engraved symbols on her pendant matched what they saw below.

"Raven's Glenn and the engraving on your pendant look similar," said Stomper.

"It is our way, the way of the Ancients and the Circle of Life," Kali explained. "Come, we must enter Raven's Glenn."

As they entered Raven's Glenn, dozens of witches dressed in robes or long dresses that fluttered in the breeze rushed out to meet them. Stomper and Lamehoof hesitated and backed up a step. Kali assured them it was safe and no harm would come to them. Relaxed, they smiled as the witches surrounded them. A woman wearing a black hooded robe approached Kali.

"Welcome home, High Priestess. Is this child the chosen one?"

"Yes Priestess Flora, Talia is home. Tomorrow, you and the other high priestesses will prepare our sacred place. We will give thanks to the Ancients. Tonight, we will celebrate under a full moon light. Talia, come with me, I will take you to your new home."

Kali smiled at Talia and whispered, "Rest today and tonight, tomorrow you will begin to learn our ways."

Raven's Glenn glowed that evening. The crackle and flicker of fires and the sounds of laughter echoed off the mountainsides. Later that night, the fires and laughter died. Sunrise would soon appear, and with the arrival of the sun, a new life waited for Talia.

Chapter Two

The glow of the full moon began to fade as the distant sun emerged over the peaks of the eastern mountains. From the still of the early morning, the sounds of an awakening Raven's Glenn brought life to the surrounding mountains and forest.

Covered with a goatskin blanket and asleep on a bed of crushed straw, Talia slowly opened her eyes. The room was dark except for a slight glimmer of light emerging from the edges of the wooden shutters that covered the nearby window. Still half-asleep, she gazed into the darkness and her thoughts were of her mother and father. She could still hear her mother's cries for mercy as the men of darkness murdered her and set fire to her house. Tears filled Talia's eyes as she climbed out of bed and opened the shutters that covered the window. She looked outside and saw several women dressed in brown robes moving from building to building.

"Talia, Talia!" a familiar voice from behind her called out.

Talia turned around and saw Kali standing in the doorway. With the sun's light behind her and dressed in a black and red robe, Kali appeared to glow. Talia wiped the tears from her eyes and looked at Kali. "Am I in Raven's Glenn?" she asked.

"Yes," Kali replied. "Come, Talia; sit next to me on the cot."

Talia walked back to the cot and sat down next to Kali. Kali took Talia's hand into hers and looked into Talia's eyes. "Talia, what you see now is your new life. Raven's

Glenn is your new home and all the people here are your new family."

"I miss my mother and father. Why did they have to die?" Talia asked.

"We do not always understand the ways of the Round of Life," Kali explained. "You must always accept what happens and follow the ways of the Ancients. You are here in Raven's Glenn, you are the chosen one ... chosen by the Ancients before you were born. Talia, someday you will rule Raven's Glenn and battle the forces of darkness. Your power will be great but you must first learn our ways and the secrets of the Ancients. Come, child, we must greet Raven's Glenn, for all are waiting to meet you."

"Kali, I do not want to meet the witches of Raven's Glenn. They will expect too much from me."

"Child, do not worry, everything will be revealed to you in due time, and you will learn our ways. Tomorrow night you will participate in giving thanks to the Ancients. Now come, everyone is waiting."

The witches of Raven's Glenn had gathered outside waiting to see the chosen one. Talia and Kali walked through the doorway and into the light outside. Dozens of witches had gathered and moved closer; the sound of hisses made by the whispers of the witches filled the area. Confused and unable to understand the witches, Talia covered her ears with her hands and closed her eyes; the witches stared at her, pointing, and sometimes laughing. Kali reached down and touched Talia's shoulder. Talia lowered her hands and opened her eyes; her eyes slightly glowed, and the witches gasped and stepped backwards.

"Kali, are they all witches? Am I a witch?"

"Yes, Talia. Standing before you are the witches of Raven's Glenn. No, Talia, you are not yet a witch."

Kali raised her hand for quiet. "Welcome, sisters; my journey was long and, by the will of the Ancients, I have found the chosen one, she who will lead us through our darkest hours."

The witches again crept closer for a better look.

"She's so young!" a witch hissed.

"She's a little girl!" said another.

Angered by the humiliation, Talia shouted back, "I am not a little girl, I am almost thirteen years old, not a child."

Flustered by the witches comments, Talia looked up at Kali, who then spoke, "We will train her and teach her our ways. The power inside her is great. The Ancients have chosen her and we will help prepare her. Blessed be the Ancients, for we are their servants."

All responded, "Blessed be."

Kali took Talia back inside; Talia rested and slept throughout the day and into the night. The next morning arrived quickly, and when the sun first peeked above the mountains, Kali awakened Talia.

"Talia, are you hungry?" Kali asked. "Come, you must eat a morning meal."

A table had been set with various fruits, cheeses, wheat bread, and a vessel of goat's milk. Located next to the fire pit, the table had a place setting for one. Talia sat down and drank from the vessel before reaching for an apple and a piece of bread. Her thoughts focused on the day ahead and what Kali was going to do with her. After eating her fill, Talia stood up and walked to the door; Kali was waiting.

"Come, Talia, we will walk the circle that connects the five points of the star, and visit the five houses."

"Kali, where are Lamehoof and Stomper? I haven't seen them since we arrived in Raven's Glenn."

"Do not worry, Talia, they are still here. Last time I saw them was this morning. I believe they are exploring Raven's Glenn; maybe later you and Stomper can go explore. We have an important ritual tonight; tomorrow you will become my maiden, and act as my servant until you are of age and start your training. Come with me, we go to the northernmost house first."

Raven's Glenn resembled the shape of a pentagram, a five-pointed star, the symbol of the witch's power. A house was located on each point of the star. There was also a house located in the center of the star. A path made of stone called the Circle of Round connected all five houses. In four of the houses lived a high priestess who ruled over her house; each house controlled a source of Raven's Glenn power. The fifth house, the northernmost house, was the House of the Ancients, a sacred place. Kali, high priestess and ruler of Raven's Glenn, lived in the center house and ruled over the other five houses.

Kali and Talia entered the northernmost house, the house of spirits, the House of the Ancients. The room was empty except for a large stone altar located in the center of the room. The walls were ten feet tall and the ceiling came to point sixteen feet high over the center of the room. Four large windows located on the north, south, east, and west walls allowed sunlight to enter and light up the room; with the daily passing of the east to west sun, a moving shadow appeared to follow and pass over the altar. A polished stone floor glittered under the sunlight.

Talia commented, "Why is there nothing in here?"

Kali responded, "This is the place where you will learn about the unknown and the source of our power. This is the house of spirits and visions. The Ancients visit us here, and from here they will guide you."

"I have to learn about visions from something I cannot see?" Talia asked.

Kali laughed and replied, "Yes, Talia, I promise you will understand. The power is within you. You will soon be able to feel the Ancient's presence, and it will become second nature for you to contact and draw from the Ancients when needed. Come, child, we must go to the second house."

The Circle of Round, the path that led to the five houses, was clean, swept daily, and easy to walk on, even with bare feet. Their walk continued to the second house; along the way, awakening their senses, sweet smells arose from the flowers and blended with the crisp morning air. Soon they entered the second house where Priestess Alisa was waiting to greet them.

Born with the powers of a witch, intelligent, and musically minded—she often played a large wooden flute— Priestess Alisa joined Raven's Glenn just before Kali became ruler. Educated in the customs of different lands by passing travelers, she offered insight into the ways of the outside world. Banned from her village for practicing witchcraft, she found Raven's Glenn and soon joined the coven of witches. Once freed from the influence of men, her powers flourished and she became protector of the upper left point of the star.

Tall, thin, with brownish blonde hair and a pale complexion, her speckled hazel-colored eyes appeared to match her colorful taste for clothing. Wearing a green and red robe with a black hood draped back across her shoulders, Priestess Alisa greeted Talia and Kali,

"Welcome, Kali, this must be the chosen one."

"Yes," replied Kali. "Talia, you will learn judgment, wisdom, and insight from Priestess Alisa."

Alisa smiled, "We can start tomorrow!"

"No!" Kali interrupted, "She will be my maiden and learn my ways; only then will I send her to you."

"Remember," Kali explained, "Talia was born with all of our powers. Her powers are great and blessed by the Ancients. We need to awaken her powers, and she must learn how to use the powers of the Five Points of the Star ... the Ancients say it is so."

Alisa bowed and walked them to the door. "Blessed be the Ancients," said Alisa.

"Blessed be," responded Kali.

The third house was located at the lower left point of the star. Walking the Circle of Round, Kali and Talia arrived at the third house.

"Be careful when you are with Priestess Sasa," Kali warned Talia.

A foot shorter then Kali, stubborn and yet wise, Priestess Sasa was the oldest of the high priestesses, arriving at Raven's Glenn long before Kali was born. The previous ruler of Raven's Glenn made her high priestess of the lower left point of the star and for many years, she protected those powers and served Raven's Glenn. Her long snow-white hair, deep black eyes, and stern deep voice commanded attention and separated her from the other witches. Those deep black eyes could see into the soul and few questioned her when she spoke.

They soon entered Sasa's house.

A stern raspy voice called out, "I suppose this skinny little nothing is my next task?"

"Yes, this is the chosen one," Kali replied.

"I see nothing special here!"

Kali frowned and said, "Priestess Sasa will teach you to have patience, strength, and persistence."

"Go, child ... leave my house!" Sasa pointed at the door.

"Kali, I don't think she likes me," said Talia.

"That is her way. You will be wise to do what she says. It is very important that you learn all you can. Someday you will take my place and rule Raven's Glenn. We still have two more houses to visit. Priestess Morra waits for us. She will teach you courage and how to defend yourself."

Priestess Morra, an expert of manmade weapons, taught the other witches how to protect themselves. Raven's Glenn—a coven of witches—used the five points of the star as their power source, was also home to a coven of warrior witches who knew how to defend themselves in case they lost their powers. Priestess Morra was large and strong for a woman—taller than Kali. Her presence intimidated even the men she came across. With thick wrist and strong, firm hands, she felt at ease with a sword or spear, and was a deadly shot with the bow. Her long black hair often covered her dark black eyes, hiding her thoughts and expressions. One never knew which angle she would strike from, giving her the edge in battle, and often surprising her enemies with a deadly blow.

Sunlight flowed in through the shutters that covered the windows in Priestess Morra's house; shadows covered the walls throughout the room. When Talia and Kali entered, an arrow swished past Talia's head and stuck in the wall behind her. Talia immediately fell to the floor, her eyes widened as she tried to see into the shadows that filled the room. Sounds of laughter roared from the darkest shadow located near the back wall. Talia watched in fear as Priestess Morra appeared out of the shadow with bow in hand.

"Get up, my child!" Morra commanded. "You will soon learn to be unafraid of such actions. Your mettle will be tested here."

Kali and Morra both chuckled at the disbelief and fear expressed on Talia's face.

"Why ... why would you shoot an arrow at me?"

"I wanted to see what you would do," laughed Morra. "You will have more control when I am done with you, and hopefully be able to sense such danger before it happens."

As they left to go to the last house, Talia heard the bow bend and turned around just in time to catch Morra aim another arrow at her. Morra, surprised by the blank stare from Talia, lowered the bow. Kali and Morra looked at each other and nodded with approval.

Priestess Flora greeted them at the last house. Wearing a reddish maroon-colored robe—a color extracted from a red berry dye—Priestess Flora stood in the doorway. Her bright red hair, braided into three pigtails and tied together behind her head with a small brown leather cord, glowed in the morning sun. As Talia approached, Priestess Flora smiled kindly and opened her arms; her soft brown eyes beckoned Talia to come closer for a hug. Talia stopped and stared at Priestess Flora.

"Welcome, Talia, what do you feel inside?"

Talia looked at Priestess Flora. "What do you mean?" asked Talia.

"You're feelings ... your emotions control your powers; if you can control your feelings, you will be able to control your powers. What are you feeling now?"

"I feel nothing!"

"You will learn our ways," explained Priestess Flora.

Kali laughed and interrupted, "Priestess Flora will teach you how to control your emotions. Come, Talia, we will go back to my house and prepare for tonight's ritual."

Before they could leave, the house started to shake. Kali's fingers tingled, alerted by an unusual, strange force of power. She looked down at Talia and shouted, "Talia, you need to calm down before you bring down Flora's house!"

Talia looked up at Kali and cried out ... "I do not understand any of this! Not long ago, I was happy and lived with my parents. Witches that demand the impossible now surround me and you want me to calm down. I do not know how to control the power you keep telling me I have."

Talia turned and ran out the door. She was so upset she did not know where she was going, running out of Raven's Glenn, she ran into a meadow full of tall grasses and flowers. Talia stopped and looked around—Raven's Glenn was behind her, mountains and forest before her. With no place to go, she dropped to her knees, then rolled over on her back and stared at the sky. A raven floating on the winds circled high above in the sky. Talia watched as the raven circled around and around; sleepy, her eyelids fluttered, then closed....

Dreaming of her mother, Talia pleaded, "Mother! Please, I want to go home, come back for me."

"Kali will help you," her mother responded. "You are on your way to greatness. This is how it is supposed to be. Listen to Kali and the priestesses of Raven's Glenn, you were born for greatness. Your father and I had to die in order for the prophecies to come true. Trust Kali, wake up daughter—wake up!"

A couple hours later, Talia awakened to the sound of her name and recognized Stomper's voice. She stood up and shouted, "Stomper, Stomper—over here!"

"Everyone is trying to find you, what are you doing here?"

"I feel so alone and confused, what am I supposed to do?"

"You will get use to Raven's Glenn, and it will become routine for you. Everything will be fine once you get used to it."

"Stomper, will you stay in Raven's Glenn with me?"

"I do not know if I can, I need to go home so I can help my father with the crops."

Talia's smile faded and tears appeared in her eyes. Stomper could sense Talia was starting to lose control and quickly said, "We can talk to Kali and my father when we get back to Raven's Glenn."

"Oh, thank you, thank you, Stomper. I will convince Kali that you should stay until I feel safe in Raven's Glenn."

"Hop on, Talia, I need to take you back to Raven's Glenn, everyone is worried about you."

On the way back to Raven's Glenn, Stomper and Talia spotted Kali standing in the meadow, watching them. "I think Kali is upset," whispered Stomper.

"Talia, thank the Ancients I found you! Where did you go? We were all very worried about you."

Stomper interrupted, "I found her over there, in the meadow of flowers, sleeping."

"Thank you, Stomper," replied Kali.

"Kali, I had a dream. My mother was talking to me and told me I would be a great witch. How did my mother know about the Ancients and what is to come?"

"Do you not remember? Your father spoke to you about Raven's Glenn. Both your mother and father knew what was to come and tried to keep it from happening by living away from our kind. Your mother was once one of us; when she fell in love with your father, she decided to leave Raven's Glenn. You have to understand, Talia, you are the chosen one, chosen before birth, and nothing can change that. I am sorry your parents had to die because of it. Your mother was a great witch and missed dearly when she left. The witches of Raven's Glenn did not support her decision to leave. They understood what was to come and when your mother left, she lost her powers and set in motion the prophecy."

Talia could not believe what she was hearing. "Why did she not mention this to me? I do not understand, why did she not tell me?"

"Talia, you are still very young, and for some reason you were meant to be here now. I am sure your mother would have told you when you were older, but the time came sooner instead of later for you to start your journey.

We know not why things happen when they do, they just happen. Your time has come to fulfill the prophecy. Come with me, child, we must go and prepare for tonight."

After Kali and Talia returned to Raven's Glenn, Kali requested that the other four priestesses meet with her at the center house. One by one they arrived, and soon everyone was present.

"Why have you sent for us?" Priestess Morra asked Kali.

Kali responded, "Talia's powers are emerging. Just by being in Raven's Glenn, she is being reborn."

"That explains how she was able to sense my arrow," remarked Priestess Morra.

"And the shaking of my house," said Priestess Flora.

"Yes," explained Kali. "It is time for Talia to know her name ... her witch name, and join us. Tonight, we honor the Ancients and Talia becomes Sorcha."

"Sorcha?" Flora repeated.

"The Ancients selected the name Sorcha," replied Kali, "It is their will, so it will be."

"Blessed be the Ancients," they all responded.

"Now go and prepare the Sacred Circle for tonight," Kali commanded. "You will stand at your points on the star and bring forth the powers of your houses. Tonight, Sorcha is born."

Kali headed towards the northernmost house, the House of the Ancients. Hidden there and protected by the Ancients was her sword, book of spells, and *athame* ... the ritual dagger. The Ancients protected the tools used for rituals, and only the ruler of Raven's Glenn knew the spells that would reveal their hiding place.

After Kali entered the House of the Ancients, she opened her robe and let it drop to the floor; now naked and alone, she stood for a moment and stared at the altar. She then walked up to the altar, removed the pendant from around her neck, and placed it on the altar. Placing both hands on the altar, she closed her eyes and softly chanted ...

"I summon thee from the bright of light, unlock the gates and release the spell, bring forth the secrets that hide so well."

From behind Kali, a small section of ground covered with polished stones appeared to melt away, a dark hole appearing in its place. Kali turned around, reached into the hole, and pulled out a black cloth bag. She removed her *athame* and a dark black and red robe. After she put on the black and red robe, palms facing upwards, she raised both hands towards the ceiling and said out loud,

"I am finished, cover and protect as before."

The gap in the ground closed and Kali placed her pendant back around her neck. Before leaving the northernmost house—the House of the Ancients—Kali gave thanks to the Ancients and then walked out into the waiting sunlight. Priestess Morra approached Kali and informed her that the Sacred Circle was ready for the ritual.

"We will meet one hour before it is time for the ritual," explained Kali. "The moon is full and our powers will be great tonight. I will have Talia prepared in the way of the Ancients. Send Talia to me, we prepare for tonight."

Back in her house, Kali placed the items she would need for later that night on the table. Priestess Sasa had made a black hooded robe sized for Talia and delivered it to Kali.

"Thank you, Sasa," said Kali as she inspected the robe. "Are the oils and herbs ready for the cleansing bath?"

"Yes," replied Priestess Sasa. "And the sandalwood incense will be delivered soon."

"Good, then we are ready. Where is Talia?" Kali asked.

"I am here," replied Talia. "Can Stomper eat with us? I am hungry."

"Stomper must leave. You need to prepare for tonight, we will not eat until after the ritual."

"Can Stomper come with us tonight?"

"No, you can see him tomorrow. Tonight is only for witches. Come, child, you need to rest."

Dusk approached Raven's Glenn. The sky was a reddish orange color. Kali stood over a sleeping Talia and whispered. "Your energy is great, Sorcha. Remember, everything around you is connected. The path lies within you and we will open the path for you. Soon, little one, the time is near."

The hourglass hung in the northernmost house; for every hour that passed after dusk, a bell would ring, until the last hour when the bell would ring twice, a signal for all to join in the circle.

This ritual will be different, Kali thought to herself. *Talia has had no training, yet she has the power of Raven's Glenn inside her. At only thirteen years of the wheel, she has all our powers. Young or not, it is time she became a witch of Raven's Glenn, it is the will of the Ancients, so it must be.*

The first ring of the bell echoed throughout Raven's Glenn. Kali looked up and walked over to the window. She stood there and stared at the sky. Knowing that her time would soon pass, she spoke to the Ancients,

"Guide my hands and words tonight, for we give birth to the chosen one." One hour later, the second bell rang. Kali smiled and lay down to rest.

As the shadows disappeared, the dark of night crept into Raven's Glenn. Kali awoke and walked over to Talia.

"Wake, child, the time is near."

"I am awake. Is it time?"

"It is time to prepare your bath."

The bell rang, and the night grew darker. Kali took Talia to a small round hut located by the Sacred Circle. Here, a large wooden tub had been prepared. The water in the tub came from the sea and rivers, delivered to Raven's Glenn in round wooden barrels. Oils and herbs added to the water gave it color. Talia undressed and lowered herself into the tub while Kali lighted the candles and sandalwood incense that surrounded the tub. Kali raised her *athame*, circled it in the air above Talia, then chanted,

"Blessed be this body and soul. Remove the thoughts that cloud the mind and cleanse from inside out the spiritual self within."

Kali then reached into the tub and pulled out a small wood plug from the bottom of the tub, and the water slowly drained.

"Close your eyes, Talia, and feel the water as it leaves the tub. Your skin will chill as the water drains; with the water goes the old ways. When the tub is empty, you will be rid of the life you had and be ready to accept our ways." Kali reached for the robe Priestess Sasa made.... The bell rang twice.

"Here, Talia," smiled Kali, "is a robe worthy of a witch. Put on the robe and come with me, the time is here."

Witches arrived from throughout the land, but only the witches of Raven's Glenn dare enter the Sacred Circle. Raven's Glenn was aglow with lit torches; visiting witches watched from nearby hills, rooftops, and some even climbed trees to get a view. The hills and mountains surrounding Raven's Glenn sung of activity.

Within the Sacred Circle, the witches of Raven's Glenn gathered around the outline of a large pentagram that covered the ground. The high priestesses took their places on the points of the star. A large altar made of river rock, mountain stone, and clay stood near the center of the pentagram. The glow of lit torches lighted the area while the makings for a fire lay to the side of the altar, waiting for its time to burn.

Kali led Talia to the entrance of the Sacred Circle, before they could enter, Priestess Morra stepped in front of them. Pointing her finger at Talia, she challenged her entering.

"Who comes to our circle?" challenged Priestess Morra.

"It is I, Talia."

"Who speaks for you?"

"It is I, Kali."

Priestess Morra continued. "You are about to enter our Sacred Circle of Stone and witness the powers that be. You are about to step between two worlds, that of what you see and what you do not see. You stand on the threshold of the Ancients. Do you have the courage to enter? For it is best to go back now than enter with fear in your heart."

"Tell her you enter with no fear," nudged Kali.

"I enter with no fear," replied Talia. Kali smiled.

Morra pointed at the Sacred Circle filled with waiting witches and said, "Then enter the circle and thus leave your world—prepare for death and rebirth."

Kali and Talia entered the circle and headed for the altar. Kali placed her *athame* and pendant on the altar, and then firmly secured Talia's hand in hers. Kali turned and faced the gathering of witches.

"Talia is no more," Kali shouted. "The Ancients have given her a witch's name. From this day forward, Talia will be known as Sorcha."

Kali led Sorcha to the upper left point of the pentagram where Priestess Sasa waited.

"Hail Priestess Sasa, guardian of the earth and its point on the star. Behold Sorcha, sent by the Ancients to be made priestess and witch."

"Welcome, Sorcha," said Priestess Sasa, and then she lit a candle and bowed.

Turning to their left, Sorcha and Kali approached Priestess Flora.

"Hail Priestess Flora, guardian of water and its point on the star. Behold Sorcha, sent by the Ancients to be made priestess and witch."

Priestess Flora kissed Sorcha on the forehead, lit a candle, and bowed. Kali and Sorcha moved on to the next point on the star and Priestess Alisa.

"Hail Priestess Alisa, guardian of air and its point on the star. Behold Sorcha, sent by the Ancients to be made priestess and witch."

"Raven's Glenn waits for you," said Priestess Alisa as she lit a candle, bowed, and pointed the way towards the upper right point of the pentagram and Priestess Morra.

"Hail priestess Morra, guardian of fire and its point on the star. Behold Sorcha, sent by the Ancients to be made priestess and witch."

Priestess Morra held Sorcha's face in her hands and looked deep into Sorcha's eyes. "Welcome to Raven's Glenn and our coven, Sorcha. We have waited a long time for this day." Morra stepped back, lit a candle, and bowed.

Kali and Sorcha continued to the uppermost point of the pentagram. Kali released Sorcha's hand and stood facing Sorcha. The other four priestesses shouted, "Hail Priestess Kali, ruler of Raven's Glenn, guardian of spirit, and protector of the House of the Ancients. Behold Sorcha, sent by the Ancients to be made priestess and witch." Kali lit a fifth candle, bowed, and guided Sorcha back to the altar.

Kali knelt at the altar and kissed Sorcha's hand.

"Are you willing to swear the oath?" asked Kali.

Sorcha replied, "I am."

"Are you willing to suffer if need be and learn of Raven's Glenn and the Ancients?"

"I am," Sorcha replied again.

Kali stood and retrieved her *athame* from the altar.

"Hold out your hand, Sorcha."

Sorcha offered her hand to Kali. Kali cut her finger with the tip of the knife. Blood oozed out of the cut and a few drops fell at her feet.

"Kneel!" Kali commanded. "And repeat after me ... say what I say."

"I, Sorcha, do of my own free will promise to protect and defend all that is Raven Glenn, and to keep secret all that must not be revealed. This I swear on my mother's grave and my hopes of future lives."

Sorcha repeated the oath and Kali shouted out, "So it must be!"

"So it must be!" shouted the coven of witches.

Kali stepped to the side and ordered Sorcha to stand. The coven of witches rushed forward and grabbed Sorcha. They lifted her into the air and carried her three times around the circle, ending at the altar. Kali placed Sorcha on the altar and the witches shouted, "Sorcha!"

Kali stepped forward and spoke, "Sorcha, the hands that touched you are the hands of Raven's Glenn; thus you are brought into our world, and thus you are brought into our coven. Behold, guardians of the points, behold Ancients of the past, and behold witches of Raven's Glenn, it is as the Ancients have willed, so it must be. Behold Sorcha!"

"So it must be!" shouted the witches.

Kali pointed at the stack of wood that was prepared earlier and shouted. "Light the fire and bring forth the vessels of wine, for we celebrate a new witch in Raven's Glenn tonight!"

The mountainsides around Raven's Glenn echoed with laughter and song, and the witches of Raven's Glen danced and drank by the fire and moonlight until early morning.

Kali led Sorcha to her house ... the centermost house of Raven's Glenn, and put her to bed. After Sorcha fell asleep, Kali started to leave—when the image of Celeste appeared in the room. The Ancients sent one of their own to deliver a warning and Celeste of Greythorn arrived to deliver it.

"Celeste ... I mean, Mother, what are you doing here?" asked Kali.

"There is danger surrounding Raven's Glenn. An evil source is searching for Sorcha. You must—and I mean must not—allow her out of your sight. Someone must be with her at all times. We do not yet know what the danger is."

"I have not sensed anything unusual, Mother—are you sure?" asked Kali.

Kali thought about the witches camped throughout the surrounding hills.

As if Celeste could read Kali's mind, she responded, "The other witches will be fine. They are only after Sorcha. Be careful—and please protect your sister. I have to go now. Heed my warning."

"I will warn the other priestesses," replied Kali.

Celeste's image and voice began to fade, and, with a faint voice, she said, "You must teach Sorcha to use her inner powers. Until then ... protect her."

Several hours had passed since Kali received Celeste's warning. The night's celebrations had passed and the sun's morning light now flickered over the eastern mountains. Kali went to find the other priestesses and found Priestess Morra in a panic ... wild with worry. Kali listened while Priestess Morra explained that Sorcha was gone ... nowhere to be found. Kali remembered Celeste's warning.

"I just had a conversation with Celeste. She had warned us not to let Sorcha out of our sight," explained Kali. "Sorcha is in great danger. There is something dark and evil searching for her. We must find her and bring her back inside Raven's Glenn where she will be safe. Hurry, we must find her."

Meanwhile, Sorcha had wandered outside the protection of Raven's Glenn. As she walked along the foothills enjoying her freedom, she heard a growling-snarling noise coming from behind a cluster of bushes. Rounding the corner of bushes, she saw a young woman crouched over with something in her hands. Sorcha, a little startled and hesitant, asked the woman if she was in pain. Startled, the woman quickly stood and hid something behind her back.

"Hello," she said, "my name is Chaela, and no, I am fine."

"Are you one of the visiting witches?" asked Sorcha.

Chaela thought about the question for a moment and hesitated, being careful not to alert Sorcha of her true intentions, she answered. "Yes, yes, I am. I have traveled a great distance to watch the ritual last night, Sorcha."

"How ... how do you know my name?" asked Sorcha.

Chaela laughed, "Everyone here knows your name. Was it not shouted at the ritual last night?"

"Why don't you come back to Raven's Glenn with me?" asked Sorcha. "I could use another friend."

"I wish I could, Sorcha, but I am afraid I am not really welcome in Raven's Glenn. That is why I am out here."

"But if you are a witch, why would you not be welcome in Raven's Glenn? All the other witches are welcome there."

"Let's keep this meeting a secret for now," replied Chaela. "If you would like, we can meet here on occasion and get to know each other a little better."

Sorcha's eyes lit up as she smiled and said, "Oh, yes, and I won't tell anyone I saw you ... I promise. I must go—someone is calling my name. Please meet me here again in two nights time, while the moon is still high and bright."

Chaela nodded and replied, "As you wish, Sorcha." Chaela watched as Sorcha ran towards the call of her name. Once Sorcha was out of sight, Chaela looked down at the rabbit in her hand and thought, *I must go further into the mountains to feed. That was too close.*

After Sorcha left, Chaela noticed her brother Aleric was hiding several yards away behind a large cluster of bushes.

"Aleric, what are you doing here?" Chaela asked.

Aleric walked out from behind the bushes and replied, "I wanted to make sure you were doing what you were told to do, and that you made contact with the little witch."

"Yes, I have," hissed Chaela. "And I will continue to meet with her till I can earn her trust, then I will bring her to you."

In a flash, Aleric grabbed Chaela by the neck and warned her, "You had better watch that tone. I will snap your neck faster than you can blink. I am the quicker of us."

With gritted teeth, Chaela replied, "I am well aware of that, Aleric, you keep reminding me. Now, if you would kindly let me go, I have a witch to watch."

Aleric let go of Chaela's neck and snarled, "I will be watching you."

Meanwhile, Sorcha heard Stomper call out her name and yelled back, "Stomper, Stomper, where are you?"

"Sorcha, there you are," replied Stomper. "The priestesses are worried about you. It is not safe for you outside of Raven's Glenn. Come, we must hurry back."

Kali spotted Sorcha and Stomper as they entered Raven's Glenn. With a stern look, Kali approached Sorcha and scolded her. "You must not leave Raven's Glenn without permission. Do not leave again."

"You are not my mother!" Sorcha yelled and ran towards Kali's house.

Kali slowly turned and whispered, "No—I am your sister."

Stomper slowly looked up at Kali and Kali realized she was overheard. "I will explain later, Stomper. For now, she does not need to know."

"It is not my place to tell her.... I will not say a word. If you do not mind, I would like to stay here in Raven's Glenn and help you keep her safe."

Chapter Three

*P*riestess Alisa's patience was just about at an end; it was time to find Kali and Sorcha. *They were supposed to be here early this morning*, Alisa thought. The sun was now straight up, and the day seemed over. Leaving her house, Alisa walked towards the center of the round, heading for Kali's house. As Alisa glanced at the mountainside, Sorcha emerged from the tall grasses at the base of the mountain.

"Sorcha, Sorcha!" Alisa shouted out.

Sorcha heard Priestess Alisa and waved. Still upset by Kali's nagging, she wondered what Priestess Alisa could possibly want with her, and decided to run away in the opposite direction. Sorcha took two steps to the left ... right into Priestess Alisa.

"How—where did you...?" muttered Sorcha.

"And where did you think you were going?" Alisa interrupted.

"How did you get here so fast? You were over there and now here ... how?"

"Grab hold of me, Sorcha, embrace me, and clear your mind of all thoughts."

Sorcha put her arms around Priestess Alisa. With her eyes closed, she cleared her mind. A white light filled her head, and her feet tingled.

"Your body feels as light as a feather," Alisa whispered. "Do not feel the ground below your feet, only feel the air around you. Focus on my house, Sorcha. Slowly open your eyes. Do you see my house up ahead?"

"Yes!" Sorcha replied.

"We need to go there, so think it, Sorcha. Focus on my house, and will yourself there."

In her mind, Sorcha could see the front door and tried to move towards it. A flash of bright light entered her mind; everything around her turned whitish blue, and then the door appeared in front of her. She reached out and touched the door.

"Very good ... very good," repeated Alisa.

Her normal senses quickly returned, and Sorcha felt as she did before the trance.

"That was fun. Can we do it again?" Sorcha asked.

"Not now, Sorcha. You must experience the room of mirrors today. Come inside and we will prepare, the sun is just about in the right position to begin."

Once inside, Priestess Alisa took Sorcha to a dark room hidden by a secret door. A bale of straw waited in the center of the room. Alisa asked Sorcha to sit on the bale of straw while she blindfolded her.

"Do not remove the blindfold until I tell you. Do you understand?"

"Yes," replied Sorcha.

"You will see me again when the time is right. Remember, do as I say—when I say it."

Priestess Alisa left Sorcha, walked into another room, and looked out a window at the sky. *The sun is just about at the right angle*, Alisa thought to herself. It was time to allow the sun's light into Sorcha's room. Alisa pulled on a rope that hung from the ceiling; a long narrow gap in the roof above Sorcha opened, and light entered through the gap, exposing the walls of mirrors.

"Remove your blindfold, Sorcha—remove your blindfold, and come to me," Alisa commanded.

Sorcha removed her blindfold and stood up. *What is this?* Sorcha thought, *I am surrounded by mirrors. Where is the door?* Trapped within the mirrors, Sorcha panicked. She shouted for help and started pushing on the mirrors. Alisa called out and told Sorcha to relax and think about her situation.

"You have an obstacle in front of you. All you can see is yourself. What do you do?" Alisa asked Sorcha.

Sorcha looked into the mirror and saw fear—her fear. She looked around at all her reflections and laughed. *How silly of me*, Sorcha thought, *the way out is behind me in the mirrors*. Sorcha started breaking the mirrors and soon discovered an open door. She walked through the doorway and found a smiling Alisa waiting for her.

"Sorcha, you have just learned that when there is an obstacle in your way, even if that obstacle is you, what do you do?"

"I break things," replied Sorcha.

"No!" Alisa replied. "You do not go around, under, or over an obstacle, you conquer your fears. Use your instinct and judgment, and find the best way to get through it. Today, you learned how to transport yourself, deal with obstacles, and see beyond yourself. It is time for you to go to Kali's house. I will see you tomorrow—on time, I hope."

"Yes Priestess Alisa, I will be on time."

Sorcha said goodbye to Priestess Alisa and headed for Kali's house. As Sorcha walked the round, a voice from behind her asked, "How was your day with Priestess Alisa?"

Sorcha turned around and looked at Kali. "Watch this!" said Sorcha, and she lowered her head and closed her eyes. A bright light filled her mind as she concentrated on the image of Kali's house. Sorcha disappeared as she traveled within the light, reappearing in front of Kali's home, with Kali standing next to her.

"I see your day went well. Remember, Sorcha, you only use your powers when you must. I will not have a lazy witch living with me. Next time, we walk home."

"Yes," replied Sorcha. "Kali, can you travel like that anywhere, or is it just here in Raven's Glenn?"

"You can travel just about anywhere like that, Sorcha. Why do you ask?"

"Is that how you found me?" Sorcha asked.

Kali, startled by this question, lowered her head and said, "I traveled that way for a while. You cannot travel undetected through the land of the dead, and there are other places where teleporting yourself will not work. It is tricky. You will learn where you can and cannot travel. I really am sorry I was not in time to save Mother. There is food prepared for you inside. You must eat and rest."

Sorcha, distracted by other thoughts, did not hear Kali's comment about her mother. After she ate her meal, she went to bed. Kali breathed a sigh of relief and thought, *I will see you in the morning. Sorcha, you have more to learn tomorrow.*

Sorcha laid awake for what seemed like hours before she heard Kali finally go to bed. *I wonder if this will work,* she thought to herself as she closed her eyes and concentrated on the place she last saw Chaela. A bright light filled her mind and a feeling of forward motion overpowered her. Traveling within the light, she was there. Sorcha looked around. This is going to be easy she thought. Maybe I will be able to sneak Chaela back into Raven's Glenn.

Her sleep filled with dark dreams, a restless Kali awakened. Covered in a cold sweat, she slowly sat up and lit a candle located on a table next to her bed. The flicker of candlelight cast strange shadows on the walls and ceiling ... holding Kali's thoughts captive. Kali watched the shadows dance across the walls and remembered her dream of a darkness that awaited Sorcha. Worried, Kali decided to look in on Sorcha.

Satisfied that she could transport herself, Sorcha, thought of her bed and stepped forward; a bright light engulfed her mind, and she was back in bed.

Kali approached Sorcha's bed. Sorcha's eyes met Kali's.

"You are awake!" commented Kali.

"I was thinking about Priestess Alisa," lied Sorcha.

"You must rest. Go to sleep, Sorcha."

While Sorcha turned on her side and closed her eyes, Kali looked over at her and whispered, "Be careful of what you do. Be very careful, Sorcha."

The early morning sun began to glow behind the mountaintops. Priestess Alisa awakened to a sound by her door.

"Who is there?" she called out.

"Sorcha!"

"Come in ... come in. In the name of the Ancient's, child, why are you here so early?"

"You said to be early and on time," replied Sorcha. "You did not tell me what time, so I am early."

Priestess Alisa shook her head and pointed at a wooden bucket by the door. "Fetch water from the well while I prepare for the day. Now go, do as I say." After Sorcha left, Priestess Alisa commented aloud, "I best take a little smartness out of that little witch."

After Sorcha returned with a bucket of water, Priestess Alisa prepared a cup of broth. "We will hike into the mountains today," Alisa told Sorcha. "You will learn that not all paths lead to the same end. What you see is not what you see, but what you see is what you see."

"What?" asked Sorcha.

"You will see," replied a smiling Alisa.

Casting morning shadows under its path, the light from a new day's sun reached Raven's Glenn. Priestess Alisa and Sorcha had already begun their journey up the mountain path. After a long walk, they came to a clearing.

"We will rest here," said Alisa.

Sorcha looked around and realized she was near the place she and Chaela were supposed to meet later that night.

Alisa called out to Sorcha. "Look around, Sorcha, how many paths do you see?"

"One!" replied Sorcha.

"There are several."

"I do not see them," replied Sorcha.

"That is because you do not see what you see."

"I do not understand," replied Sorcha. "Where are these paths?"

"The paths are hidden by spells cast by the witches of Raven's Glenn. You have the insight to see through most spells and the power to undo their magic. Close your eyes and feel the warmth from the sun, feel the earth under your feet, feel the breeze as it flows through your hair. Smell the air, touch the air, reach out and touch the air that is around you."

Sorcha began to relax. Her senses seemed to come alive. She could hear the sounds of birds flying above and the grass swaying at her feet.

"Open your eyes," ordered Alisa, "and see for the first time."

Sorcha opened her eyes and the sights before her came into focus. The images were crisp, clear, and vivid. What was far away was now close, what was close was now larger. Six paths appeared in front of her, each leading in a different direction.

"Select a path, Sorcha, and go explore. I will wait here for you."

Before Sorcha decided which path to take, she thought of Chaela. *The center path should lead to our meeting place*, she thought. Taking the center path, Sorcha found Chaela waiting at the place where they first met.

"Chaela, we are not supposed to meet until tonight. What are you doing here?" asked Sorcha.

Chaela smiled and called for Sorcha to come closer. "What are you doing here?" asked Chaela.

"I am with Priestess Alisa, so I can't stay long. Will you meet me here tonight—like we planned?" asked Sorcha.

Chaela quickly asked, "How long have you lived in Raven's Glenn?"

Sorcha responded, "I have seen the full moon come and go several times, I am entering my fourteenth year of age.

The witches of Raven's Glenn watch and care for me constantly, meeting you again after tonight might become more difficult. Do not forget, when the moon is high and bright, meet me here tonight."

"I will be here, Sorcha, do not worry."

"Sorcha, Sorcha!" Alisa called out. "Where are you?"

"Priestess Alisa looks for me, I must go."

"I am here!" cried out Sorcha, and soon, the two met on the path.

"It is time to return to Raven's Glenn," said Alisa. "Today, you learned how to sense and see through a spell. You have released the sight within you and you can see what you do not see."

"Do we have to walk back to Raven's Glenn?" Sorcha asked.

"Yes, Sorcha. Remember, we only use our powers when we must."

Sorcha and Priestess Alisa began their walk down the path towards Raven's Glenn. When they passed an area of tall grasses, Sorcha stopped.

"I hear movement in the grass," whispered Sorcha and pointed towards the area where the grass was parting. "See, it's over there!"

Alisa turned to look just as a wolf emerged from the tall grass and ran off in the opposite direction.

"That was close," said Priestess Alisa.

"I do not feel that the wolf meant to harm us," argued Sorcha. "The wolf was just watching and following me."

"Nonsense," replied Alisa.

"You taught me to see these things. I know what I felt and saw."

"Come, Sorcha, it is late, and we must hurry. Priestess Kali is waiting."

Night had started to settle over Raven's Glenn. The torches glowed, and the fire pits were ablaze when Sorcha and Alisa arrived. Sorcha looked ahead and commented,

"I see Kali coming this way."

Alisa grumbled, "We are late, Priestess Kali will be upset with us."

"Your training in the mountains went well today?" Kali asked.

"Yes, Sorcha is ready to move on to the next house," replied Priestess Alisa. "On the way back, we came across a wolf and Sorcha insisted the wolf was following her."

"Oh, a wolf?" Kali asked ... her eyes wide. "We must keep closer hands on Sorcha. The night has a feel to it, and I feel we are being watched."

As the night grew darker, Chaela arrived at the place she would meet with Sorcha. Circling the ground, she marked her spot and fed on a freshly killed rabbit. A white haze of light appeared in front of her and the voice of an Ancient sounded from within the haze.

"We know what and who you are, Chaela, and we have the power to destroy you where you stand."

In a blur, Chaela was on her feet, blood dripping from her now visible fangs. "I am not so easy to kill," she replied.

"You are on Raven's Glenn soil. Your power is limited here—behold!"

The area around Chaela lit up as if the sun had awakened. Chaela screamed out in burning pain, "Stop ... help me ... stop it!" She cried out. "What do you want of me?"

"Do you know of Sorcha?" the Ancient teased with the question.

"Yes, she is my friend, I wish her no harm," cried Chaela. "Please! Stop the pain. I am dying."

The brightness of the light faded and the voice from within the haze continued, "You must promise never to try and harm Sorcha, and you must protect her from your kind. Do you understand?"

"She is my friend," Chaela responded. "I have no reason to harm her. How can I protect her during the light hours?"

"While on Raven's Glenn soil, you will be protected, and the light that shines will never fully reach you. Harm Sorcha and you will die in the light's burning fire."

Chaela looked around; the haze vanished, and she felt a cool breeze sweep over her.

"Chaela," a voice called out.

"Sorcha! You are early."

"I told Kali I was taking a walk and must return soon. Will you meet me here later than planned?"

"Yes, Sorcha. Let us meet two hours past the witches' moon. Everyone should be sleeping by then."

"The priestesses look for me. I must go," Sorcha replied.

Chaela watched as Sorcha disappeared on the path back to Raven's Glenn, and as she looked around, she thought to herself, *What am I going to do about Aleric?*

Kali greeted Sorcha as she entered the center house. "Come, Sorcha, your dinner waits. Tomorrow, Priestess Alisa will take you to Priestess Flora's house. Tell me about the wolf you saw today."

"Priestess Alisa said I am wrong but I know that wolf was following me."

"When did you notice that the wolf was following you?" asked Kali.

Sorcha thought to herself ... *Right after I left Chaela*, but said aloud, "When we were on the path home."

"Eat your dinner and go to bed early tonight," replied Kali. "You have a full day tomorrow. I will spend the night in the northern house. The Ancients and I must discuss matters. Goodnight, Sorcha."

Sorcha watched Kali leave and knew she was up to something, but that would have to wait for another time. Right now, it was time to meet Chaela. Sorcha closed her eyes and visualized the clearing by the path where she and Chaela had been meeting. A cool breeze swept across her face and, in an instant, she was there—as was Chaela. Chaela had just transformed from wolf form and was wiping blood from her lips when Sorcha arrived.

"Chaela ... Chaela! What are you doing?" asked Sorcha.

Chaela froze, and then lowered her head. "Sorcha, I am sorry, you were not meant to find out like this."

Sorcha looked at Chaela and said, "Chaela, please ... it's okay. I knew you were not a witch. It was you following me in the form of a wolf. Why didn't you just tell me?"

"You are right, Sorcha, I should have told you. There are things I cannot control, and I don't know where to begin."

"You can start with telling me what you are," said Sorcha.

"I am a vampire." Chaela replied. "I was turned when I was eighteen, over 200 years ago. I came from a royal family. I could not help it. I was young, and he was so handsome...."

Sorcha realized Chaela's mind was in the past but waited patiently while she told her story.

"By the time I knew what was happening, it was too late. I remembered waking up with the strangest feeling, and there he was. I asked him what had happened, and that was when he told me what he was and what he had done. I have spent the last 200 years running from him, only he keeps finding me ... I haven't the strength to hide from him."

Sorcha took a deep breath and asked, "Who is the other one with you?"

Chaela's head popped up at the question. "You know there is another?"

"Well, yes, there is a presence similar to yours—who is it?" asked Sorcha.

"Aleric" said Chaela. "He is here to make sure I bring you to Volac."

"Volac—is he the one who turned you?" asked Sorcha.

"Yes. I do not know what to do. You are my friend. I don't know how to hide from him, and I can't take you to him either."

"I will figure out how we can hide you, but for now you have to act like you are still going to take me to Volac. We will figure this out, but you will have to give me time. I have to go, it will be morning soon, and I really need to get back to Raven's Glenn before they discover I am gone.

Meet me here at the same time in two days and, hopefully, I will have something figured out."

"I will be here," Chaela replied.

Sorcha felt restless and tossed around in her bed. A few minutes ago, she had made a promised to help Chaela—but how? Maybe tomorrow she would find the answer.

"Wake up, Sorcha!" a voice called out from the doorway. Priestess Flora and Alisa entered her room.

"Priestess Flora is here to take you to her house," Alisa explained.

"Come with me, Sorcha," Priestess Flora commanded. "You need to learn how to control that temper of yours— we start today."

Kali entered the room. "Why are you all here?" she asked.

"We have come for Sorcha. She is late," the Priestesses replied.

Kali looked at Sorcha and decided to say nothing, but thought, *We must watch her. She leaves us during the night.*

"Come with me," said Priestess Flora, "my house waits for us."

Kali watched as the three walked away towards Flora's house. The morning dew on the round path mirrored their reflections, and Kali realized Sorcha was almost the same size as Flora and Alisa. All three images appeared to waver in their own reflections as they walked away.

The air had a slight morning chill to it as they walked in silence. When they approached Flora's house, Sorcha glanced to her right and saw several witches throwing stones and beating on Stomper with branches, attacking

Stomper. Her eyes widened in shock and disbelief as she pointed towards the witches.

"Stop them! They are hurting Stomper! Stop it!" shouted Sorcha.

In a blink, Sorcha grabbed the closest witch. "Stop it!" she yelled.

The ground began to shake under them as Sorcha's anger increased. A slight glow appeared in Sorcha's eyes.

"Now," whispered Priestess Flora. The two priestesses grabbed Sorcha and tossed a sheepskin sack over her. The trap had worked.

The sudden acts of aggression took Sorcha by surprise. Fear overpowered her emotions, and the darkness within the sack led to panic. Sorcha started to kick and scream, her powers blocked by her own confusion.

"Calm yourself, Sorcha," whispered Priestess Flora. "Calm yourself and control your fear and anger."

Sorcha controlled her breathing first, and slowly began to accept there was nothing to fear. With her anger now diminished, and in control of her fear, her powers returned. In an instant, Sorcha was standing next to Priestess Alisa and Flora, all three staring at the empty sack.

"Well! What took you so long to get out of the sack?" Priestess Flora asked.

Alisa laughed, and then pointed at Sorcha, "You sounded like a crying baby goat."

Both priestesses started laughing at Sorcha. Again, the anger started to build within her.

"No, no, no!" Priestess Flora shouted out. "Watch that anger.... Remember the sack."

Alisa fell down laughing. Sorcha realized what had just happened and started to laugh also. *Control* ... Sorcha thought to herself. *Feel it, know it, and always control your fears and anger.*

As if reading Sorcha's mind, Priestess Flora commented, "Remember the sack."

"Stomper! What about Stomper?" Sorcha asked.

"That was a trick," responded Flora. "We needed to make you angry and then cloud your anger with fear to weaken your powers."

"And it worked!" Alisa laughed aloud.

Priestess Flora interrupted, "Sorcha, will you come to my house with me? A guest waits for you at my house—enough teasing."

The smell of incense greeted them as they entered Priestess Flora's house. Flora asked Sorcha to sit in front of the fire and watch the flames flicker. Sorcha sat and stared at the flames while Priestess Flora sprinkled a bluish powder over the flames.

"Clear your mind, Sorcha. Behold."

The room filled with a white and yellow haze. A voice from the fire called out ...

"Talia, Talia."

"Mother!" Sorcha called out.

The voice became clearer, and the image of Sorcha's mother appeared.

"Mother!"

"Child, the Ancients are pleased with you. Remember, I am always with you."

"Mother, come back!" Sorcha cried out, but the image faded, and the crackling sounds of the fire returned. Sorcha stood and turned towards the door and there stood Kali.

"Kali, my mother was here."

"It is time to go," Kali replied.

A tear fell from Kali's cheek and melted into the dirt floor. *Someday soon*, Kali thought to herself, *I will tell Sorcha the truth about our mother*.

Sorcha and Kali returned to Kali's house. Stomper was there waiting for them.

"Stomper!" Sorcha shouted. "Are you all right? Why did you let them do that to you?"

"Yes, I am all right. I needed to let the witches pretend to hurt me so that you would learn to control your emotions.... It was their plan. I had to make you think they were hurting me. If you do not learn to control your emotions, you will not be able to control your powers, and you could hurt those who you care about."

Sorcha looked at Stomper and replied. "I guess you are right. I will try to control myself."

Later that evening, Sorcha and Stomper went for a walk, and Stomper asked, "What are you thinking? You seem distracted. Is everything all right?"

Sorcha stopped walking and looked at Stomper before she responded, "I have a secret, but I need some help. If I tell you, will you promise not to tell Kali?"

Stomper rubbed his chin with his hand and replied, "I cannot promise, but I can promise to do what I can to help you."

Sorcha took a short gasp of air and replied, "I have a friend who is in trouble and needs my help."

Stomper asked, "Why is that a secret? I am sure Kali can help. Which one of the witches is it?"

"That's the problem, Stomper. She is not a witch. She is a vampire."

Stomper stared at Sorcha. He could not decide if she was telling him the truth or just joking with him, trying to get even for what happened earlier that day. Finally, he decided she was telling him the truth.

"Where ... how, did you meet a vampire, and when?"

"I met her the day after the ritual. I was walking in the mountains and there she was. I have been secretly meeting her at night. She has become my friend, and now she is in trouble."

"A vampire—I find that hard to believe. What kind of trouble can a vampire be in?"

"Are you done doubting me? Listen to me. Her name is Chaela—she was sent here by a vampire named Volac."

"VOLAC!" Stomper shouted, "Did you say Volac? 'Land of the Dead ...' Volac. Sorcha, this is not good; you cannot keep sneaking off to meet a vampire. If Volac is near, we must tell Kali."

"Listen, Stomper, Volac is not here. He sent Chaela and a vampire named Aleric to watch over Chaela and make sure she follows his orders. Chaela is not strong enough to hide her presence from Aleric, and I am afraid of what might happen if I do not help her. I need to find a concealment spell or something until I can figure out what else to do. Please, Stomper, she is my friend."

"When do you meet with her again?" Stomper asked.

"Come with me, I will show you our meeting place," Sorcha replied.

From the House of the Ancients, the northernmost house, Kali summoned the other high priestesses to discuss her suspicions about the wolf that was hiding in the surrounding hills and about Sorcha sneaking out at night. "Sisters, I feel I am failing in keeping Sorcha safe. I cannot keep an eye on her all times of the day, and it is not safe for her to be sneaking out during the day or at night. I need to put a spell on her room so she cannot use the powers she possesses. It will have to be a very powerful spell in order for her not to break it. I have called you here to help me. With all our powers, we will create such a spell. I am sure that the wolf Sorcha saw and her sneaking around late at night are related. Until I know for sure what Sorcha is up to, a spell on her room is our best option."

The other four priestesses from the Points of the Star agreed.

"Priestesses," Kali continued, "with all five of our combined powers, we can cloak Sorcha's powers,"

Priestess Sasa reminded the others, and added, "We five are the powers that come from the points of the star, and we are the protectors of Raven's Glenn. It is the way of the Ancients, the way of Raven's Glenn."

"Then it is settled," Kali replied. "We begin now, before it is too late."

The five priestesses gathered in a circle near the center of the room. Holding hands so as not to weaken their powers, they walked in a circular movement to the left.

Kali chanted ...

"We the power of five, circle to the left, we combine our powers to halt Sorcha's quest."

After they complete several circles, Kali changed direction and chanted ...

"We the power of five, circle to the right, we cloak Sorcha's powers from working at night."

After several circles to the right, they stopped, and Kali moved to the center of the circle. Holding her hands above her head, slowly spinning to the right, Kali chanted in a soft voice,

"Under the moon's glow we ask of thee, Sorcha's powers will no longer be. With the rising sun of each new day, restore the powers we took away."

All the priestesses raised their hands towards the sky and chanted together.

"We ask the Ancients to hear our plea, to protect the chosen one, it must be."

A great white light engulfed the room and faded as fast as it appeared.

"It is done," said Kali. "Now we must discover what Sorcha has done, for I sense she is in danger."

Near the edge of the mountain, Sorcha was taking Stomper to where she and Chaela meet.

"Sorcha, how far are we going?" Asked Stomper

"Just over the next hill," Sorcha replied. "I do not know if she will be there. It is daylight."

After a few minutes, they reached the clearing where Sorcha and Chaela had been meeting.

"Chaela!" Sorcha shouted. "Chaela, you are safe! I brought my friend Stomper with me, and I promise you he will not harm you."

Sorcha and Stomper heard a rustling noise coming from an area of tall grasses. The grasses parted and a wolf appeared.

"Sorcha, stop, do not go near it!" Stomper warned.

"Nonsense," replied Sorcha. "Chaela, please, you are safe, I promise."

In a flash, there stood Chaela. Stomper quickly took a few steps back and stared at her.

"Stomper, are you okay?" asked Sorcha.

"I did not know vampires could change into wolves," Stomper replied.

Chaela smiled and explained, "Actually, vampires can change into any animal they choose. My choice is a wolf. I find it harder to be found but, unfortunately, not impossible."

A sinister deep rich laugh surrounded them. Stomper yelled for Sorcha and Chaela to hop on and hold on tight.

"Hold on tight, we're getting out of here!" Stomper cried out.

At a full gallop, Stomper tried to run down the hill and into the open meadow, but slowed to a crawl.

"Stomper, what is it? Why are we not going anywhere?" Sorcha cried out.

"I ... I can't move," Stomper replied. "Some kind of invisible wall is holding me back."

"Wait!" Chaela shouted.

Chaela hopped off Stomper and ran into the meadow; suddenly, she stopped and stared across the open meadow. A voice from across the meadow cried out,

"You cannot hide from me, Chaela!"

"Aleric," Chaela whispered.

Aleric appeared on the other side of the meadow. When he tried to enter the meadow, the same invisible wall stopped him.

"Very clever ... little witch," Aleric snarled.

"But I'm not doing it," Sorcha replied.

"If you did not create this barrier, who did?" Aleric demanded.

Sorcha saw a shimmer of light out of the corner of her eye and turned to look.

"Kali ... how ... how did you find us?" Sorcha asked.

"It is not hard when you know what to look for. It is a good thing I decided to look for you. I expected more from you, Stomper. You were sworn to protect Sorcha, and here you are in the middle of a vampire feud."

"It is not what it looks like," replied Stomper.

Sorcha interrupted. "Stomper, stop.... Please, Kali, it is not Stomper's fault. I brought him here, hoping he could help me. I can't explain right now."

Aleric laughed and pointed at Chaela. "You are smarter than I give you credit for. Volac will not be happy."

Chaela started to respond, but Aleric vanished.

Not taking her eyes off Chaela and with a stern look on her face, Kali approached Sorcha and Stomper.

"Stomper, I want you and Sorcha to head back to Raven's Glenn. I will follow shortly."

Sorcha panicked and replied, "Kali ... please, you can't hurt her, she is my friend, and I know she will not hurt any of us."

"Sorcha, I am aware of that. I will do what I can to help Chaela. She plays a big part in your future, and I must keep her safe, at least until I can talk to the Ancients about her. Now, go!"

Sorcha jumped on Stomper's back and took one last look at Chaela before they galloped off towards Raven's Glenn. Priestess Flora and Alisa were waiting, and greeted them when they arrived.

"Where have you been?" Alisa asked Sorcha.

Stomper quickly responded with a lie, "We took a walk so I could tell Sorcha about the trick we played on her."

The priestesses laughed. "Come with us, Sorcha," demanded Priestess Flora, "we have something at the house for you."

"Can Stomper come with us?" Sorcha asked.

"Not now, you can meet with Stomper later in the day," Flora replied.

After arriving at Flora's house, Alisa signaled Flora that she had something to tell her and asked Flora if she would walk her home so she could discuss the day's events with her. Priestess Flora nodded in agreement, and asked Sorcha to wait outside until she returned. As the two witches departed, Sorcha heard a voice coming from inside Flora's house and walked over to the window to peek inside. As she approached the window, Sorcha heard her name mentioned and snuck under the window to listen.

"Oh, that Sorcha!"

"You mean the little brat."

"Kali's little pet for sure."

Sorcha could hear several witches inside talking about her so she peeped into the window and listened.

A hooded witch stoking the fire commented next. "If that little brat was a rat, she would be owl food in a witch's blink."

"As dumb as a dead oak branch for sure," another claimed.

"Kali's pet dog," another said.

"The chosen one!" They all laughed.

"She still wets herself, like a baby," another witch commented aloud.

"Sorcha has been with us for three years." The witch stoking the fire said, "She is now sixteen passes on the wheel of life and she still acts like a little girl, future ruler of Raven's Glenn ... my rear end." Again they laughed.

"Sorcha!" A voice from behind her called out.

"What are you doing?" Priestess Flora asked.

Sorcha turned around, her eyes full of tears, a pain in her chest. "They all hate me!" Sorcha cried out.

"Who hates you?" Priestess Flora asked.

"The witches of Raven's Glenn hate me, the witches in your house," Sorcha whimpered.

Flora looked in the window and said, "I see no witches."

Alarmed, Sorcha jumped to the window and looked inside.

"But I heard them talking about me. They said awful things about me."

"And you're crying because your feelings are hurt?" Priestess Flora asked. "What if you overheard the Lord of Darkness making fun of you, or that he wanted to kill you ... would you still cry?"

"No!"

"Then why cry now?"

"I do not know."

"You do not know because you let what is inside you take over and you did not control yourself. Of what importance is there to what you think you heard?

"I do not know," Sorcha replied.

Flora wagged her finger at Sorcha and explained, "There is no importance to what others say about you, unless you allow it. The ways of the dark world will use this trick on you many times."

"I feel so stupid," Sorcha replied.

"Have you learned to control the emotions inside you?" Flora asked.

"Yes," Sorcha replied.

"Then my teachings are over and it is time for you to visit Priestess Sasa. She will be waiting for you tomorrow."

Sorcha felt confused about the witches who were there but not there. Clearing her mind, she decided to visit Stomper, only to find him gone. Deciding to go back to Kali's to rest for a while, Sorcha lay in bed and thought about Chaela. Would it be safe to visit her that night? With that thought, she fell asleep. Later that night, Sorcha awakened to a noise outside her window. Quietly, Sorcha walked over to the window. Sorcha looked outside the window, but nothing was there. She then closed the shutters. *Oh, well,* she thought, *time to leave and visit Chaela*. Concentrating on the area where she would meet Chaela, Sorcha tried to transport herself out of her room, only to discover she could not.

"Well, this is strange!" Sorcha said aloud. "Why can't I use my powers?"

Sorcha tried again—nothing happened. She kept trying, and after several failures, finally gave up. In disgust, she sat down to calm herself and thought, *Maybe it was lack of control due to a difficult day*. After a few minutes, she tried again; still, nothing happened. Confused and upset, she walked back to the window and tried to open the shutters. When the shutters would not open, she tried the door. The door would not open.

"I am trapped in my room," Sorcha mumbled. "This cannot be, I have to find out if Chaela is safe."

Frustrated and not knowing what else to do, Sorcha went back to bed. *I will talk to Kali in the morning*, she thought to herself, and fell asleep.

Waking with a start, Sorcha realized she needed to visit with Priestess Sasa. With a loud sigh, she stood and walked to the door. Remembering last night's attempts to leave, she stood in front of the door for a few minutes and wondered if she could get out. Slowly, she reached for the door and pulled it open. *Was I dreaming last night?* Sorcha thought to herself. *Oh, well, I will figure it out after I visit with Priestess Sasa*. Wearing a blood-red hooded robe and a new pair of calfskin sandals, Priestess Sasa greeted Sorcha when she arrived at her door.

"Are you always late?" Priestess Sasa shouted.

"I am not late," responded Sorcha.

"Is it light outside?" Sasa replied.

"Yes!"

"Then you are late!"

"When should I be here—when it's not light outside?"

"Did I say that?" Priestess Sasa sneered.

"No, but you...."

"But you ... I suppose now you think you can also tell me what I'm thinking."

"No.… No!"

"Now, what…? Well, speak up!"

"You will not let me finish!" shouted Sorcha.

"Finish what?"

"What I am trying to.…"

"You are trying to do what?" Priestess Sasa asked.

"I am trying to ask you when I should be here!" shouted Sorcha.

"Don't shout at me, you poor excuse for a witch."

"What?"

"Come back tomorrow, and be on time," scolded Sasa.

"But...!"

"Go! Come back tomorrow."

Sorcha walked away and thought to herself, *How can I be on time? I do not know what time I am supposed to be here*. A voice from behind her rattled her thoughts.

"Be here before daylight and after darkness!" shouted Priestess Sasa.

"What!" Sorcha mumbled.

The next morning, Sorcha awakened and looked out the window and smiled—it was still dark outside.

Kali and Alisa had made Sorcha a new hooded robe and just in time, since her old robe was falling apart and much too small. The material, much lighter than wool, had come from a distant land and cost Kali two goats. Sorcha tried on the robe—*A little large*, she thought. The color was the deepest black she had ever seen, and the black and red belt was a nice touch. Now dressed, Sorcha looked at herself.

"This will do just fine!" Sorcha said aloud.

Arriving at Priestess Sasa's, Sorcha hesitated at the door. *Am I on time?* she thought to herself. A glimmer of light hid behind the mountains. *It is before daylight, and the glimmer of light makes it after darkness—I must be on time.* A voice from inside Sasa's house called out,

"Are you going to stand out there all day?"

Sorcha lowered her head and walked inside.

"We visit the caves of Raven's Glenn today," a smiling Sasa warned Sorcha.

"Caves?" Sorcha asked.

The sun's rays now glowed over Raven's Glenn and Sasa could see the new robe Sorcha was wearing.

"What beggar did you steal that robe from?" Sasa asked.

Sorcha replied. "I did not...."

Sasa interrupted. "You did not what?"

"I did...."

"You did! So you're a thief also."

"No! I am...."

"So you're a thief and a poor excuse for a witch. Come here, Sorcha, and take my hand."

Sorcha did as she was told and reached for Sasa's hand. When her hand touched Sasa's hand, a dim blue light filled her mind. The room appeared to spin out from under her, and then a faraway darkness approached, coming closer and closer. In the blink of an eye, Sorcha found herself surrounded by the rock and dirt walls of a very dark and cold room. Sasa lit a candle. Exposed by the flickering flame of the candle light, their shadows covered the ceiling, floor, and walls of the cave.

"Where are we?" Sorcha asked.

"I could say we are in the caves of the mountains that surround Raven's Glenn," Sasa replied, "but then, where do you think you are?"

Sorcha looked at Sasa and, for the first time, saw a humorous gleam in her eyes, and realized how dumb her question was.

"There are candles on the floor and a small vessel of water over there," Sasa pointed at a dark corner.

"Why are we here?" Sorcha asked.

"We are not here," replied Sasa, and she vanished into the darkness. From the darkness, Sasa echoed a warning ... "Your powers will not work in the cave."

Five days had passed since Sasa left Sorcha stranded in the cave. The candles and water were gone. Sorcha sat on a rock and questioned her fate. Hunger pains clouded her thoughts, and her strength weakened with each passing hour. She heard voices ... her mind was starting to play tricks on her.

"Chaela!" Sorcha called out ... no answer.

"Kali!" she called out again ... no answer.

Her lips were now dry and cracking, her eyes dim and shallow. She dug into the dirt with her hands. *What is this?* Sorcha thought to herself ... *The soil is moist.* Digging faster, she hoped to find water, but instead found rock. Holding a handful of moist dirt in her hands, she squeezed out a few drops of water across her dry lips. The water tasted bitter, awful, and the water burned her lips. Ready to give up, Sorcha lay on the ground; the cool dampness of the soil felt comfortable as she submitted to the deep black darkness that surrounded her.

A white light engulfed her mind and, with no will to live, the light slowly began to fade.

Seven days had passed. Unable to walk or speak ... her powers useless, Sorcha submitted to her fate and closed her eyes. From somewhere deep within, a voice beckoned her to awake.

"Get up, get up!" the voice cried to her. "Do not give up. Fight, fight for your life!"

With all the strength she had, Sorcha stood and started clawing at the walls. Surprised at how easy the dirt fell, she worked faster. Soon, the wall crumbled and a hole into another cavern appeared. Sorcha crawled through the hole and into another room.

Lying on the floor, Sorcha sensed she was not alone. As she looked up, candles lit and the room filled with shadows. Sorcha rubbed her eyes ... before her sat Kali, Alisa, Flora, and Sasa.

"It's about time! What took you so long?" a smiling Sasa asked.

Sorcha, her throat too dry to speak, pointed at Sasa, and whispered,

"You!"

Priestess Sasa laughed and said, "Sorcha, at a loss for words ... how wonderful!"

Priestess Kali stood and walked over to Sorcha with a small wooden bowl of water.

Kali grinned and handed Sorcha the water. "Drink slowly, you have passed Sasa's test. You now know how to reach inside your soul and find the strength to overcome life and death."

Sorcha looked at Kali with disbelief in her eyes.

"You will need to rest for a few days and regain your strength," Kali continued. "Priestess Morra will come for you when you are ready."

Sorcha passed out; when she woke, she found herself in her own bed, food on a nearby table, and sounds of life, the sounds of Raven's Glenn, flowing through her window. She smiled and closed her eyes.

Hours later, Sorcha awakened and, after she ate, decided to find Kali and discuss Chaela. While she was searching for Kali, she found Stomper.

"Sorcha, I was so worried about you," said Stomper. "They said you would be fine, but I did not believe them."

"I am fine, Stomper. A little sore and bruised, but, I will be fine. Have you seen Kali anywhere? I need to know about Chaela."

"Kali has been keeping an eye on Chaela," replied Stomper. "Your time in the cave took a little longer than the priestesses thought it would."

"Are you telling me I have permission to visit Chaela?"

Stomper chuckled and replied, "Yes, and I am here to take you to her. Kali had mentioned that your meeting place was too far away. Kali wanted her closer for both your safety. She cannot allow Chaela into Raven's Glenn until the powers of Raven's Glenn can control Chaela's vampire issues. Until then, the priestesses have selected another meeting place."

Sorcha was so startled she could not respond.

Stomper looked at her and said, "Hop on, I know Chaela is anxious to see you."

As they approached the area where Chaela was hiding, Sorcha looked around. The area was not familiar to her.

"Stomper, where are we?" Sorcha asked.

"We are heading to an old ruin that very few know about, and those that do stay away. I have heard this place is haunted."

"Haunted? How could anyone believe something is haunted?"

Stomper laughed and replied, "The witches claim the ruins as their own. Travelers once used the building for shelter; now, the buildings have decayed, and travelers are not welcome, so the priestesses have it well protected with spells. No one comes here or disturbs the place. Kali figured it was the safest place for Chaela to hide, and no one will be able to detect she is there."

"Remind me to thank Kali for her kindness. I was really worried she would drive Chaela away, or worse, kill her."

"Believe it or not," Stomper replied, "Kali said Chaela is a big part of your future. I do not know how and neither does Kali, but Kali was instructed by the Ancients to protect Chaela.

"The Ancients already protect her from the sun as long as she stays near Raven's Glenn, and Volac's powers protect her for short periods. Kali and the Ancients are working on something to protect her from the sun at all times. Apparently, she will need it if Chaela is to stay in Raven's Glenn. Here we are ... Chaela hides over there in the ruins. I will wait here for you."

Sorcha ran up several rock steps and through a deteriorated doorway. Under a partial roof, and standing in the shadows of a decaying corner of the building, stood Chalea.

"Sorcha, what happened to you?" Chaela asked. "You look like someone took a stick to you."

"Priestess Sasa had fun with me."

"I was worried. Kali visited and said you would be fine."

"I was afraid Kali would not allow me to be friends with a vampire, and I think Kali put a spell on my room. I could not get out of my room on the night before my visit with Priestesses Sasa; I thought I was going insane. I have to find Kali and find out what was done to my room."

"Do not worry, Sorcha, I am sure you will find out."

A few hours later, Sorcha left the ruins and arrived back in Raven's Glenn with Stomper. Sorcha spotted Priestess Morra walking the round and called out to her,

"Priestess Morra ... wait!"

Priestess Morra stopped and turned around, "Sorcha! I see you are almost well enough to visit me."

"Yes," replied Sorcha. "I would like to start tomorrow if that is good for you."

Priestess Morra looked at Sorcha and said, "Good! I will see you tomorrow."

Sorcha started to walk away and stopped—she turned around and asked, "What time should I be there?"

Priestess Morra replied, "When the sun's light shines on your bed, you should already be at my place."

Sorcha looked at Priestess Morra and mumbled aloud, "Can't anybody in this place give me a straight answer ... just once!"

Deep in sleep, darkness arrived early that night. Awakened by the sound of rain, Sorcha opened the shutters and looked out the window. The smell of rain filled her senses. Reflections of Raven's Glenn mirrored in the puddles, added color to the puddles of water the rain was leaving on the ground. Sorcha looked out over Raven's Glenn and said,

"What mysteries hide within the rain? I love the rain."

A gust of wind opened the door. When Sorcha stepped outside, rain flowing from the roof soaked her back and neck. Sorcha stepped back and tried to transport herself to Priestess Morra's. Her powers gone, a frustrated Sorcha pulled up her hood and stepped outside, right into a large puddle. As she looked down, she saw a reflection of herself. A voice from the puddle called her name,

"Sorcha, what you see is your fate, what you see is you."

Sorcha looked down at the puddle of water. Her reflection faded then appeared again, clearer and vivid, with bright deep rich colors, her image stared back; her eyes started to glow within the image, and the torches of Raven's Glenn flared as darkness, fire, and horrid screams emerged from the images. Alarmed, Sorcha jumped back, the horror of what she just saw burning into her memory. Shaken, she continued on the path to Priestess Morra's.

As if aware of Sorcha's vision, Priestess Morra was waiting at the door when Sorcha arrived.

"You look different, Sorcha,"

"It is nothing," replied Sorcha.

"Good! Then come inside, I will teach you the weapons of men."

Once inside, Sorcha asked, "Why do I need to learn of such things? I am a witch with powers ... I need no weapons."

"What if you cannot use your powers and you are attacked with such weapons?" Morra replied. "You are a

young woman now, almost seventeen years ... not a child."
Morra retrieved a sword from behind the door. "I will teach
you how to use the sword and bow; within time, you will
learn how to use other weapons."

"Defend yourself!" Morra cried out.

Morra tossed Sorcha a sword and attacked her. Sorcha
fell back, the sword a strange weight in her hand. Morra
swung her sword at Sorcha. Sorcha raised her sword and
blocked the sword's forward motion. Again and again,
Morra attacked. Sorcha's sword became lighter and the
sword soon felt like an extension of her arm and hand. Able
to thwart Morra's advance, Sorcha attacked.

"Stop!" Morra shouted. "Take the sword home with
you and practice."

Sorcha left, and over the next two cycles of the moon,
practiced. Soon, she was able to best Stomper, and even
Kali appeared fearful of her blows. Assured of her skill,
Sorcha returned to Morra's. With Sword in hand, Sorcha
walked through Morra's doorway.

"Good ... good!" Morra cried out. "Attack me!"

Back and forth, they fought. Soon, Morra tired, and
Sorcha was faster. Sorcha swooped inside the thrust of
Morra's blade. Knocking Morra's sword to the side ... she
hooked Morra's leg with her own and pushed. Morra went
down and hit the floor, hard. Sorcha stood above her and
pointed her sword at Morra. Morra looked up and started
laughing.

"You learn fast ... very good."

Sorcha smiled and lowered her hand to help Morra up.

"Look out the window, Sorcha. Do you see that piece of
firewood lying on the path?"

"Yes," Sorcha replied.

"Good.… That will be our target."

Morra walked over to the wall and removed a bow and a quiver of arrows that were hanging from a wooden peg.

"You hold the bow like this," explained Morra, and she extended her arm with the length of the bow vertical.

"You rest the arrow on the spot between your hand and the bow. Now hold the arrow tight up against the bowstring. Use these two fingers and pull the string back; keep the arrow tight on the string or it will fall. Now, watch me!" Morra aimed at the target ... swoosh ... thud! A perfect shot. "Now you try, Sorcha."

Sorcha took the bow and arrow and repeated what Morra showed her. She pulled back the string and released—the bow snapped as the arrow fluttered and fell to the floor, the string nicking the inside of her arm.

"That hurt!" Sorcha cried out.

Morra laughed and handed Sorcha another arrow. After a dozen tries, Sorcha was able to shoot the arrow but not hit the target. Morra whispered to Sorcha,

"Concentrate! See nothing else, feel your target; now feel your arrow, see your arrow hit the target."

Sorcha pulled back the string and released. Swoosh ... thud! A perfect shot. Morra jumped forward with another arrow.

"Do it again!" Morra shouted.

After each shot, Morra handed Sorcha another arrow. Faster and faster Sorcha loaded and released the arrows, each a perfect shot. After the last arrow found its mark, Sorcha looked at Priestess Morra.

"You did well," complimented Morra. "You have learned well today, and when Kali returns she will be proud of you. What is that noise outside?"

Three arrows flew through the open window. Appearing struck by an arrow, Morra fell to the floor. Sorcha turned towards the door. Three intruders dressed in black robes and masks rushed into the room with swords in hand. Sorcha leaped for her sword as the intruders attacked her. Sorcha ducked the first swing as the blade sliced the air above her head. Holding her sword tight, Sorcha attacked. The first intruder fell quickly and as Sorcha turned to face the others, they ran from the house.

"Morra!" Sorcha cried out as she ran to her side.

Sorcha looked down at Morra. Priestess Morra opened her eyes and winked at Sorcha. Startled, Sorcha jumped back.

"What! Are you okay?" Sorcha asked.

Morra started laughing. "You show courage, Sorcha, you have handled the challenge well."

Sorcha was angry. "I could have killed those people!" she yelled out.

"It was a trick to test your skill and courage," replied Morra.

Sorcha laughed and said, "When will you priestesses leave me alone?"

"You are old enough now ... we will see," replied Morra.

A little calmer, Sorcha prepared to leave.

"Wait!" Morra shouted. "You forgot these."

Morra handed Sorcha a sword and bow with a quiver full of arrows.

"You are giving these to me?" Sorcha asked. "Why?"

"They used to belong to the high priestess, the ruler of Raven's Glenn before Kali. I am sure she would want you to have them."

With bow and sword in hand, Sorcha departed from Priestess Morra's. Unaware of her surrounding and deep in thought, Sorcha bumped into Kali.

"It's time we had a talk," Kali whispered.

"I agree," Sorcha replied.

Together they walked to the uppermost house ... the north point of the star, the House of the Ancients.

"Why did we come here?" Sorcha asked.

"We will not be disturbed here and I have something to show you," replied Kali.

Together they entered the House of the Ancients and sat on the stone benches by the altar.

"Listen to me, Sorcha. I want you to listen to me and please try not to interrupt. What I am going to tell you is going to be hard enough as it is. Can you do that for me?"

"I will try," Sorcha replied.

"As you know, you were born with the powers bestowed upon you by the Ancients. Your mother also had powers and was a very powerful witch. When your mother met your father, she gave up her powers to be with your father. She knew about the prophecies and guessed that you were the chosen one. Your mother gambled. She thought that if she left Raven's Glenn and did not practice witchcraft anymore, then you would be safe. As you can see, that did not happen. All she did was set in motion what was to come. I did everything I could to get to your village in time, but failed. I was not supposed to make it in time, for that would have changed the outcome.

"Your mother also had another child, and that child replaced her as ruler of Raven's Glenn. Your mother—*our mother*—is now one of the Ancients. When a ruler of Raven's Glenn dies, her spirit transfers over, and she joins the past rulers of Raven's Glenn. The Ancients are the past rulers of Raven's Glenn."

Kali stopped for a minute to see how Sorcha was reacting to the information she was just given. Sorcha stared at Kali as if she were insane. After a few minutes of silence, Sorcha finally responded,

"So ... so you are telling me you are my sister and that our mother is an Ancient?"

"Yes," replied Kali.

"That is how you knew all about me and where to find me. Well, that makes a little more sense. I am here to learn the ways and someday become ruler of Raven's Glenn."

"That is only part of it," replied Kali. "You have the powers, yet you did not know how to use them. The lessons and challenges we put you through over the past several years released your inner self and allowed for your powers to surface. Your powers are growing stronger ... soon, you will be ready."

"What about Chaela?" Sorcha asked.

"Chaela was a complication and one I did not know about, which is why I went away. I needed to figure out what to do about her. Now I know she is a part of your future and I know Chaela needs our protection. The Ancients and I have created a pendant for her. As long as Chaela wears the pendant, the sun will not harm her, and other vampires will not be able to detect her. I was on my way to see her when I ran into you. She is still safe, so do not worry. We have also worked out a way for her to come into Raven's Glenn safely, as long as she wears the pendant. If she takes the pendant off while in Raven's Glenn, she will perish. Tomorrow we will go get her and the other priestesses and I will take the spell off your room. With Chaela in Raven's Glenn, I will no longer have to worry about you sneaking out at night."

"So that is why my power weakens when the sun is not shining. I thought I was just going insane," whispered Sorcha.

Kali laughed. "You are not going insane. It is getting late. First thing tomorrow morning we will take the pendant to Chaela.

After a full night's rest, Sorcha awakened anxious to see Chaela; pacing back and forth in the room was Kali.

"What are you doing?" Sorcha asked.

"Stomper watched over Chaela last night; there was an intruder at the ruins. All is well, and so is Chaela. We need to go and invite Chaela to join us here in Raven's Glenn. Come, we leave now!"

An hour or so later, they reached the ruins where Chaela was anxiously waiting.

With a worried voice, Chaela said, "I am so glad Stomper decided to stay last night or I am not sure what would have happened. I think Volac's spies have found me."

Kali interrupted, "Chaela, I have a gift for you from the Ancients. Wear this pendant at all times. It will protect you from the sun and hide you presence in Raven's Glenn.

However, if you take it off in Raven's Glenn, you will perish."

Chaela took the pendant and replied, "Thank you ... I am a natural enemy and yet you have not befriended me. What can I do in repayment?"

Kali answered, "Use your skills as a vampire, and watch over Sorcha. Dark days are ahead and soon you will need each other."

Stomper started to get restless and spoke, "We had better go, someone is coming."

Sorcha's eyes darkened. "It is Aleric and someone else, someone very powerful. I can sense them. Hurry, Chaela, put on the pendant, you must mask your presence."

Kali raised her arms, palms of her hands facing the sky; a slight breeze followed, and the view around them became hazy and distorted. Within seconds, they vanished and reappeared in Raven's Glenn.

Aleric was searching for the ruins he was sure Chaela was hiding in. This time, he had Volac with him.

"Aleric, I am tired of these games you insist on playing. Where is she?" commanded Volac.

"She was here last night, I know she was. Something is masking her presence," replied Aleric.

"I can't believe you let witches outsmart you. You are a vampire. You are better than they are. I cannot believe Chaela has taken up with witches. She was to be by my side. Find her and bring her back to me in one piece. If you do not, that will be the end of you. Do you understand?"

"Yes!" Aleric sneered. "I promise the next time you see me I will have her with me. She will regret ever taking up with those witches."

Back in Raven's Glenn, Kali was very impressed with Sorcha's ability to sense danger. Kali also sensed there was danger approaching.

"I cannot believe Volac came so close to Raven's Glenn," Kali commented. "Chaela, do you know why Volac is here?"

Chaela lowered her head and said, "He is looking for me. I was supposed to bring Sorcha back to him, but I could not do it. I want nothing from him. His very name scares me. I was supposed to marry him over 200 years ago and still he will not let me be. Volac knows Sorcha is the chosen one and he cannot allow the prophecies to come true. He wishes to kill her."

"I see!" Kali replied. "Do not to worry. We will do what we can. You have the protection of the Ancients, and now of Raven's Glenn."

Kali looked at Sorcha and asked her to find the other four priestesses.

"Meet me at the northernmost house within the hour," Kali ordered.

As Kali walked away, Sorcha called out to her, "Thank you, High Priestess, ruler of Raven's Glenn ... Sister."

Kali turned around and met Sorcha's smile with her own. Their eyes locked and Kali said, "Go now.... Do as I ask."

That special time of day was approaching Raven's Glenn; the sun was low in the western sky and just before the arrival of the approaching darkness, an orange glow would cloak all of Raven's Glenn. Everything you see would appear so clear and colorful. Kali stretched her arms outward, her head back; a soft breeze flowed through her hair and cooled her face.

"I am Raven's Glenn!" Kali shouted and, for a second, all sounds ceased as the echo of her voice dulled the sounds of the wind blowing through the trees. Kali looked upward and saw a raven circling in the sky above. Raising her arm, she signaled for the raven to come to her. Arm stretched out, the raven landed and locked eyes with her.

"Watch the skies and land," Kali told the raven and then released the hold she had over the bird. Kali then closed her eyes and visualized the northernmost house. As if riding the wind ... she was there. Sorcha and the four priestesses soon arrived. Kali had everyone join in a circle with her and hold hands.

"Sorcha, Stand in the center!" Kali commanded.

Kali and the other priestesses started circling to the left. Faster they turned as Kali chanted.

"We the power of five, circle to the left and ask of the Ancients to hear and bequeath."

Kali stopped the circle and continued again, moving to the right while chanting.

"We the power of five, circle to the right, remove the spell that cloaks the night."

Kali released her hold from the other priestesses and joined Sorcha in the middle of the circle. Holding Sorcha in her arms, she spun to the right and let go of Sorcha while raising her arms upward, chanting,

"From the house of the Ancients we ask of thee, remove the spell, and set Sorcha free."

A strong breeze entered the room and as it swirled around the high priestesses; the room turned dark ... then light again, and Kali whispered, "It is as it was."

The four priestesses departed and Kali turned to face Sorcha.

"Come, Sister, sit with me on the altar of the Ancients."

Sorcha sat on the altar next to Kali and Kali spoke,

"Raven's Glenn is hundreds of years old. You and I are of the bloodline that founded Raven's Glenn. Each generation shares our story with the next generation. Now, it is your turn ... so listen and remember.

"Long ago, a powerful witch from a land beyond the mountains discovered this place. She walked across this exact spot when the color of the day was at its best. So impressed with the orange glow the sunset produced, and the beauty of the plants and flowers, she decided to stay and built a hut right where we are sitting. The first night, she slept on the ground under the open sky; awakened by the sounds of ravens flying above her, she named this place Raven's Glenn. Each day she would practice her craft and soon the land, birds and animals called to her and she became one with all. Because of a powerful evil darkness that stalked this land, she cast the first spells of protection. Each ruler since has added spells of protection, making Raven's Glenn the safe place it is today. Her name was Mirra, also known as Queen Mirra, the first high priestess and ruler of Raven's Glenn. We are descendants of her as all the rulers of Raven's Glenn have been."

Interrupting Kali, Sorcha asked, "We are related to her?"

"Yes," replied Kali, "as was your mother and her mother."

Kali continued, "When our life dims, we do not enter the Summerlands; instead, we join our ancestors and become one of the Ancients. It is our way—the way of our ancestors, and the source of our power. After Mirra died, the other witches built a house to honor her. This house became the House of the Ancients. The altar is the same altar Mirra used in her hut. The altar has never been moved; this is also our most sacred place, for the Ancients visit us here and protect this building."

"So this building was once Mirra's hut?" Sorcha asked.

"Yes!" Kali replied. "Now let me finish with the story!"

"Word of a powerful witch and an open coven soon spread, and witches came to visit. Only the most powerful could stay, and soon Raven's Glenn flourished. Because men kill what they do not understand, we—the high priestesses of Raven's Glenn—do not allow them to live here. We have little use for them. When the time is right to ensure our bloodline continues, we disguise ourselves and search for a mate outside of Raven's Glenn. Your mother fell in love with a man this way and gave up Raven's Glenn to be with your father. She lost her powers when she left Raven's Glenn and, after several years, found a new home in a small village called Greythorn. I was next in line and took control. Soon, the powers of darkness will try to destroy us. You are the chosen one, the one who will conquer the light and dark, the one chosen to lead us through the battle that is to come, and you will rule after I am gone."

"I am ready!"

Kali laughed, "Not yet, Sorcha, you still need to learn more, and my time is not yet over. Close your eyes, Sorcha, and be at peace. Find the light inside you and clear your mind—relax. I will return in a few minutes."

A white dense fog slowly filled the room. Images of several witches wearing long white hooded robes, faintly visible in the dense fog, appeared before Sorcha. A soft, clear, woman's voice from within the fog called to Sorcha.

"We are your ancestors, Sorcha. We know of the past and the future, we will be there when you need us. You need only seek us and we will appear. Remember, Sorcha, only the living can change the future, only you can correct the past."

Sorcha pushed herself off the altar and walked into the fog in disbelief; she rubbed her eyes and the images were gone, the fog appeared to follow the images of the Ancients and vanished.

Kali returned and asked Sorcha about her visit with the Ancients. "I will be with them someday," commented Kali. "You need only seek their advice and the Ancients will appear in image or voice."

"I thought I heard our mother," said Sorcha.

"Although our mother gave up Raven's Glenn, she was of Mirra's bloodline. When her spirit left her body, she took her rightful place with our ancestors. We are done here, Sorcha; this house is always open to you, and it is your home also."

Chapter Four

$\mathcal{K}$ ali left the house of the Ancients to watch over a band of traders that arrived at Raven's Glenn. Sorcha decided to stay for a while and inspected the building closely. The building was large and round, with polished flat stone flooring and smooth rock walls. There was a large single window on the north, south, east, and west walls of the building, and only one doorway in and out. The roof came to a sharp peak and a large stone altar was in the center of the room.

The room had an airy feel about it and Sorcha felt at home. She closed her eyes and danced around the room while humming a tune she learned from her father. She bumped into the altar and noticed one of the flat stones on the top of the altar was loose. Feeling the ridges of the stone, she pulled it forward and the stone moved, exposing a secret compartment. Reaching inside, she pulled out a large book with a leather covering, and after laying it on the altar ... opened it.

What is this? Sorcha thought. The book contained a list of animals and plants with a description of how to use them when making spells. Sorcha opened to the middle of the book and found numbered pages full of spells.

"This must be Kali's book of spells," Sorcha said aloud.

Startled by a noise from outside the window, Sorcha looked out the window. Walking up the circle of round towards the House of the Ancients was Stomper and Chaela. Sorcha smiled as she waved.

"I'm in here! Wait! I will be right out!" Sorcha shouted as she ran back to the altar and put the book back into the secret compartment. After replacing the stone, she turned and ran outside.

"Where are you going?" asked Sorcha.

"The traders are here," replied Stomper. "Chaela and I are going to see what they have brought to Raven's Glenn."

"I have nothing to trade!" Sorcha commented.

"Oh! Just come with us, Sorcha, it will be fun and we can talk," replied Chaela.

Sorcha thought for a moment and remembered that Priestess Kali was also visiting with the traders.

Sorcha looked Chaela in the eyes and smiled. "Let's go see what the traders have brought to Raven's Glenn. Maybe it will be fun. Besides, I need to talk with my sister."

The traders had arrived by the southern route. The southern path into Raven's Glenn ended and only the witches knew how to proceed. The area at the end of the path was scattered with tents, carts, and animals. Since men could not enter Raven's Glenn, the traders had made camp at what they thought was the entrance. To outsiders, this was the southernmost entrance into Raven's Glenn.

Sorcha hesitated before entering the camp and looked around. She saw Priestess Kali standing on a small cliff overlooking the activities at the entrance.

"Chaela! You and Stomper go ahead; I am going to talk with Kali for a few minutes."

Sorcha followed a well-worn animal trail up the side of the mountain and joined Kali on the cliff.

"Why do you watch from here?" Sorcha asked.

"Those men are strangers, they can be anyone," Kali explained. "I rule and protect Raven's Glenn and I sense something is not right down there."

Sorcha was looking at the cluster of witches and traders below when she spotted Chaela.

"Is it safe for Chaela to be seen by strangers while hiding here at Raven's Glenn?" Sorcha asked.

They both were staring at Chaela when Sorcha noticed two men following her.

Sorcha pointed at the crowd and commented, "See those two men wearing brown hooded robes standing behind Chaela? I think they are following her."

Kali looked and noticed a bright reflection from something hidden within the gap of one of the men's robe. The men moved closer to Chaela and stood right behind her; the taller of the two reached into his robe and pulled out a sword. He raised it above Chaela's head. Sorcha screamed and vanished.

As the sword slashed through the air towards Chaela's neck, Sorcha appeared before the man and grabbed the man's wrist, redirecting what was sure to be a fatal blow. Spinning inwards, Sorcha pulled his arm and sword downward and used his forward motion from the strike to push the sword into his midsection. Kali reached for the second man, but he dropped to the ground, rolled, and disappeared into the crowd.

"What!" Chaela cried out as she turned around.

"He tried to kill you!" yelled Sorcha.

"The other one escaped!" Kali shouted.

"Look! This one still lives," Sorcha sneered and then jumped on him and pushed the sword in deeper.

"Stop!" Kali shouted as she pulled Sorcha off the man. "We must know what he knows. Who sent you? Speak! Who sent you?"

The man smiled. Kali placed the palm of her hand on the man's chest. His body lit up, engulfed in fire.

"Who sent you?" Kali asked.

The man started screaming in pain.

"Who sent you?" Kali repeated.

"Lord Volac!" the man screamed before he died.

"This is not good," Kali whispered. "One murderous spy has escaped and Volac is sure to find out that Chaela lives with us. Chaela must stay within Raven's Glenn or Volac's forces will kill her. We must all be very careful. Those men are devoted to Lord Volac and will stop at nothing in order to please their master."

"Where is Stomper?" Sorcha asked.

"Here he comes now," replied Chaela.

"What happened here?" cried out Stomper as he came galloping up to Sorcha.

"Volac has sent men to kill Chaela," replied Sorcha. "One man has escaped and we are now sure that Lord Volac knows that we protect her."

Kali heard a raven's call and looked towards the sky. A large raven circled above.

Kali touched Sorcha's shoulder and said, "Take Chaela back into Raven's Glenn."

Sorcha tried to respond to Kali but Kali had vanished, so she turned towards Chaela and noticed her eyes were darker and her complexion had turned a slight whitish blue.

"Chaela!" Sorcha whispered

Chaela tried to respond but in doing so exposed her fangs and quickly covered her mouth with her hand. Startled, Sorcha looked at her friend.

"Calm down, Chaela," Sorcha said. "We will go to Kali's house, you will be safe and can relax there."

Back in Raven's Glenn, Chaela transformed back to normal. They walked to Kali's house and once inside, Sorcha laughed aloud.

"You almost lost your head!" laughed Sorcha. "Do not worry, Chaela, when Kali gets back, we will figure this out."

Stomper started mumbling about needing to do something. Volac was near and they were all in danger. Sorcha just stood in the middle of the room and looked at her friends.

"I am open to ideas, does anyone have a plan?" Sorcha asked.

Chaela took several deep breaths and replied, "A plan to do what? We need to gather an army. Volac is very powerful and he will stop at nothing until he has what he wants. Right now, Sorcha, he wants you and me. I could go to him, but that still would not be good enough."

"No!" Sorcha replied. "You will stay in Raven's Glenn."

Stomper interrupted, "Someone needs to stop the man that got away. Why are we just standing here? We should go after him."

At that moment, Kali appeared and said, "The man is dead. A raven led me to him and I killed him, but I fear he managed to get a message to Volac. We are safe for now. He cannot enter Raven's Glenn for the protection spells of the Ancients are powerful; however, the other priestesses and I must consult with the Ancients to find a way to reinforce the protection for the lands surrounding Raven's Glenn. No one is allowed to leave here till further notice, understood?"

"But ... but!" replied Stomper.

"But?" Kali asked. "Are you ready to take on Volac and his army? I know I am not, and neither are the witches of Raven's Glenn. We need to gather reinforcements and that is going to take a while. Volac has tried for hundreds of years to destroy Raven's Glenn. With the arrival of Sorcha, he has no option but to attack us. Chaela is a traitor in his eyes and he wishes her dead. So in the meantime, stay in Raven's Glenn."

Stomper interrupted, "Kali, I have been sworn to protect Sorcha, but I cannot do that if I remain here doing nothing. You must allow me to go back to my home. I can do more from there than sitting around here doing nothing. I am only asking this instead of just going because you have been most gracious in letting me stay, but now it is time for me to go."

"I have no right in keeping you here against your will," replied Kali. "I will see to it that you make it back to your home safely. You can leave tomorrow morning."

The next morning, Stomper stood in front of Kali's house, spear, and shield at the ready. The morning sun glittered off Stomper's shield. Sorcha and Chaela approached and said goodbye.

"We will see each other again, but it is necessary that I go home," explained Stomper, "We need to ask my father and the other centaurs for help. I can do nothing from here."

Sorcha looked at Stomper and said, "I understand ... I will miss you. Now go, and be safe."

Out of nowhere, a swirl of wind surrounded them, and Kali appeared. Reaching out, she touched Stomper's shoulder and, under a cloak of invisibility, they both vanished. Stomper and Kali reappeared at the outer edge of Lamehoof's farm. Stomper turned to say goodbye to Kali and asked,

"Why could we not be invisible on the way to Raven's Glenn?"

"The use of our powers can sometimes be detected. I could not take the chance of Volac knowing exactly where we were."

Stomper gazed at Kali and asked, "Will you send for me when the time is right?"

"You will know when the time is right," Kali replied. "The armies of darkness will pass this way. Gather as many of your kind as you can and be ready.

Sorcha was waiting for Kali's return when a breeze flowed through the doorway. Dried leaves from outside the doorway circled the room and when they fell, Kali appeared.

"You're back!" said Sorcha.

"Yes I am, and Stomper is safe at home."

"We must let the other priestesses know you have returned," commented Sorcha.

"They know! It took all of our powers to stay invisible while crossing over the land of the dead. Tomorrow we will gather and discuss what to do about Volac."

"Is there any word from our spies?" asked Volac.

Gorgan, Volac's servant, a hideous creature with long pointed teeth and red fiery eyes, approached his master.

"Lord Volac! We have received word that both of our spies are dead."

"What!" replied Volac,

"They are dead, my lord, but a spy was able to send a message that Chaela lives within Raven's Glenn.

"Where is that accursed brother of hers?" Volac asked.

"He still hides in the mountains around Raven's Glenn trying to capture her, my lord!"

"What! Send for him. I have other plans and will deal with Chaela later."

"But my lord, Chaela is protected by a witch named Sorcha! She and Chaela are good friends and...."

"Yes! Sorcha, I know of that name. She is the one their Ancients speak of, the one who will someday destroy me, ha! I will taste her blood soon enough and Raven's Glenn will flow red with the blood of their witches.

Startled, Sorcha awakened and found Chaela standing over her bed with bloodstains on her mouth.

"I needed to feed," explained Chaela. "Your protection magick does not feed me."

"I hope we do not find a dead witch," Sorcha replied.

Chaela laughed and said, "No, but you have one less rabbit."

Just then, Priestess Alisa stuck her head in the door and shouted, "Kali wants us all to meet with her at the northernmost house!"

"We are on our way," Sorcha replied.

Kali greeted each of the high priestesses as they entered and started the meeting with the statement, "Volac now knows Chaela is protected by us and will come for her soon."

"Is Chaela worth the destruction of Raven's Glenn?" Priestess Morra asked.

Kali responded, "That is not the issue anymore. Volac knows of Sorcha and what the Ancients have foretold, he will come for both of them."

Priestess Sasa asked, "Are we not protected?"

"Yes," Kali replied. "But what would happen if Volac figured out a way to get through our protection spells? Can we defend ourselves without using our powers?"

Priestess Morra spoke. "I will tend to the defenses of Raven's Glenn. How many witches do we have who will fight with us?"

Kali thought for a minute and replied, "We have but thirty witches living within the protection of Raven's Glenn and another one hundred and fifty witches living in the hills around us."

"Good!" Morra replied. "We will start building our defenses and start training today."

Kali looked at the high priestesses and said, "Go! Warn the other witches and tell them a battle will soon be here."

Later in the day, the priestesses returned to inform Kali on their progress.

Priestess Flora spoke first, "We have visited the surrounding witches and most will be here within the hour."

"We are going to need to figure out where to house everyone," Priestess Sasa said. "It will not be safe outside of Raven's Glenn for anyone if Volac finds out what we are doing,"

"Sasa," Kali replied, "you will work on building shelter for our guests. Flora, you will help her. Morra is still working on the defenses around Raven's Glenn. Alisa and Sorcha are setting up areas to store food and water. We will all meet at the House of the Ancients when the sun sets."

An hour later, the witches from the surrounding hills started to arrive; they were told to gather within and around the Circle of Stone. A dense white smoky haze covered and masked the Circle of Stone; uneasiness and fear spread among the witches and they were reluctant to enter. Kali arrived and walked into the haze and vanished. Startled, the witches gazed into the haze, their voices becoming louder as they questioned Kali's disappearance. Fear and panic began to settle in; then the haze faded, and standing in the middle of the Circle of Stone was Kali and Celeste, Kali's mother—an Ancient.

Celeste spoke, "Thank you for joining Raven's Glenn in her time of need and coming to our defense. As most of you now know, we have a vampire staying with us. She serves our purpose and is here to stay. Volac is out to capture both Chaela and Sorcha. We must ensure he fails. Our priestesses will help train you to fight not only magically but also with a sword and bow. The prophecies are upon us and our way of life is at stake. We must not fail."

Celeste caught Kali's eye; she nodded her head, smiled, and vanished. Priestesses Morra and Alisa immediately gathered several witches and instructed them to enter the forest and gather fallen branches.

"Only bring back branches that are thick and at least six feet long," Morra explained to the witches.

Soon there were hundreds of branches stacked in a pile, and several of the witches started shaping the branches into long poles with very sharp points. Priestess Morra asked Alisa if she would find Priestess Sasa and have her make a poison for the points on the poles.

"The poison must be powerful enough to stop Volac's creatures or at least slow them down," said Morra.

"We can use the poison on our spear tips also," responded Alisa, "and on our swords and arrowheads."

"Good," replied Morra. "Make the poison!"

Sorcha was looking for Kali and found her on a hill overlooking Raven's Glenn. As Sorcha approached Kali, Kali asked,

"Look below, Sorcha, what do you see?"

Sorcha thought for a minute and responded, "I see what the spies for Volac see."

"You are correct! Volac still has to gather his forces. The attack could be a full wheel of the year away. We must prepare but prepare in secret."

"I will go and tell the witches to be more careful," Sorcha replied.

"Wait! Sorcha, you are now of age to rule Raven's Glenn. In my absence, you will take charge. Now go and warn the witches and stop the chaos below."

Sorcha moved from hut to hut explaining what to do and soon, Raven's Glenn was quiet and peaceful. All activity slowed, as it was before.

"Volac! Aleric has arrived."

"Bring him to me!" Volac demanded.

Volac stared at Aleric as he approached.

"My lord I...,"Aleric muttered.

"Be quiet!" Volac demanded. "I have a mission for you. If you fail me again, I will tear out your heart and feed your wretched body to my dogs."

"Anything! I will do anything," responded Aleric.

Volac continued, "There is a place several hundred miles east of here named Hatana. A powerful witch of the black arts named DeMorra rules over Hatana. DeMorra and her coven of evil witches can aid us greatly in defeating the spells that protect Raven's Glenn."

"My lord, I ... " Aleric interrupted.

"You will ask her to join us. Tell her I march on Raven's Glenn. Go!"

Stomper was explaining the recent events that happened at Raven's Glenn to his father, Lamehoof.

"We need to gather our kind and prepare to defend Raven's Glenn," stated Stomper.

"We have little choice," replied Lamehoof. "We can either live as we do now under the control of Raven's Glenn or become part of Tir Na Marbh and slaves of Volac."

"Tir Na Marbh?" Stomper questioned.

"The Land of the Dead," replied Lamehoof. "What choice do we have but to defend Raven's Glenn?"

"Chaela!" Sorcha called out." Let's take a walk in the hills."

"Are we looking for spies?" asked Chaela.

"Always! And we need our own spies; but who will spy for us?" asked Sorcha.

"I will," replied Chaela.

"No! You must stay here, but I have an idea. I know where Kali keeps her book of spells and magic. We can create our own spies."

"What will Kali do when she finds out?" asked Chaela.

"When Kali is gone I am in charge. We can do it then," Sorcha replied.

Night was approaching and Sorcha commented to Chaela, "I am tired and hungry. Would you join me for a meal by the fire tonight?"

"Your food does not appeal to me, Sorcha. Allow me to stay here in the hills while you rest and eat."

Sorcha agreed and left her friend as she headed home. Alone, Chaela looked around. *Yes, I am hungry*, she thought to herself and transformed into a wolf. Her howl echoed throughout Raven's Glenn as she began the hunt.

An early morning fog blanketed Raven's Glenn as an eerie quiet set in. Sorcha, awakened by the stillness around her, walked outside. The fog dampened her face with moisture as she tried to see through it. Approaching in front of her at a fast speed was two small glowing lights illuminating within the fog. *What is this?* she thought to herself, when out of the fog appeared a wolf, and then ... Chaela.

"Chaela! You startled me, where is everyone?" Sorcha asked.

"Morra is training them in the caves," Chaela answered. "She takes advantage of the fog."

"This is good!" Sorcha replied, "Morra is keeping the training secret."

While the fog slowly melted under the piercing rays of sunlight, the witches slowly returned to Raven's Glenn.

"Has anyone seen Kali this morning?" Sorcha asked.

Priestess Alisa said, "I saw her leave for the mountains early this morning."

Sorcha signaled for Chaela to follow her. "Come, Chaela, we must find out what she is up to."

Sorcha and Chaela headed for the mountains and, after several hours, found Kali on a high plateau overlooking the countryside.

"Kali!" Sorcha called out.

Kali turned to face Sorcha and signaled for Sorcha and Chaela to join her.

"What are you doing?" Sorcha asked Kali.

Kali looked into Sorcha's eyes. "Close your eyes and tell me what you feel, Sorcha."

Sorcha closed her eyes and her flesh turned cold. Darkness filled her mind and a cold breeze from the east swept over her. She opened her eyes and said,

"A great evil from the east comes this way."

"DeMorra!" Kali replied. "We must go back to Raven's Glenn and check on our defenses."

Sorcha asked Kali, "What of the witches who are still in the surrounding mountains? Shouldn't someone try to convince them to join us in Raven's Glenn?"

"Yes," Kali replied. "I will talk with the other priestesses, but remember we must appear like everything is normal. We will figure something out."

After a while, Kali found Priestess Alisa and they had a brief conversation about the witches who still lived in the surrounding mountains.

"Sorcha!" Kali called out. "I am leaving with Alisa. We will see what we can do about those who stayed behind. Remember, you are in charge while I am gone."

After Kali and Alisa departed, Sorcha searched for Chaela,

"Chaela, there you are, I have been looking all over for you. Kali is away with Alisa to see if they can bring the remaining witches back here to Raven Glenn; now is our time to look at her book of spells. We must hurry!"

Back at the northernmost house, the House of the Ancients, Sorcha and Chaela started looking through the black leather-covered book Sorcha found earlier.

"Look, Sorcha, here is one on creation. Maybe we can create something with these spells. What do you think?"

Sorcha panicked and said, "Quick, put everything back! Someone is coming, I feel it."

They quickly put the books back and pushed the stone over the hidden area.

"Let's go!" Sorcha said.

As they turned to leave, Priestess Flora entered.

"What are you two up to?" Flora asked. "Oh, I see, this place does warm the spirit, doesn't it? You know you are supposed to be keeping an eye on everything. If Kali finds out you are snooping around, she will hang you for sure."

"We were not snooping!" Sorcha sneered. "We were trying to talk with the Ancients to see if they had any more information for us."

"Any luck with that?" Flora replied.

"No, I could not concentrate enough to make contact with them," Sorcha replied.

Kali found Sorcha a few hours later and told her, "We managed to get most of the remaining witches to come back with us. I think mainly due to the fact they were too scared to be on their own. It is good some of the witches stayed in the mountains, otherwise Volac will know we are all here and preparing for him."

Kali looked at Sorcha with concern and commented, "I think we were not the only ones who felt DeMorra's presence earlier today. Some of the witches have scattered and I am not sure where they have gone to, it makes me fear for them. Alisa is still out there looking for them and I hope she finds them. What is this I hear about you trying to contact the Ancients?"

Surprised, Sorcha looked at Kali.

"Just because I leave you in charge does not mean the others are not keeping an eye on things also."

"Kali!" A panicked Alisa called out.

"What is wrong, Alisa?" Kali asked.

"I have found some of the missing witches. They have been tortured and burned to death. What are we to do?"

Sorcha looked at Chaela and said, "I know what to do—we hunt!"

Sorcha and Chaela soon arrived at the disfigured bodies of the burned witches. The witches had been tortured, layers of skin removed and set on fire.

"Smell them out!" Sorcha yelled at Chaela, and Chaela transformed into a wolf.

The scent was weak but strong enough to follow. Faster the wolf ran in pursuit, Sorcha close behind. Soon the wolf was gone, much too fast for Sorcha to keep up. Having stopped to catch her breath, Sorcha heard a horrid scream and hurried to the spot. Standing above a mutilated body with its throat ripped apart was Chaela.

"The others got away, but I took care of this one," smiled Chaela.

"Search him!" demanded Sorcha as her eyes scanned the forest for others.

"Nothing, I found nothing!" Chaela replied, "Wait! Look at his ring, it shows the crest of Volac."

"We must return to Raven's Glenn and warn the others," whispered Sorcha. "Volac's spies will now torture and kill our witches. We must stay close to Raven's Glenn and within our protection spells."

Night had fallen over the land as Aleric boarded a ship destined for Hatana. With strict orders not to be disturbed, he resided himself to a small enclosed room within the hull of the ship. Six days passed before the knock on his door.

"We anchor within the hour," cried out a raspy voice.

"Is it nightfall?" Aleric asked.

"Yes!"

The lit torches of Hatana were visible from the ship. Aleric stood on the dock with the cargo as the men hurried to return to the ship. The glow of lit torches weakened the dark night as Aleric walked towards the lights. A passing farmer on a mule-driven cart appeared out of the darkness, stopped, and asked him if he was lost. Aleric attacked him, fangs piercing his neck ... Aleric drank. Arriving in Hatana, he searched for DeMorra not realizing what awaited him. An old man crossed his path and Aleric asked him if he knew of DeMorra.

"She lives in the castle, but no one is allowed to disturb her," the old man told Aleric.

"Where is this castle?" Aleric demanded.

"The path out of town will lead you there, but she is not to be disturbed."

"Enough!" shouted Aleric, and headed for the castle.

The castle was easy to find; the tall stone wall that surrounded the castle made Aleric laugh—he easily jumped over it, landing in a courtyard full of witches. Startled, Aleric announced who he was.

The witches laughed, "You foolish vampire, you come to certain death. DeMorra waits for you on the other side of that door." They all pointed at the same door.

Aleric walked through the gathering of witches. The witches hissed at him. Fangs out, he hissed back. Startled, the witches backed up and gave him room. He opened the door and walked inside, right into a cage made of thick iron bars. The door slammed shut, trapping him.

"What! Let me out!" Aleric screamed.

A tall woman with pale skin, thin lips, and deep black eyes approached. Her long black hair covered her shoulders and the hood of her dark red robe.

Aleric panicked and shouted, "I was sent by Volac to seek your aid."

"I know! And I know of Volac," DeMorra replied.

"We march on Raven's Glenn. Why have you caged me?" Aleric cried out.

"I have no love for Queen Kali or her coven, and have long desired her death. You have broken our laws and killed without my permission and must be punished. I have sent a message to Volac ... that you will be killed."

Volac received word of Aleric's fate.

"We must secure DeMorra's aid at all costs. If Aleric broke their laws, then so be it. His fate is in their hands."

"He is one of us, my lord," Gorgan replied.

"He *was* one of us," Volac smiled.

"Summon the priestesses," DeMorra commanded. Soon, the room filled with witches, all staring at Aleric.

"We will go to the aid of Volac," DeMorra explained. "I have long wished for the destruction of Raven's Glenn and the power of their Ancients. They have been a curse on me for way too long. As for you, Aleric, Volac can not help you here, every day, a few seconds of sunlight will burn you until the darkness within you fails, at which time you will be left for the birds of Hatana to feed on. Come, sisters, we prepare for a long journey."

"Kali," Sorcha cried out. "We killed one of Volac's spies, the one responsible for burning our sisters."

"Sorcha, you must be careful and not take it upon yourself to do such careless things," Kali replied.

"I will rule as a queen and a warrior if need be. That will be my way," Sorcha replied.

Kali walked away shaking her head and thought to herself, *It is what the Ancients said it would be.*

"Chaela!" Sorcha whispered, "Kali leaves for a while, we must get back to her books."

Once inside the House of the Ancients, they retrieved the book and started going through the pages.

"This spell will work," said Sorcha, "Let us try this spell."

Laying the open book on the altar, Sorcha took a step back and raised her arms; palms facing upwards, she chanted,

"From within and without, from there to here, open the door and reappear."

Sorcha chanted the spell three times and lowered her arms.

"Look!" Chaela yelled out.

Suspended in the air, above and in front of them, a small spinning black hole appeared and slowly started to grow larger. The twirling winds and deafening sounds of a major storm soon filled the room and spun counterclockwise around the growing black hole. Chaela and Sorcha jumped back and watched with amazement and fear as their spell developed before them.

"What have you done?" Chaela screamed.

"I ... I can't stop it!" Sorcha cried out.

"Look!" Chaela shouted, "something is trying to climb out of the hole."

Sorcha panicked and screamed, "I don't know what to do!"

"Can't you just use a spell and close the hole?"

"I didn't look to see if there was one."

"I wish Kali were here!" Chaela yelped. "She would know what to do!"

"Stomper!" Lamehoof called out. "Today when the sun is straight up, our kind will gather at the three hills in the meadow,"

"Will they all come?" Stomper asked.

"Yes!" Lamehoof replied. "Their lives depend on it. Go; tell your mother we leave soon."

Two hundred centaurs gathered at the selected meeting place. Most came armed with spears, shields, and swords. A look of hate and determination in their eyes revealed their inner thoughts as they gathered, talked among themselves, and waited for Lamehoof to speak.

"Raven's Glenn will soon come under attack by the forces of Volac!" Lamehoof shouted above the noise of the crowd. "We can either surrender to Volac and become his slaves or fight with Raven's Glenn. What shall it be?"

"Fight…! Fight!" the centaurs shouted.

"Then we must be ready to meet our fate on the battlefield," Lamehoof shouted. "Go! Prepare! We will meet here when word arrives that Volac approaches."

Priestess Kali prepared to visit with Queen Isle and the water witches. Still thinking about Sorcha and Chaela's brutal encounter with Volac's spy, she smiled. *Yes, Sorcha will make a great ruler*, she thought to herself.

Appearing out of nowhere, Kali startled the water witches as they were working by the banks of the river. Queen Isle approached Priestess Kali with open arms and soon the two were in deep conversation. Kali reminded Queen Isle, "You are our first defense. Volac will pass through here first and destroy all that is in his path."

"We have no quarrel with Volac, nor he with us," Isle replied. "Why would he attack and destroy us?"

"Because this land is part of Raven's Glenn, controlled and protected by me," Kali replied. "Volac wishes to destroy Raven's' Glenn, and you are the first in his path. When he arrives, Queen DeMorra will be at his side and you know what her witches will do here."

"Queen DeMorra! What choice do we have?"

"Then you will stand with us?"

"Yes."

Kali and Isle summoned the other witches and explained the fate that awaited them. A few decided to leave, fear having grasped their spirits and weakened their will. Others responded with anger and committed themselves to the survival of their coven and Raven's Glenn.

"When the dark day comes, we will do what we can," pledged Isle.

"Prepare your witches, Queen Isle, I will send word when the time is near. There is a strange force coming from Raven's Glenn and I must return immediately. Blessed be Isle."

"Blessed be Kali."

Kali returned to Raven's Glenn and appeared in front of the northernmost house. As she approached the door, Chaela screamed.

"Sorcha, what have we done!" screamed Chaela.

Alarmed, Kali darted through the door and into the twirling winds of a displaced angry storm. Covering her face with her arm, she looked up in time to see several imp like creatures float out of a large, suspended, spinning black hole. Raising her arms and with the sound of her voice echoing off the walls, she shouted, "Be still!" As if lost in time, the room spun to a halt.

"Sorcha! What are you trying to do?" asked Kali.

Kali looked around at the mess and saw that her book lay open on the altar.

"Sorcha! You have not answered my question. What are you trying to do?" asked an irritated Kali.

Sorcha looked over at Kali and said, "I was just trying to help gather an army. I was thinking that if we created an army, nobody would know they were helping us. Only I don't know what I did."

"Sorcha! You have opened the door to another world and released creatures that do not belong in our world. You must be very careful with these creatures. While they are very loyal, they are very mischievous creatures with magical powers we do not fully understand. You opened the door, Sorcha, only you can close the door. Gather up the creatures!"

With all the imps frozen in a semisuspended state, it was easy for Sorcha and Chaela to find and place the imps on the floor under the black hole. Kali released her spell of stillness and told Sorcha to read the spell she used backwards. While Sorcha chanted the spell backwards, the winds slowly decreased, and the black hole started circling in the opposite direction. One after the other, the imps rose from the floor, immediately, they were sucked back into the black hole. The winds continued to decrease, the hole became smaller, and suddenly, the hole closed with a loud ... thurp!

"Umm ... Sorcha, Kali, we have a small problem," said Chaela as she looked around frantically.

"What seems to be the problem?" asked Kali.

"We are missing one imp," replied Chaela.

"What!" said Sorcha. "How can we be missing one?"

"Well," replied Chaela, "the imps sucked back into the hole were brownish in color. The one we are missing is greenish in color, chubby, has large, round, yellowish, googly eyes, huge ears that are larger than his head and slightly pointed, and a long hooked snout type nose. He is only a couple feet tall with web feet, three long fingers, and he has a thin long tail that points upwards. He really is kind of cute, in a mysterious sort of way."

Kali laughed and said, "Sorcha, it looks like you have a friend."

"What! What do you mean?"

Kali laughed and pointed to a spot behind Sorcha where the creature stood mimicking her. Kali took a few deep breaths, tried to control her laughter, and chuckled.

"Sorcha, we can use your new friend. I think he will make a useful spy. Are you listening to me, Sorcha?" Kali asked.

Sorcha turned around laughing and said, "I think I will call him Kreador, what do you think?"

Chaela looked at Kali and said, "I think he is going to be a distraction and a whole lot of trouble."

Kali responded, "I agree. Let's hope Sorcha will not regret this."

Aleric grabbed the bars of his cage and tried to bend them apart. The thick cold metal in his hands refused to give way. Trying to take a different form failed; he frantically slammed his body into the sides of his cage, rage took over, as his fangs grew larger.

"You have no powers here," came a voice from within the room.

"I will rip apart your neck!" Aleric shouted at the witch now standing in front of him.

"If you call me Priestess Morta, maybe I will kill you a little faster," laughed the witch.

Priestess Morta called upon several witches to aid her.

"Come, Sisters, we must move the cage in front of the window."

Several witches joined in to help push the cage across the floor and positioned the cage in front of a large covered window. Reaching through the bars and clawing at the witches, Aleric tried to grab hold of a witch. They laughed at his fate.

"Tomorrow at sunrise, Vampire, you will take your first bath in sunlight."

Aleric exploded in rage, beating on his cage and cursing the turn of fate that had befallen upon him.

"My master will destroy you!" Aleric screamed out.

"Your master Volac has betrayed you," laughed Priestess Morta.

Sorcha, awakened by the sound of angry voices, jumped out of bed; a quick look around the room told her Kreador was gone.

"Kreador! Where is Kreador?"

Into the room stomped Priestess Morra. "I take it this thing belongs to you!" she yelled, and with her right hand around his neck, held up Kreador, shaking him in front of Sorcha.

"Kreador! What…?" said Sorcha.

Priestess Morra interrupted, "This devil was eating my sandals—my new sandals," and tossed Kreador towards Sorcha when, Poof! Kreador vanished.

"Were did he go?" asked Sorcha.

Priestess Morra looked around, "I don't know, he was right here."

"Sorcha, Sorcha!" Chaela called out. The voice came from outside the house.

Sorcha ran to the door and saw Chaela pointing towards Priestess Sasa's house.

"Kreador just ran into Priestess Sasa's house!"

"Oh, no!" shouted Sorcha. "We have to catch him before Priestess Sasa finds him."

BANG!

They hear loud noises coming from Sasa's dwelling. Sorcha and Chaela stopped and looked at each other.

"Oh, no, we are too late!" said Chaela.

Sasa was standing in her doorway, dripping wet.

"Sorcha, where are you...?" Sasa called out, and then muttered, "You good for nothing witch!"

Looking around, Sasa spotted Sorcha and Chaela.

"I know that good-for-nothing imp must belong to you!" shouted Sasa. "It is just the sort of thing you would do."

Sorcha was always at a loss for words around Sasa and lowered her head.

"Yes, Priestess Sasa, it belongs to me."

"I knew it. I just knew it. Imps do not belong in this world and yet you bring one here. Just wait until Kali finds out about this. Maybe then she will believe what I have been telling her.... There is no way you could be the chosen one ... the chosen one—HA!"

Mumbling to herself, Sasa walked off towards Kali's house.

Chaela looked at Sorcha and said, "Do not worry, we will find Kreador, and we will have to find a way to do something about those powers of his. Maybe Kali can help spellbind him, then Kreador will only be able to use his powers when they are truly needed. She did something like that on you, did she not?"

Sorcha smiled and replied, "That is a great idea, let's go find Kali. I just hope Sasa doesn't find her first."

They arrived at Kali's house and found Priestess Sasa outraged as Sasa explained what the imp did to her place. Kali looked over at the door and, seeing Chaela and Sorcha standing there, told Priestess Sasa,

"I already know about the imp, Sasa. Be glad I returned when I did; otherwise, there would be several more of them running around. Kreador was one we did not get back into the portal and now we will have to deal with him. It is too soon to open the portal again, I am afraid we would have more than we could deal with if we did. I am sorry for the mess he caused and I am sure Sorcha will help you clean it up."

"I want that good-for-nothing witch nowhere near me or my house. I never could stand her. She thinks she is better than the rest of us just because she is the ... CHOSEN ONE! She thinks she can get away with everything. Well— I will show you!"

Sasa stomped out of the house, and when she passed Sorcha in the doorway, shouted, "You will see ... Sorcha will be the destruction of Raven's Glenn and all of us yet!"

Kali looked down, shook her head, and reminded Sorcha that Sasa was not a witch to tangle with and that Sasa was very upset that the time for the Chosen One had arrived while she was still alive. She was rather hoping that she would be long gone before another ruler took over.

"Where is Kreador?" asked Kali. "We must do something about that imp's powers."

"Kreador! Kreador!" Sorcha called out, "where are you?"

Sorcha searched throughout Raven's Glenn. Tired and out of places to search, she decided to take a nap. Within minutes, the darkness of sleep overcame her, her problems with Kreador now seemed so far away.

At first, the tug on her robe went unnoticed; again, another tug—Sorcha stirred slightly. Upset by the lack of a response, Kreador grabbed the robe and pulled with all his strength. Within the blink of an eye, Sorcha was on her feet.

Startled, Sorcha yelled out, "Who dare...! Oh, Kreador, where have you been?"

Jumping up and down while clapping his hands, Kreador greeted Sorcha with a large smile.

"uoy rof gnikool saw I." Kreador laughed.

"What did you say?" asked Sorcha.

"uoy rof gnikool saw I," Kreador repeated.

"I do not understand you, and why are you causing me such grief?" Sorcha asked.

"tluaf ym ton," explained Kreador.

Sorcha reached for a rope and tied one end around Kreador and the other end around her wrist.

"There! Until I can trust you, you will stay tied to me."

Kreador smiled as he slightly pulled on the rope and then dashed around Sorcha twice. Tangled up in the rope, Sorcha spun in the opposite direction, freeing herself. Stunned by the quick response, Kreador clapped his hands and laughed. Sorcha started laughing and petted Kreador on the head.

"I think we will become good friends, Kreador."

"sey," replied Kreador

Sorcha sent word to Kali that she had caught Kreador and had him under her control. In disbelief, Kali sent for Sorcha. *This I must see*, Kali thought to herself. Sorcha arrived with Kreador in tow. Irritated by the constant tugging of the rope, Sorcha screamed at Kreador and told him to stop it. Kreador looked at Sorcha; his smile faded and he lowered his head.

"You call that control!" laughed Kali

Sorcha answered, "Yes, I do, and this is not easy, but we are becoming friends."

Kali laughed, knowing you could never fully trust an imp.

"su ta gnihgual ehs si?" asked Kreador.

"What?" Sorcha replied. "See, Kali, he talked to me."

Kali started laughing. "You did not understand what he said ... did you?"

"Well! Maybe just a little," Sorcha fibbed.

Chaela arrived and commented, "I see you finally caught the little imp."

Kreador looked up at Chaela and dashed under Sorcha's robe.

"eripmav!" He squeaked as he poked his head out from under the robe.

"Kreador! Stop it!" Scolded Sorcha, and then tried to pull him out from under her robe.

"eripmav dab,dab!" Kreador cried out.

"What a squeaky little voice, and you are wrong about me," laughed Chaela.

Stunned, Sorcha looked at Chaela and said, "You understand him?"

"Well, yes, and you do not!" Chaela replied.

"I ... I think I do."

Kali laughed. "Sorcha does not know how they speak. Should we tell her or let her figure it out for herself?"

Embarrassed, Sorcha demanded, "Tell me what?"

Chaela shook her head and said, "In the otherworld, imps speak backwards from us."

Shocked, Sorcha looked at Kreador, "Is this true, Kreador?"

"sey!"

Sorcha laughed and said, "Well! I guess now I will be able to understand you. You need to promise me you will stop causing so much mischief, otherwise we will have to bind your powers. Understood?"

"sey...."

"Good, now maybe I can relax for a little while without worrying about you."

Chaela looked at the rope attached to Kreador and said, "Shouldn't you take the rope off of him? He did promise, which means he has to keep his word."

Sorcha reached down and untied the rope.

Kreador looked up at Sorcha and said, "yaw sti no si live."

Kreador's statement alarmed the three. Kali ... vanished. Sorcha and Chaela rushed outside.

"We must search the mountains and forest," whispered Sorcha.

"Yes! Before sunset," Chaela responded. "It is not safe outside of Raven's Glenn after sunset."

"I agree," said Sorcha.

Arriving at the edge of the forest, Sorcha asked Chaela to take wolf form and search for any signs that show even a glimpse of a threat. At twice the speed of a normal wolf, she covered the deepest sections of the forest first. All appeared as it should and no strange smells alerted her senses. As she approached the southern perimeter of the forest, a strange scent filled the air. Tracking the scent, she came to a narrow dry ravine that wrapped around the southern portion of the forest. Once in the ravine, the strange scent became stronger. Chaela howled ... a long and deep sound, the sound of a wolf on the hunt. With the smells so strong and clear, Chaela started to run; faster she ran, as if chasing the smells, her paws barely touching the soft dirt as she glided over the ground. The ravine ended at the base of the mountains. Chaela stopped and circled the ground, sniffing. Once before, Chaela had explored this area while hunting and was aware of the caves ahead. It was time to inform Sorcha of her findings.

"We must search the caves," Sorcha replied after hearing of the strange smells.

"This can be very dangerous; shouldn't we just inform Kali and leave?" asked Chaela.

Kreador shook his head in approval.

"We go to the caves," Sorcha commanded.

As the three approached the southern base of the mountain, Chaela pointed out where the ravine ended and the path leading upward towards the caves began. The crude path mainly used by mountain animals proved difficult to follow as they advanced towards the first cave.

"Look! Is that Kali?" Sorcha whispered as she pointed towards the cave.

Standing before the entrance to the cave, arms extended upwards and shouting with a voice that echoed off the mountainsides, stood Kali.

"She's casting a spell," informed Sorcha.

"Maybe so, but look, she destroys the cave," said Chaela.

A bright beam of light glowed from Kali's hands and attacked the entrance walls of the cave. With a loud, "CRACK!" the walls fell, and the entrance filled with dirt and stone.

Without turning around, Kali shouted, "Sorcha, come here!"

Sorcha and Chaela looked at each other while Kreador shook his head and pointed at Kali.

"Why are you not in Raven's Glenn?" Kali asked, "You are in charge when I leave; what if we are attacked and neither of us are there ... then what?"

Sorcha looked at Kali and tried to explain that she was just searching the areas around Raven's Glenn, ensuring they were safe.

"You did well by finding this cave," praised Kali. "Several humanlike creatures, large hideous beasts covered in grey-colored skin with black wings, hands like claws, and yellow eyes are now either trapped or dead within the cave." Raising her arms, Kali transported everyone back to the safety of Raven's Glenn.

"It is time we send our own spies to Volac's land," said Kali as she stared at Chaela and Kreador. "I would not ask you to spy for us if you were not the best choice. You know the land and can move from place to place without being detected."

"But I will be detected! They will sense I am there and kill me," responded Chaela.

"Even in wolf form?" Kali asked.

"As soon as I change they will know I am there. Volac will sense me in any form."

"She is correct!" interrupted Sorcha. "As soon as she steps outside of our protection spells, Volac will know and start searching for her."

Raising her eyebrow as she pointed a finger at Chaela, Kali whispered, "Then we must change her appearance from the inside out. An imp ought to do."

Kreador looked up and said, "tahw!"

While Kali, Sorcha, and Chaela discussed transforming Chaela into an imp, Kreador listened closely, sometimes rolling his eyes in disapproval and at times clapping while nodding his head in agreement, but most of the time he just stared in amazement with his tongue slightly hanging out.

The dark of night was close, and a thunderstorm had crept over Raven's Glenn. The sound of rain outside increased and cloaked their conversation. Kali decided the time was right to perform a transformation spell and asked everyone to join in a circle around the smoldering fire pit and hold hands. Kreador immediately dashed for the door, only to find Sorcha there first. As Kreador kicked and squeaked, Sorcha dragged Kreador back to the fire pit and forced him to hold hands. With his eyes closed, he whimpered and shook as Kali began the spell.

Kali produced a pouch filled with a white and blue speckled powder from beneath her robe and sprinkled the powder over the fire, then she pointed at Chaela and Kreador and chanted.

"On this side is what you were. On this side is who you will be, no differences between you will the eye or spirit see."

Kali crossed her arms. A flash of blinding light, and the sound of a loud "CRACK!" filled the room. Chaela instantly appeared as Kreador. Sorcha looked at Kreador who was three feet off the ground, feet spinning, and heading for the door. Sorcha smiled and reached for Kreador, who screamed out a loud squeak, slipped out of her grasp, and dashed for the door. In the blink of an eye, a blur of motion, Sorcha was there first and stopped him.

"I think we scared several years off his little imp life," laughed Kali.

Sorcha massaged Kreador's neck and ears, calming is inner spirit, and then whispered to Chaela and Kreador that they must enter Tir Na Marbh, spy on Volac, and report back with any information that involved anything to do with Raven's Glenn. Chaela and Kreador decided to leave just before sunrise. Sorcha agreed to stay with them until they reached the outer boundaries of Raven's Glenn.

That night, dreams filled Chaela's head, with visions of a life she once had. How she missed the privileged life of royalty, the love and belonging of a family, and the simple things she learned as a child. Everything changed that night ... the night Volac entered the castle under false pretense and cornered her in her chambers. They buried her the next day. Dug up by Volac's men, she was supposed to serve him forever ... that was until she met Sorcha.

"Wake up, wake up," whispered Sorcha as she lightly shook Chaela.

"Is it time already?" asked Chaela,

"Yes!" came the reply

Kreador was already awake and pacing back and forth. Sorcha could see the fear on his sad green face.

"It will be okay, Kreador. It will be okay," Sorcha told Kreador as she rubbed a spot behind his ears trying to calm his nerves. "You and Chaela look exactly alike. Use this to your advantage, and keep your wits together. I will be with you, as will Kali. You will be back soon."

"Do we leave now? Chaela asked.

"Wait," replied Sorcha. "Kali wishes to speak with both of you."

Kali arrived and stood in the doorway, her hair and robe flowing forward as a breeze from behind her passed and filled the room. Sorcha looked at her with admiration. As she entered the room, her shadow lay before her ... dancing on the walls and floor, her blowing hair matching the flickers of candlelight as she moved forward.

Reaching beneath her robe, Kali pulled out a small leather pouch and handed it to Chaela.

"When you arrive at Volac's lair, remove what is inside and place the contents someplace high so as to view all before you. Do not open the pouch before you are inside. Do you understand?"

Chaela nodded in agreement.

"Then go! Blend in with Volac's creatures and find out what his plans are. Remember the pouch and return safely."

Hiding during the day and traveling at night, Chaela and Kreador arrived at the outskirts of the Lands of the Dead, the place called Tir Na Marbh. Hearing the sound of hoofs pounding the dirt and voices from an approaching mule-driven cart, they hid behind several large rocks.

"Look," whispered Chaela. "Are those imps I see?"

Kreador nodded his head in acknowledgment as they slid lower behind the rocks. The cart stopped.

"I have an idea," whispered Chaela.

As the cart tried to move forward, two imps stood in its path.

"emoclew!" Kreador shouted out at the riders in the cart.

"emoclew ... emoclew," came the response from the cart.

"em wollof" Kreador shouted out and waved the cart forward towards himself.

Soon, Kreador and Chaela were leading the cart of imps through the gates of Tir Na Marbh and into the dark world of Volac.

"We made it inside," said Chaela. "No one sensed who I really am. We made it! That was a good idea leading the cart through the gates. Who would suspect two imps?

"uoy knaht" replied Kreador.

"Look, over there by the fire—is that a gathering of imps?" asked Chaela.

Chaela and Kreador joined the imps and soon learned that Volac had been gatherings his vampires and other creatures from the Land of the Dead for an attack on Raven's Glenn.

Chaela spoke softly to Kreador, "They wait for the evil Queen DeMorra and her witches."

"kool ... kool" responded Kreador,

Volac approached, kicking the imps out of his pathway. When Volac passed Chaela and Kreador, he stopped and sniffed the air. Chaela held her breath and Kreador began to shake. Volac's eyes focused on a group of vampires who were torturing a witch, a witch captured from the mountains around Raven's Glenn. He passed without noticing them.

The screams from the tortured witch sent chills up Chaela's spine as she watched in horror. Volac ripped layers of flesh from the witch's naked body. Tied to a post, her robe at her feet, the witch pleaded for mercy. Volac laughed and, with razor-sharp fingernails, tore at her flesh and tossed small chunks of bloody skin and meat to his pets, the wild dogs of the dead.

We must hide Kali's pouch! Chaela remembered. Looking around, she spotted a flat ledge high above and overlooking the area. Holding the pouch in her teeth, she and Kreador climbed up and emptied the pouch on the ledge. Shocked, Chaela gasped and jumped backwards. Starring at the contents, Kreador looked and whispered, "ees I seye owt."

While blending with the other imps, Chaela and Kreador slowly made their way out of the courtyard and out of Tir Na Marbh.

"We must return to Raven's Glenn and tell them what we know," Chaela told Kreador.

Kreador nodded in agreement and soon they were back on the same path they used to enter the Land of the Dead.

"We must hurry!" Chaela said in haste.

The mountains around Raven's Glenn were a welcome sight.

"Over here, Kreador. Here is the path to Raven's Glenn!" Chaela shouted

As they walked up the path, they noticed smoke coming up through the trees, and Chaela looked at Kreador and said quietly, "We must see who it is."

Kreador nodded his head in agreement and they quickly snuck down the hillside towards the fire. As they got closer, they could hear voices arguing,

The younger voice said, "Volac has told us not to return without her."

The older one responded, "I am aware of that, but how do you expect to be able to get into Raven's Glenn, find her, and sneak back out?"

The younger one replied, "I don't know! There has to be a way in. Are you sure we have circled Raven's Glenn completely?"

"Of course I'm sure," replied the older one.

Chaela turned and quietly motioned for Kreador to follow her. When Chaela was sure they were far enough away and could not be overheard, she told Kreador,

"We must hurry and return to Raven's Glenn," Kreador nodded his head in agreement.

They finally reached Raven's Glenn. The images of Volac's torturous ways burned in their memories, and now with the news of spies camping in the forest, they dashed into Kali's house, hoping to find someone there. Instead, they found it empty.

"Where did they go?" Chaela asked.

Kreador looked at her and said, "em wollof." Kreador ran to the northernmost house with Chaela close behind him.

The door flew open with a loud "CRASH!" Kali and Sorcha both jumped and turned, ready to defend or fight, they rushed towards the door. The blur of two green imps rolled through the doorway and past their feet.

"ilak, ilak," the imps yelled, they both started talking at once.

"SILENCE!" Kali shouted. They both stopped and stared at her.

"Well, now, I am glad you're back and safe. What have you...."

Both Chaela and Kreador started talking at once; again, Sorcha interrupted,

"Kreador! Chaela can speak both languages, let her speak and be quiet."

Kreador lowered his head and mumbled, "oot ereht saw I."

Sorcha looked at Chaela, "What news do you bring us of Volac?"

Chaela told of the witch being tortured and that Volac was gathering his forces from throughout the Tir Na Marbh. He will move on Raven's Glenn once his forces have assembled and DeMorra arrived with her coven of witches.

"As I fear," responded Kali.

"What was in the pouch you gave me?" asked Chaela.

Confused, Kali looked at Chaela. "You did not see?" she asked.

"I saw two eyes!" replied Chaela.

Kreador's eyes widened as he remembered what he saw. "oot em," he interrupted.

Kali explained, "The Ancients created the eyes so we could spy in the dark lands of Volac. Someone had to deliver and place the eyes in Volac's lair. You did a good job, Chaela."

Kreador started jumping up and down and pointed at the door.

"What's wrong?" asked Sorcha.

"seips, seips," Kreador shouted.

Lost in conversation, Chaela had forgotten about the two men in the forest. Alarmed, Kali walked outside and summoned the spirit of the forest.

"Sprits of the forest I command of thee, bind the intruders to the nearest tree."

Sorcha and Kali closed their eyes, lowered their heads, and vanished.

Stoking the fire, the younger of the two did not see the thin lower branches from a nearby tree come alive and slide across the ground. From behind, a branch quickly wrapped around his legs and pulled him towards the tree, then other tree branches quickly wrapped around him, firmly tying him to the trunk of the tree. Screaming, he yelled for help. The older of the two turned just in time to watch a branch flip around his waist. Trapped, the branches dragged him over the ground and secured him next to the younger man. Immobilized and at the mercy of the trees, the two men struggled to free themselves.

Sorcha and Kali appeared and approached the two intruders.

"Why are you here?" asked Sorcha.

The men refused to answer, so Sorcha asked again, and again they refused to answer.

"We should torture them as Volac would," commented Sorcha.

"No!" replied Kali. She pointed towards the campfire, "Watch!"

The fire began to twirl and take form. Kali controlled its movement and pointed at the younger of the two. The fire leaped towards his feet. His clothes now on fire, his words flowed freely.

"We were sent to either capture or kill the chosen one!"

"What else?" demanded Sorcha.

"Volac wants the head of Chaela."

"Shall we kill them?" asked Sorcha.

"No!" Kali replied, and she commanded the fire to return to the pit. "The ravens will eat today. They deserve no mercy."

Kreador and Chaela were still at the northern house when Kali and Sorcha reappeared.

"Did you catch them?" asked Chaela.

"They have decided to hang around for a while," laughed Sorcha.

Kali smiled and glanced out the window, looking upwards and over the treetops. Off in the distance ... above the forest, a flock of ravens had gathered and started to descend. Kali told Sorcha to look up and pointed at the ravens; they both laughed and together walked over to the altar. Kali placed a large shallow bowl on the altar and filled it with water, then asked everyone to gather around and watch.

"Look into the water," Kali told Sorcha.

As Sorcha stared at the water, the image of Volac's domain appeared.

"Be quiet—watch, and listen," instructed Kali.

A voice from someone not seen by the eyes informed Volac, "DeMorra's ship will be here soon, my Lord."

"krow seye eht," squeaked Kreador.

"Yes, they do!" Kali responded.

Sorcha looked up at Kali and said, "What do we do now? DeMorra is almost there."

Kali shook her head and said, "I was hoping for more time, but unfortunately time is running out. Volac is not waiting. Someone will have to stay here at all times and watch what is going on, keep an eye on what our eyes see. Chaela, Kreador, and the other priestesses will take turns watching and relay the information to me. Volac still has to gather the rest of the creatures from Tir Na Marbh. We must take advantage of this time and prepare ... the battle is near."

Sorcha was about to ask a question when Kali vanished.

Chaela looked at Sorcha and said, "How are we supposed to let her know if we cannot find her? She keeps disappearing."

Sorcha shook her head and chuckled, "Chaela, have you not learned anything yet? Kali is my sister and I have a link to her. I am beginning to be able to tell where she is at all times. I am also starting to feel what she feels—that I do not like so much. She is under a great deal of stress right now, and I get dizzy when I sense her feelings. Anyway, I think it would be best if you stay here with Kreador and in imp form, they are less likely to find you in imp form."

Kali appeared outside of Priestess Morra's house and explained the current events to her. Kali explained about Volac and the tortured witch, DeMorra taking sides with Volac, the gathering of Volac's forces, and the two men in the forest she left for the ravens to skin. She then told Morra to warn the other priestesses and those who have agreed to help.

"The time draws near," explained Kali, "let them know it is time to prepare."

When Kali finished with Morra, she headed for the northernmost house where she would call upon the Ancients once again.

A grayish-white misty fog filled the room when Kali entered. Floating in the fog waited the image of her mother. Surprised, Kali approached Celeste. Celeste raised her hand, signaling for Kali to stop. The fog in the room thickened while Kali waited and listened. From within the fog, Kali heard voices using the old language, a language used hundreds of years ago. The voices talked with her mother. Celeste looked up and signaled Kali to move closer.

"Mother, I fear the time is near where we will either survive or Raven's Glenn will perish."

"Kali, Volac has enlisted the aid of DeMorra. She is as powerful as you, maybe even greater. She can undo the spells that protect Raven's Glenn. You must be very careful when you meet her."

"Mother, you know of DeMorra?"

"Yes! DeMorra is my sister."

"Your sister!" Kali replied.

"She is of our blood, yet her heart is dark and evil and she will destroy you and Raven's Glenn if you do not stop her."

"How can I stop her?" asked Kali.

"You will need to trick her. You do not have the power to stop her, we the Ancients do. Remember, this is the place of the first house, the beginning of Raven's Glenn; from here, we have the power to destroy her. You need to set a trap, but be careful, it could cost you your life."

"What trap ... how?" Kali asked as the image of Celeste began to fade.

Celeste's fading voice responded, "Bring her here!"

Under the light of a full moon, DeMorra's ship arrived. Nine witches departed for shore. DeMorra stayed on the ship's deck and looked out through the night's darkness at the place called Tir Na Marbh, and smiled. Raising her hands, she lowered her head and vanished.

"Lord Volac! Lord Volac, DeMorra has arrived," the lookout cried.

"Then where is she?" Volac demanded.

"I am here!" a voice responded.

A tall woman dressed in a black hooded robe emerged from the shadows and approached Volac. Volac stared into the witch's cold eyes and, for the first time in over three hundred years, he felt fear. DeMorra stepped forward and Volac's guards scattered out of her path.

"Welcome, DeMorra, I have been waiting a long time to meet you," Volac said with a smile.

"You, your vampires, and all these hideous creatures mean nothing to me, Volac. I am here for only one reason and you just happen to offer a solution for something I have long desired. Keep your pets and vampires away from my coven of witches or I will destroy you as well as Raven's Glenn. My witches tire from the long journey, where do we rest?"

Anger and disdain crept over Volac as he stared at DeMorra. *How dare she talk to me in this manner?* Fangs showing, his eyes a blood curling red ... he leaped at her.

DeMorra saw the blur approach—with the wave of her hand, she stopped Volac's attack. Her hands now glowing yellowish-red, she reached out, grabbed Volac's neck, and held him while she used her fingernail to peel a small strip of skin from his face and then tossed Volac on the ground. Licking her fingers and tasting his flesh, she spit on Volac as he tried to crawl away.

Standing above Volac, she warned him, "If you ever try to attack me or my witches again, I will cut off your head and feed your heart to my witches. Now take me to my resting place."

Volac signaled for his guards to escort DeMorra to the highest peak on Marbh.

"There are caves there that you will find suitable," Volac told DeMorra. "You can almost see Raven's Glenn, even though it is almost three hundred miles north of here."

"Volac! You could surprise me yet!" laughed DeMorra.

A large fire pit warmed the largest of the three caves. DeMorra and her coven of witches decided that the cave was suitable for their needs and unpacked the trunks they brought with them. Unpacking a large black book, DeMorra sat as she started scanning through the pages. The dark red ink, made from the blood of those who have defied her, appeared to crawl across the pages as she searched for the right spell.

DeMorra stood and, with a voice that could pierce any soul, demanded, "Where are my belongings? I need the black case from my trunk."

Priestess Iris quickly dragged her trunk in front of her. "Here it is, my Queen, I have guarded it with my life since we left Hatana."

DeMorra, her eyes aglow, said nothing while she opened the trunk. She removed a long black case, and then looked up at Priestess Iris,

"Fetch my bow!" DeMorra commanded.

DeMorra opened the black case and removed a long black arrow. The arrow was over three feet in length, the arrowhead made from a dragon tooth, the feathers on the arrows shaft from a fallen birdman that had once crossed her, and the arrows shaft, bathed in the blood of her enemies. Holding the arrow, she smiled then placed the arrow in the fire and raised her hands.

"*Arrow of darkness defeat the light, follow a path to Raven's Glenn tonight.*"

DeMorra reached into the fire and removed the arrow.

"Bring me my bow!" DeMorra commanded again.

DeMorra left the cave and walked to the edge of the cliff. Priestess Iris appeared with a bow over seven feet in length and handed it to DeMorra.

It was late and the night air warm. Sorcha and Kali transported themselves to the cliffs overlooking Raven's Glenn. The night air was much cooler up there and all of Raven's Glenn glowed below. The glow from the huts and the lit torches formed an outline of a giant star, a star shaped hidden village, the place named Raven's Glenn.

"How peaceful Raven's Glenn appears," commented Sorcha.

The torchlight and moonlight mix gave off a yellowish orange glow, illuminating all of Raven's Glenn; even the shadows appeared brighter. Startled, Kali looked southward.

"What's wrong?" asked Sorcha.

"Do you not feel the change?" replied Kali.

Sorcha paused and let her senses take over. They both heard a strange noise coming from above and looked up when, out of the sky ... "SWISH ... THUD!" a large black arrow pierced the ground between them. Kali quickly reached down and pulled the arrow from the ground, but dropped it as quickly as she grabbed it, her hand now smoking from flesh burns.

"DeMorra has arrived!" whispered Kali, and they both glanced towards the south.

Chapter Five

*D*eMorra smiled as she handed Priestess Iris the bow and walked back towards the cave. Waiting inside the cave, the other eight witches had formed a circle around the fire pit. DeMorra approached and told them to hold hands, warning them not to break the chain. Holding her arms outright, hands and palms upward and looking downward, DeMorra chanted,

"Lord of darkness our guarding light, put forth my image in Raven's Glenn tonight."

DeMorra raised her head and saw that she was on a cliff overlooking Raven's Glenn. While watching the activities below, she noticed two tall witches enter the center house. As if riding a blanket of air, DeMorra glided down the mountainside and over the land to within five feet of the door. Standing there, she heard a noise from behind her and turned around.

"live live hctiw" cried out a squeaky voice.

Kreador jumped up and down and pointed at DeMorra. DeMorra quickly turned back towards the door and found herself face to face with Sorcha.

Realizing she was seeing an image, Sorcha laughed aloud.

"The great Queen DeMorra sneaking around like a bug looking for crumbs," said Sorcha.

Kali appeared behind the image.

"Welcome, DeMorra," said Kali.

Kali raised her arm and opened her hand, exposing a white powder. Taking a deep breath, she blew the powder over DeMorra. Instantly, her image was ablaze.

With a loud scream, DeMorra opened her eyes and found the witches before her staring in surprise.

"What's wrong?" the closest priestess asked.

DeMorra waved her away and walked back to the edge of the cliff. Looking north, she pointed towards Raven's Glenn,

"Your magick tricks will not stop me, Kali ... next time!"

The next morning, Stomper and Lamehoof arrived in Raven's Glenn.

"Stomper, Lamehoof, what news do you bring?" Priestess Morra called out from behind them.

"We are looking for Kali and Sorcha. Do you know where they might be?"

"They are at the northernmost house. I tell you they never leave that place. Come, I will take you there."

They arrived at the northernmost house, the House of the Ancients, and as soon as they reached the door, they could hear yelling and high-pitched squeals coming from inside. Morra opened the door; there in the middle of the room stood Sorcha holding Kreador upside down above Chaela. Chaela, still in imp form, was shaking her fist at Kreador. Kali was standing by the altar, laughing. Morra looked around in disbelief while Stomper shook his head and chuckled.

"Stomper, Lamehoof, it is good to see you again," said Sorcha. "It looks like it is time to change Chaela back to herself. It will only take a moment and then we can visit."

Stomper looked around and then realized that Chaela was the frazzled imp standing next to Sorcha.

"Sorcha ... you will tell me how you managed to transform a vampire into an imp, won't you?" Stomper asked.

Sorcha chuckled and said, "Of course I will, and Chaela will too, but first Kali will change my dear friend back."

Kali raised her arms and chanted,

"*From now you are to once you were, remove the spell and reappear.*"

The room grew dark ... then light. Chaela appeared as before.

"Finally, I am back to myself," said Chaela. "Now, where is that Kreador?"

Chaela lunged for Kreador and, just at the last second, Kreador jumped out of the way, and Chaela crashed to the floor empty-handed. Chaela glanced up at Kreador,

"Just wait; you have to sleep sometime."

With that said, Chaela got up and brushed herself off, and then stomped out the door. Kali was quick to speak,

"Sorcha, why don't you and Stomper go see if you can calm Chaela. The last thing we need is an upset vampire on the loose. Lamehoof, we can talk here. What news do you bring from the meadows and your kind?"

Lamehoof began to tell Kali about the meeting he attended when Priestess Alisa walked in the room.

"Kali," Alisa interrupted, "the eyes have informed us that DeMorra and her witches will be here soon. They come to weaken our defenses."

"Who is watching the water mirror?" Kali replied.

Priestess Alisa explained that she left Priestess Sasa watching the water mirror and that the two of them overheard Volac talking with DeMorra.

Lamehoof interrupted, "Sounds like we need to set a trap or two."

"DeMorra travels with nine other witches," said Alisa. "Her power flows through them. We need to kill one or two and weaken her power."

Sorcha raised her hand and pointed outside.

"Then let's set a trap and surprise our visitors," said Sorcha. "We should prepare now."

Confusion took hold as everyone tried to explain his or her idea for a trap. After several minutes of arguing, Sasa shouted aloud.

"I know what we can try!"

Sorcha looked at Sasa and asked, "Well, are you going to tell me?"

"Let's set up an ambush—we will lure them in and slay them," Sasa replied.

"Just wonderful, and how are we going to do that?" asked Sorcha.

"Like this: First, spread the word not to engage the witches; instead, hide from them—abandon your homes and hide. Second, spread a rumor that there will be a large gathering of witches at a certain location. They will come for sure to attack us. Third, we will circle the area and prepare it so they cannot escape. We must select a location within the forest so the trees can help us. Priestesses Morra and Alisa can see to the details."

Volac sent for Queen DeMorra.

"Ask DeMorra if she has the time to visit with me," Volac told his guard. "Be careful; do not offend her or you will pay dearly."

DeMorra soon appeared before Volac and asked, "Why do you wish to see me?"

"When are you planning to attack Raven's Glenn? My men are getting restless."

"I am sending three from my coven tomorrow. They will strike a blow that will cripple Raven's Glenn. Ready your men, Volac. You will be in Raven's Glenn soon."

DeMorra gathered her three most powerful witches and told them, "Destroy the witches who live around Raven's Glenn. Torture them, leave their bodies in the trees, and burn their homes. Send a message of fear, break their spirits, and their protection spells will follow."

Sorcha told Lamehoof and Stomper that they must go home so that they could help set a trap for Demorra. Sorcha explained that more than likely, DeMorra's witches would come through their lands before reaching Raven's Glenn. Act surprised to see them, treat them with respect and let them know about the gathering of the witches, then show them the way to the center of the forest and to where the old house that belonged to Priestess Flora is located. Stomper and Lamehoof agreed and departed for home.

"I hope the witches come through our lands," Stomper said to Lamehoof.

"They will, Stomper, and we will be ready for them."

Kali sent a message to Queen Isle: Bring several barrels of sea salt to Flora's old house in the forest. Hide and do not engage DeMorra or her witches when they arrive. Queen Isle would have none of it and refused to hide.

"I will stay and help with the trap," Queen Isle assured Sorcha. "I will send word to my coven to avoid the witches of DeMorra at all cost. But we are not afraid of DeMorra."

"You are welcome to stay and help," replied Sorcha. "Be sure your coven hides. They are no match for DeMorra. We need them alive to fight another time."

After opening the salt barrels, the witches sprinkled the salt on the ground, forming a large circle around Flora's old house. Next, they covered the salt with loose soil, hiding the salt from detection. Several of the witches made large wooden crosses the size of fully-grown people and covered them with hooded robes. Kali liked the idea of using the fake witches, and told them,

"This will make us many and they will not know who is who. Place the fake witches over there, and there, and there! Put a few in the house. Once they have crossed the lines of salt, we have them. Summon the high priestesses. I need them here ... now!" ordered Kali.

Priestess Flora arrived with the other priestesses and brought news from the eyes that were spying on Volac. Flora told Kali that DeMorra was not coming and that she was sending her three most powerful witches instead.

"Kali, all the high priestesses have gathered. What is your plan?" asked Sorcha.

"We will wait until the witches sent by DeMorra have all crossed into the circle we made of salt. Once inside, their powers will be useless; our spells of protection and the salt line will rob them of their powers. Once they are all inside the circle of salt, Sorcha, you will attack the first witch closest to Flora's house. The other priestesses will attack the second, and I will take the third. Once they are inside the circle, we can attack with spells, magic, and weapons. We must kill all of them. It will be our doom if they escape or make it back to the other side of the salt line."

Repairing a slightly damaged spear, Lamehoof looked up and saw Stomper approaching at a full gallop.

"Father, Father! Three witches camp on the other side of the three hills. They have arrived!" yelled Stomper.

"They wait for the dark of night. Go! Warn Kali and Sorcha. I will approach them just before nightfall, and lead them to you."

Stomper soon arrived at Flora's house in the woods with word that tonight DeMorra's witches would arrive. Kali and Sorcha showed the priestesses where to hide, and gave a stern warning not to attack until all three witches have crossed the circle of salt.

"Sorcha, you, and I must prepare the spells and command the trees to help us," said Kali. "We will destroy these witches and send their useless empty souls back to DeMorra."

Together, Sorcha and Kali held hands and entered a trancelike state. Their powers combined, they cast spells of the inner circle, spells that would rob DeMorra's witches of their powers once they crossed the circle of salt. While under their induced trance, they summoned the spirit of the forest and solicited the power of the trees so no escape was possible.

The end of the day came quickly; yet, the sky fought the arrival of night and slowly changed color. Sorcha and Kali waited impatiently for the shades of daylight to pass and nightfall to arrive.

"It's time," said Lamehoof.

Stomper was right. Lamehoof found the three witches behind the three hills in the meadow and approached them. The witches moved forward and prepared to attack Lamehoof as soon as they saw him.

"Wait! I mean you no harm," shouted Lamehoof.

"Why do you approach us?" they asked.

"I farm this land. I did not notice you," explained Lamehoof.

"How well do you know this land and the place called Raven's Glenn?" a witch asked.

"I have lived here all my life. I know these places very well."

"He lies! Kill him!" one of the other witches screamed out.

"Wait! Lamehoof pleaded. "You must be here for the witches gathering."

"What gathering?" they all asked at once.

"I have heard that the witches of Raven's Glenn meet tonight at an old house in the center of the forest. Spare my life and I will show you the place…. You are here for the meeting?"

As the witches discussed the good news, the tallest of the three laughed,

"How simple and easy can this be," she whispered. "We can kill all of them. DeMorra will be so pleased. Show us the way. If you lied or try to escape, we will kill you."

Darkness always arrived first under the branches of the trees in the forest. The blend of light and darkness allowed the witches of Raven's Glenn to find easy hiding places. With their hoods pulled up over their heads, they waited. "SNAP!" A dried twig splintered….

"They come!" whispered Sorcha. All eyes now scanned the surrounding forest, watching. Kali saw a shadow move forward.

Lamehoof stopped in his tracks,

"I fear my large-hoofed feet will give us away," he explained to the witches.

"You can leave us, we do not need you anymore," said the tallest of the witches.

"Look! I can see light from the house," whispered another witch.

The three witches slowly approached the house and stopped. One by one, they pointed out the defenses before them and muttered among themselves.

"Over there, I see someone standing by the tree, and over there are a few more at the well, and I counted four inside the house."

The tallest witch raised her hand and signaled for silence. She then looked into the eyes of each witch and told them what to do.

"Here is our plan: You will circle around and kill the witches by the tree. You will hide in the shadows and attack the witches by the well. I will enter the house and kill those inside. Go and be careful, show no mercy, and kill them quickly."

"Here they come—they fell for the trap," whispered Sorcha.

The first witch crossed the circle of salt and headed for the well. The second witch moved closer to the trees unaware of the fake witches and soon crossed the circle of salt. The tall witch snuck up to the house and was soon at the door, also crossing the circle of salt. The trap was set!

Sorcha stood and, with sword in hand, moved forward. Hiding in the shadows, she was only feet away when the first witch raised her arms and, with the palms of her hands facing forward, attempted to shower the fake witches by the well with fire. Nothing happened; she tried again, still no flame from her hands. Yet again, she tried.

"What is...?" she started to say aloud when from behind her, a voice quietly said,

"Welcome to Raven's Glenn!"

She quickly turned around and faced a smiling Sorcha with sword raised above her head. Blinking in disbelief, she did not see the sword as it glided through the air and through her neck. Her head hit the ground and her body burst into flames, falling on top of her head.

"A welcome gift for you, DeMorra," Sorcha commented as she stood back and watched the body burn. With the first witch to cross the line of salt eliminated, Sorcha headed for the trees.

Unaware of what just happened, the second witch approached the witches by the trees. Noticing that none of the witches around the trees had moved, she drew a large knife and stabbed the closest witch.

"Fakes!" she said aloud, and quickly tried to escape.

Several witches rushed towards her as she turned and ran into forest.

"What happened to my powers?" she cried out.

Confused and frantic, she ran and tripped over an exposed tree root. The sounds of moving branches startled her, as small branches wrapped themselves around her ankles and legs, securing her and keeping her from escaping. Soon, larger branches reached out and wrapped themselves around her. There was no escape.

Arriving first, Priestess Morra stared at the captured witch.

"Have mercy," the captured witch pleaded.

Priestess Morra looked at her and said, "Would you have mercy for me or would you enjoy killing me? You came here to kill us and weaken Raven's Glenn. There is no mercy inside you, so I give you no mercy."

Priestess Morra pulled a sword from under her robe and, with a well-aimed swing, sliced off the captured witch's right foot. Before the captured witch felt any pain, a spear pierced her heart. Morra turned around and saw Queen Isle.

"Look!" said Queen Isle, and she pointed at the witch.

Morra turned just in time to see the witch ignite in flames. Sorcha appeared from out of the shadows.

"Where is Kali?" Sorcha asked.

Morra and Isle looked at each other.

"We must find her now!" Sorcha demanded. They ran towards the old house.

Kali was standing in the shadows along the inside wall waiting for the witch to walk through the door. As Kali watched, the door slowly opened, and the witch walked in. Kali's voice greeted her.

"Hello, Rasha."

Rasha turned towards the sound of the voice and saw Kali step from the shadows.

"Kali—finally, we meet. I'm looking forward to this. DeMorra will be pleased you are finally out of her way."

Kali chuckled and shook her head. There was a sound from outside; someone was approaching the outside of the doorway. Morra, Sorcha, and Queen Isle rushed into the room. Morra stopped so quickly that the others did not have time to stop and ran right into her.

"Morra, what is it?" asked Sorcha.

Morra stared at Rasha and said, "You were once my friend."

Rasha laughed, "That was a long time ago, Morra. Today is another day, and today I will enjoy killing you."

"Do not be so sure of yourself!" sneered Morra.

Rasha laughed and said, "Well, well, well, let's see now: I get to kill, Kali, the queen of those stupid good-for-nothing water witches, my dear sweet friend, and oh ... the chosen one."

Rasha raised her hands and started chanting ... nothing happened. She tried to vanish ... and she could not. Her powers were gone and, for the first time in many years, she felt fear and jumped towards the door. Trapped within the spells of Raven's Glenn, her movements slowed and she became suspended in midair. Rasha screamed out ... "DEMORRA!"

"Let us see what DeMorra has to say about this!" Kali shouted.

With a snap of her fingers and a flick of her wrist, Kali pointed at Rasha, and Rasha burst into flames. Immediately, the house started to shake.

"What was that?" asked Sorcha.

"DeMorra," answered Kali.

A voice echoed throughout the room.

"NOOOOO! I will kill you for this, Kali—do you hear me? It is not over. Raven's Glenn will be mine, and you will watch as your precious little coven is destroyed."

The witches of Raven's Glenn laughed at DeMorra's threats, but Kali cautioned them.

"Sisters, it is not over and the worst is yet to come. We outsmarted them tonight, next time will not be so easy. Keep a watch on the water mirror, for the eyes will tell us when they come again."

Sorcha looked at Kali and saw that familiar look in her eyes.

"Are you leaving us again? I can tell," Sorcha asked.

"Yes," replied Kali. "There is something I must do and while I am gone, you will be in charge of Raven's Glenn."

Kali looked upwards and, with arms extended outward, vanished into the night.

The night was changing into day, and as the darkness began to fade, once again a witch slowly raised the curtain covering the window. With no place to hide, Aleric crouched in the corner of his cage. Covering his head with his arms, he pleaded for mercy.

"No ... no! Not again! Please, stop!" Aleric cried out.

The two witches watching over him laughed at his torment and teased him.

"Soon, Vampire, we will feed you to the birds and laugh as they clean your bones."

The witches shook the cage and used pointed poles to poke Aleric. They did not notice what appeared behind them.

Aleric's eyes widened as he looked past his tormentors. The two witches turned to see what he was looking at and saw a tall woman in a hooded black and red robe with glowing eyes staring at them.

"Who are you?" they demanded.

"I am Kali, high priestess and ruler of Raven's Glenn. You will release this vampire immediately!"

Both witches laughed, the high pitch of their voices echoing off the walls in the room. With no fear and the hungry look of a mad dog in their eyes, they slowly circled Kali. Kali stood with both arms and hands pointed at them. The witches moved closer; Kali smiled at them—and they attacked. The sounds of their screams echoed throughout Hatana when their bodies exploded in flames. From the pile of ashes on the floor, Kali removed the keys that unlocked the cage. Approaching the cage, Kali asked Aleric,

"Your sister will need you soon. If I release you, will you help defend Raven's Glenn and thus protect your sister?"

"Yes ... yes! Let me out, I will do anything," replied Aleric.

Kali tossed the keys in the cage and vanished.

"Alisa, where is Sorcha?" Kali asked.

"She went to the House of the Ancients to see what the eyes see."

Kali arrived at the House of the Ancients and found Sorcha and the other high priestesses staring at the water mirror. Sorcha looked up and stepped back.

"Welcome back, Kali," said Sorcha. "The eyes show us DeMorra's rage. She will kill everything in her path when she comes here. We must move quickly."

"What have you done to everyone?" Kali asked Sorcha.

Sorcha looked around and said, "Oh, yeah." With a quick move of her hand, everyone was moving again.

"Sorcha, you should not freeze your friends."

"I know," Sorcha replied, "but it was too loud, they were all arguing about what we were going to do and I could not concentrate on what was going on."

"I see," laughed Kali. "Suspending everyone in time does work."

Kali started to walk towards the door and saw Chaela. "Chaela, your brother is now free and should be on his way here. Next time you see him, remember he is now on our side."

"We will travel at night and camp just outside Raven's Glenn," Volac told DeMorra.

"I will already be there waiting for you," replied DeMorra.

"Good! You and your nine ... I mean six witches," Volac smiled as he turned his head so DeMorra could not see that he felt good that she suffered over her loss of three.

"You and your six witches will break the spells that protect Raven's Glenn and then I will attack."

"Wait! You must not just attack," DeMorra replied. "Raven's Glenn uses the power of the star. You must attack each of the five houses on the points of the star at the same time. You and I will attack the northernmost house together, that is where Priestess Kali and the chosen one ... that Sorcha, will be."

From within the water mirror, the eyes revealed Volac's plan to Sorcha and Kali. Sorcha took a step backwards and looked at Kali and said,

"We need another plan, Kali. They will attack us soon."

Kali responded, "I agree. Gather the high priestesses. We will all meet at the northernmost house within the hour. Send for Queen Isle, Stomper, and Lamehoof, they will be part of our plan and need to be here also. Chaela must not hear of our plans.

"Why not?" interrupted Sorcha.

"Once the protection spells are broken, so are the spells that protect her," Kali replied. "She will be as before and Volac will be able to reach inside her mind. For our safety and survival, she must not know what we plan to do."

Sorcha and Kali continued to stare into the water mirror while the room filled with the priestesses. After a few minutes, an irritated Morra spoke up.

"You wish to talk with us, Priestess Kali ... Kali! You wish to talk with us?" Morra asked.

Kali turned around and looked at all the priestesses.

"We will soon be under attack," Kali told the priestesses. "Volac will come at night and attack our five houses at the same time. All our spells of protection will weaken, and their magic and spells will also weaken."

"Will not the Ancients protect us?" asked Priestess Alisa.

Kali replied, "The Ancients powers will weaken if our five houses fall. We will have to do the fighting. If any house begins to fall, you will retreat to the House of the Ancients, which is where we will make our final stand, if need be. Sorcha and I have a plan, so gather around and listen."

Sorcha winked and smiled at Stomper as she began to talk.

"Queen Isle, you and your water witches will be the first attacked. Use all your powers and kill as many as you can. DeMorra at some time will rob you of your powers.... When that happens, use your bows and poison arrows to kill as many as you can. Do not surrender or let them destroy you. Retreat to Raven's Glenn when you feel the battle is lost."

"Why not fall back to Lamehoof and the centaurs?" Queen Isle asked. "They will be the next ones attacked."

"No!" Sorcha replied. "Come here and let them think you have run away. I need them to think you were defeated so they will act careless.

"Lamehoof! They will enter your lands after defeating the water witches. Use your spears and arrows as they pass. Hide within the night and, when they slow their advance, attack once and charge through them. Kill as many as you can, then retreat to Raven's Glenn. DeMorra and her witches will save most of their powers to attack Raven's Glenn and not consider you a force to deal with. We need to slow them down so they will have to wait another day to attack us at night. Now go and prepare. The Ancients are with all of you and blessed be those that die, the doors to the Summerlands are open today."

Later that day, Priestess Morra approached Sorcha.

"We have gathered all the witches from the mountains and surrounding areas and await your orders, Sorcha."

Sorcha replied, "Divide the witches by five and build your defenses around your houses. Dig shallow ditches around your houses and fill them with tar and oil. Create rings of fire to trap the enemy. As they pass over the ditch, light the oil. Remember, if your house is defeated, retreat to the northernmost house."

Kali interrupted, "The forest will help us for a while, but DeMorra will soon weaken our spells and the forest will be of little help."

"Yes!" Sorcha replied. "But we can have then form a wall and lock their branches so when our spells have weakened, the wall remains, blocking any retreat."

"Good idea," commented Kali. "Sorcha, follow me. I have something for you."

Kali walked over to the altar and pushed in a stone located on the upper front of the altar, releasing a latch that allowed the side of the altar to open. Reaching in, Kali pulled out a brown cloth bag. Inside the bag was a pair of black leather breeches, commonly called *bracae* by the tailors who made them. Also in the bag was a black belted tunic that hung below the hips, a red leather vest, a large red and black hooded cape ... the underside of the cape was red in color, the outside black, and a pair of black leather knee-high boots.

"These clothes belonged to our mother and her mother; they are stained with the blood of enemies from long ago. Here, put on these clothes and dress for battle. Let's defend what's ours."

Sorcha replaced her clothes and when fully dressed, twirled where she stood. The leather pants fit snug around her waist and just tight enough on her legs to fit inside the boots. The belted tunic hung just below her hips, the belt fitted tight around her waist, the vest was short-sleeved, with extra padding on the shoulders and tied together in the front with leather straps; the vest was slightly adjustable but fitted Sorcha perfectly. The wide, thick belt fitted snug around her waist and had a metal clap attached to carry a sword. Sorcha leaned forward, reached out, and stretched the clothing, which fitted snug and felt like a second skin. Kali placed the cape over Sorcha's shoulders and tied it loosely around her neck; the cape fell inches from the ground. Sorcha pulled the hood over her head and folded the sides of the cape across her front, concealing herself. She then flung her arms outward while grasping the cape, like a giant bird spreading its wings. Kali shook her head.

"No ... no ... no, Sorcha.... Your vest is not tied correctly.

"Push your cape back over your shoulders; the red of your vest and cape will conceal your blood if you're wounded. Tie your cape behind you until you need the cape to conceal your movements. Attach your sword to your belt with the metal clasp, tighten your vest, tie your hair back ... there, you now look like a warrior and are ready to lead us into battle. Let us go and check our defenses."

Sorcha put her hand on Kali's shoulder and said, "I must see Stomper and Lamehoof one more time before Volac arrives."

"And Chaela?" responded Kali.

"Chaela will fight by my side," Sorcha replied.

"Then go!" said Kali. "We will meet at the northernmost house when the attack begins."

Sorcha asked Chaela and Stomper to walk with her so she could talk to them.

"I don't know what is going to happen when the battle begins. The prophecy tells us that I will rule the realms of both the light and dark. I feel this battle is a turning point and something will happen that sets the prophecy in motion. Chaela, you and Stomper will fight by my side. I do not want Volac anywhere near you, Chaela."

"I can take care of myself," Chaela replied. "I am practically invincible. If we were fighting in the daylight, there could be a chance I get hurt, but they will probably attack at night. I might not have any magick, but I am twice as strong as DeMorra."

Kali overheard part of the conversation and told Chaela she could destroy her like that, "SNAP!" She snapped her fingers. Looking deep into Chaela's dark, cold, vampire eyes, Kali reminded Chaela that DeMorra might be more powerful than she was since DeMorra was once from Raven's Glenn and was her mother's sister.

"With Volac at DeMorra's side, Chaela, you alone, would not stand a chance against them."

"I guess you are correct," said Chaela. "I just was trying to...."

Kali interrupted, "Do not go into this battle with false hopes—you can be killed. Remember, when Volac does see you, he will attack you, so be very careful. Do we understand each other?"

"Yes!" Chaela replied.

"Then go and prepare with Stomper and Sorcha, we only have one more day at most before they arrive. Kreador! Go and check on the water witches."

Having returned to the river located in the southernmost lands of Raven's Glenn, Queen Isle summoned her coven. When all her coven had gathered, Queen Isle asked for silence.

"Tonight we will be attacked by a force that is more powerful than we are. We will hold them off as long as possible. Remember, our powers will weaken and we will need to fight with our weapons. All of you who survive will retreat to Raven's Glenn. We need to appear as if we are running away. I am your queen and I will fight side by side with you. If I fall tonight, remember me in your songs and stories. May the Ancients protect us."

As the witches prepared for the night's battle, Queen Isle walked among them, touching those who showed fear and helping all who needed it. With her senses alert and a watchful eye on the other side of the riverbank, Isle watched as her coven worked.

"They will cross here, for the water is at its lowest!" shouted Queen Isle. "Dig a deep long trench here and place stakes pointing upward from its bottom ... quickly! Archers, you will form a line at the tree line and hide back among the trees until I signal for you to shoot. The rest of you will form three lines over here—now, spread out. I want the shortest witches up front with spears pointing upwards. The average size witches will be in the next line with spears pointing forward; the tallest witches in the last line with spears pointing downward. This will be our battle formation and I will stand with you. We are ready; rest ... nightfall will be here soon."

As the white clouds and blue sky gave way to a reddish sunset, Queen Isle studied the transformation above. Staring at the sky, she sensed her fate. *I will die tonight*, she thought to herself, as a tear slid off her cheek and dampened the ground at her feet. *Many will die with me, and I hope those we die for will remember our sacrifice tonight*. She looked around at her coven as they prepared.

Wiping the tears from her eyes, she picked up her spear and sword. Night was closing fast, it was time to hide and wait.

Out of the darkness on the other side of the riverbank, several torches ignited. Standing on the riverbank appeared a tall woman wearing a dark black hooded robe; on each side of her were three other women, all wearing black hooded robes. Light from the torches behind them made their shadows appear larger than normal. Their shadows appeared to grow and covered the riverbank. Leaning on a long spear, her hood removed, the woman in the center shouted out,

"I am DeMorra, high priestess, queen, and ruler of Hatana. I come to claim these lands as mine. Surrender and join me, or die."

All six witches with DeMorra raised their arms upward and a dark smokelike fog quickly moved in and immediately covered the area. Once the fog swept over the water witches, their powers ceased and their spells became useless. Kreador stood among the witches, yet his powers remained intact. Queen Isle shouted at Kreador to leave and let Kali know the battle has begun.

"Steady yourselves!" Queen Isle shouted at her witches.

"I am Queen Isle, ruler and high priestess of the water witches. I serve only Raven's Glenn. If you want our land, come and take it!"

The six witches parted and a horde of half-man, half-animal, and demon-type creatures dashed into the river. Isle signaled the archers to open fire. Many of Volac's forces fell as the river turned red, colored with blood. The charge soon reached the water witches' line of defense. The spears did their work; the water witches held the line while Queen Isle stood among her coven and shouted,

"Pull out ... thrust ... pull out!"

The creatures' bodies fell, but they kept coming; soon, the brave line of water witches began to fail. Surrounded and with sword in hand, Isle fought as if she were possessed; swinging her sword madly, she kept the creatures away. The water witches began to fall, their dead bodies covering the ground around Queen Isle; her witches had fallen around her, and the bodies of her enemies piled at her feet. A spear suddenly pierced Queen Isle's leg and she stumbled forward; a sword blow opened the skin on her arm and her sword fell to the ground.

"Retreat!" Isle shouted.

"Do not kill her!" DeMorra commanded as she approached Queen Isle.

"Raven's Glenn will be mine and your death will mean nothing," said DeMorra, and she pulled out a knife from under her robe.

Stumbling to stay standing, Queen Isle reached down and picked up her sword. "They will remember me—and Raven's Glenn will never be yours."

Queen Isle tried to raise her sword, but could not. DeMorra smiled and moved closer, "Your Summerlands wait for you," laughed DeMorra, and the light in Queen Isle's eyes faded when DeMorra's knife sliced into Queen Isle's heart.

Falling to the ground, Queen Isle's last words were, "You will die."

The dark night appeared to grow darker when Queen Isle fell to the ground. The creatures from the Land of the

Dead surrounded her body and clawed at her flesh, ripping her apart.

Kali faced the eastern mountains; sunrise was approaching, and the morning light slightly glimmered over the tops of the mountains. Out of nowhere, a cool breeze flowed over Kali and through Raven's Glenn. Kali looked to the south—a sharp pain pierced her heart and, with tears and sadness, told Sorcha, "Queen Isle is dead. DeMorra and Volac are now heading towards Lamehoof and will be here tomorrow night."

Sorcha pointed towards the forest and said, "Look! Here come the water witches! Go help them."

Priestess Morra, Alisa, and Flora ran out to greet the water witches and help with the wounded.

"Take me to Priestess Kali," a water witch demanded.

"I am here!" replied Kali.

"My queen died for you and Raven's Glenn tonight. She fought well and killed many. Her last request was not to forget her or those who died."

Kali lowered her head and walked away. "I never will," she replied.

Sorcha was very saddened by what had happened. As she stood there staring at the water witches, she felt a pull on her robe. She looked down to see Kreador jumping up and down.

"nepo si latrop," said Kreador.

"What! Why?" asked Sorcha.

Kreador responded, "latrop eht nepo pleh nac elpoep ym"

It took Sorcha a few minutes to realize what Kreador had said and then she ran off in search of Kali. Kreador was right behind her. Sorcha found Kali by the well and caught her breath before she told Kali that Kreador did not lose his powers when the water witches did.

"He did what he could but was afraid Volac's forces would discover who he was. Queen Isle ordered him to leave and warn us. Therefore, he came back here to tell us what had happened. He said if you open the portal, his people are ready to help us."

Kali thought about this for a minute; she looked at Kreador and asked,

"What do you mean your people?"

"dlrow ym ni ecnirp a ma I," said Kreador.

"You're a prince!" replied Sorcha. "Well, that explains a lot. What do you think, Kali, it is worth a try, right?"

"Yes," said Kali, "but I will supervise this time."

"Probably a good idea" said Sorcha. "Let's go to the northernmost house."

They reached the northernmost house and prepared themselves.

"Now!" said Kali.

Sorcha took a deep breath and chanted,

"From within and without, from there to here, open the door and reappear."

Sorcha chanted the spell three times and lowered her arms. The room filled with twirling winds of a major storm and a small spinning black hole appeared before them, growing larger. Out of the portal stepped a dozen or so imps. Sorcha repeated the spell backwards and the portal closed, leaving the imps that came through.

Sorcha commented, "A lot less messy this time."

Kali looked at Sorcha and said, "I did nothing—it was all you. See what happens when you concentrate on the spell."

Kali looked at Kreador and said, "We have brought you your people—they are your responsibility. Explain to them what we are going to do and what you need to do. Sorcha, I am afraid that Lamehoof and his kind will fall back here soon ... we must be ready. Tomorrow night, the battle comes to Raven's Glenn."

Chapter Six

The thick black night air settled in with the smell of blood and death in the air, daylight would soon arrive and end the night's horrors. Lamehoof gathered his weapons and, under the light of lit torches, talked to his fellow centaurs.

"Several witches have passed through and told of Queen Isle's death. Isle and the water witches have been defeated, but they killed many and did what they had to do. Now it is our time to show what we can do. Remember the plan! When they reach the narrow part of the meadow, use your arrows and spears to shower Volac's forces, and then fall back. I will lead a charge from the front and once I engage, you will attack the sides again with swords and spears. We must slow them down. Raven's Glenn needs one more day. Go! Get ready. They will be here soon."

DeMorra approached Volac. "See! Without their powers, you can defeat them."

Volac smiled and commented, "Kali and Sorcha will not be so easy to kill. Raven's Glenn has many secrets."

DeMorra replied, "My witches and I leave now for Raven's Glenn. When you arrive, their magic will be gone and their protection spells weakened—then you can attack."

"Good!" said Volac. "Then I move on towards Raven's Glenn."

"Lord Volac!" a guard cried out. "Our spies have spotted the centaurs setting up a trap!"

"When and where is this trap to take place?" asked Volac.

"When we enter the narrowest part of the meadow," replied his guard.

"Good!" Volac replied. "Then we will have a surprise waiting for them. We must move forward, it will soon be daylight."

Appearing more like an angry assortment of creatures than an army, Volac's forces moved forward and entered the meadow. Within minutes, they reached the narrowest point.

"Here they come!" shouted Lamehoof. "Wait ... wait ... attack!"

From behind the hills and trees, the centaurs attacked. The sky above Volac's creatures filled with arrows and spears. Volac stood back and watched as arrows and spears rained down on his forces.

"Now!" shouted Volac.

Volac's forces separated and a large gap between the warriors appeared down the center of his forces. Divided, the two sides turned and faced the centaurs. Slowly, each side moved towards the centaurs, and, as they got closer, they picked up speed. Wielding weapons and screaming, no longer surrounded, they attacked with a full charge. Confused, and outnumbered, the centaurs ran.

"What ... stop!" Lamehoof shouted at his fellow centaurs.

At a full gallop, Lamehoof caught up to his retreating forces.

"Stop!" Lamehoof shouted. "Turn around and fight!"

Regaining their senses, the centaurs turned around and charged into Volac's advancing forces. Outnumbered and with the element of surprise gone, the centaurs, were soon surrounded by Volac's creatures. Lamehoof ordered half of those with him to escape and warn Raven's Glenn; the other half would stay and fight. With spears fixed at their sides and swords waving over their heads, they charged into Volac's creatures.

DeMorra arrived outside of Raven's Glenn and positioned a witch close to each of the five houses of the star.

"You, Latria, will stay by my side," ordered DeMorra. "When Volac arrives, I will give the signal and all of us will use our powers to cloak Raven's Glenn with a cloud of spells and darkness that will reverse their protection spells. Latria and I will attack the northernmost house where we will meet up with Volac."

Lamehoof charged towards the center of Volac's forces. He felt a burning pain from his side and noticed the cuts left by the razor-sharp fingernails of the creatures as they tried to grab him. Spear gone—buried in the belly of a birdman—he used his sword and hoofs to kill as many as he could. Having reached the center of the circle, his heart stopped: Before him lay the dead bodies of his kind. Shaking his head to clear his thoughts, Lamehoof shouted out to the remaining few,

"Follow me! Hurry—follow me!"

"Lord Volac, the battle is ours, look ... they run," laughed a servant.

"Do not chase them," Volac replied. "It will be daylight soon; we must hide deep in the forest before the light shines on us and weakens our powers.."

"DeMorra waits for us at Raven's Glenn," Volac's servant replied.

"Then she will have to wait!" an angry Volac snarled back.

"Look!" said one of DeMorra's witches. "Several centaurs are coming through the forest toward Raven's Glenn. Should we attack them?"

"No," DeMorra replied, 'it will be easier to kill them when they are all together. Let them pass. What happened to Volac—where is he?"

"He hides from the light of day and takes refuge in the forest," replied the witch.

"So now we have to wait for nightfall!" said DeMorra. "I should have killed him when we met. He will be the death of me if I do not kill him first."

Kali addressed Raven's Glenn. "We are surrounded; tonight, many of us will die, but Raven's Glenn will not fall. Remember, we fight for our way of life and the house of five. The Ancients have guided us and will not fail us now. Be brave; tomorrow will be a new day."

Kali turned and looked at Sorcha. Knowing what was about to happen to her, she hugged her sister and tears formed in her eyes.

"It will be okay," whispered Sorcha.

Kali stepped back and, for the first time, doubted the Ancients.

In front of each of the five houses of the star stood a high priestess with her selected band of witches, ready and waiting to defend their house. Kreador and his band of imps found hiding places around the northernmost house. Chaela and Stomper armed themselves and arrived at Sorcha's side. Arriving wounded, Lamehoof lay in the center house with two witches tending his wounds. The day was short and the sun slowly began to fade. As darkness approached, Kali called on the forest to create a wall made of branches, to trap Volac's forces after they pass.

"Let them come and try to destroy us," said Sorcha.

Kali smiled.

Night had arrived and so had Volac. DeMorra signaled her witches, and they all stood with arms raised. Suddenly, a large black cloud formed and moved over Raven's Glenn.

"We are ready. Tell Volac to attack," commanded DeMorra.

All five houses were attacked at once. Swarms of Volac' creatures emerged from the surrounding hills and forest. Priestess Flora and her witches were the first attacked. Swinging her sword like a wild lunatic, she sliced through the first wave of creatures. Then the fire came; her house now ablaze, she stood alone with the bodies of her witches scattered on the ground around her. Surrounded and with no chance of escape, Flora picked up a spear and charged into the creatures; as if running into stonewall, she fell backwards and landed on the ground. One of DeMorra's six witches approached as Flora lay there with blood dripping from her mouth and a spear stuck in her chest.

"It is time to die, Priestess," said the smiling witch.

Flora looked up and, for the first time that night, noticed how bright the stars appeared. Trying to stand, Flora saw the glitter of a knife blade, then fell into the darkness of death.

Her house now burning, her witches all dead, Priestess Alisa escaped to Morra's house. Fighting like wild cats, they were able to repel the assault.

"We beat them!" Alisa shouted.

"No, they are regrouping in the forest; watch out for archers ... get ready," Morra replied.

"THUD ... thud ... thud!"

Morra turned around in time to watch Alisa fall as three arrows found their mark. Morra ran to Alisa's side and held her head in her hands.

"The Summerlands are beautiful," whispered Priestess Alisa.

Surrounded, Priestess Sasa stood alone. As she readied for the assault, the cries of the approaching creatures surprised her, and she watched as the creatures fell. *What is this?* Sasa thought to herself. Kreador and his imps appeared from below the creatures; having sliced open the creatures' legs, it was easy for them to stab and hack the creatures to death. Kreador and the other imps stood there smiling.

"What are you doing, Kreador?" yelled Sasa. "You are supposed to protect Sorcha! Go!"

Volac was the first to reach the northernmost house.... DeMorra was close behind. Volac's creatures were no match for Sorcha, Kali, Stomper, and Chaela ... who appeared to be killing at will as the creatures littered the ground.

"There you are," Volac said to Chaela as he grabbed her by the neck and tossed her on the ground.

Stomper quickly ran a spear through Volac's body. Volac laughed and pulled out the spear. Stomper's eyes widened. Volac was about to kill him with his own spear when another spear cut into Volac's chest.

"Father!" cried out Stomper.

Badly wounded, Lamehoof shouted, "Hurry, Stomper, follow me!"

"Into the house!" shouted Kali, "They prepare their arrows."

Sorcha ran towards the house, killing every creature in her path.

"Kali! You run from me."

Kali turned around and stood face to face with DeMorra. DeMorra raised her hand and pointed at Kali. Just then, a voice from above sounded,

"Welcome back, DeMorra."

"Celeste! It's been a long time," DeMorra replied.

"You will fight Kali without your powers," Celeste informed DeMorra. "We the Ancients have sealed your fate. Prepare for that dark hole you call the underworld."

DeMorra screamed as she lifted her sword and attacked Kali. Reaching up, Kali grabbed DeMorra and pulled her to the ground. With DeMorra on top of her, a wave of arrows landed on the ground around them; several arrows pierced DeMorra's body. Pushing DeMorra's body off her own, Kali stood.

"Where is Sorcha?" Kali shouted

"She is alone in the house," Stomper replied

"You have no powers to stop me," Volac told Sorcha as he approached her.

Sorcha raised her sword just as Kreador and two imps entered the room.

"ahcros evas!" Kreador shouted and then jumped on Volac.

Volac grabbed Kreador and threw him at the wall. Sorcha dashed to Kreador's aid and Volac ran towards Sorcha and right into Aleric, who had just arrived from Hatana and was hiding in the shadows. Tossing Aleric out the door, Volac approached Sorcha.

Forgetting Volac for a second and leaning over Kreador, Sorcha had her back turned towards Volac when he attacked.

Volac snarled and grabbed Sorcha. "I have you now ... you little fool, I am going to enjoy this very much!"

Volac sunk his fangs into Sorcha's neck ... drinking deeply. There was a sudden sharp pain in his chest and he let go of Sorcha and watched her crumple to the floor. Looking down at his chest, he saw a branch sticking out of it.

Volac turned around and saw Aleric standing there with smoke coming from his hands. He looked back down at the branch and said,

"White ash—but how ... why?"

Aleric laughed and said, "You left me to die with those witches. I did everything you asked and still you left me. Now it is your turn to die."

Volac slumped to the floor with his hand out, as if asking for help.

Kali and the others came rushing in and found Sorcha lying on the floor.

"I tried but I was too late. I am sorry Kali." Aleric hung his head in shame.

Sorcha sat up with her hand covering her neck and said, "No, it is my fault. I turned my back on him and this is my payment for it."

Chaela looked over at Sorcha and said, "You will be fine, Volac is dead. That means we should all be normal again."

At that moment, Volac shot up and leaped for the door, screaming, "This is not over! I will still kill all of you!"

Chaela looked at the door and said, "But how can that be? He should be dead."

"Volac is more than just a vampire, I am afraid. He is from the Land of the Dead where a greater evil controls and protects him. We will have to find out how to kill him and kill him for good," said Sorcha.

"That just became more difficult," Chalea muttered. "Sorcha, he drank your blood and gave you his blood. Outside of Raven's Glenn and the reach of her protection spells, sunlight will now do little to stop Volac."

"What I am to do, am I going to turn into a vampire?" asked Sorcha.

Chaela looked at Sorcha and replied, "You already have, can't you feel it?"

Sorcha turned white and threw up. Kali in the meantime was losing blood. Trying not to faint, she ended up passing out and falling to the floor.

"Kali!" screamed Sorcha.

The smell of blood filled Sorcha's nostrils as she made her way over to where Kali lay passed out on the floor.

"Kali! Wake up." Sorcha slightly shook Kali. "Kali, what is wrong?"

Kali slowly opened her eyes and as Sorcha leaned over Kali, she saw the bloodstained chest guard. Sorcha removed the chest guard, revealing a knife wound underneath.

"You have been stabbed," said Sorcha.

"I used DeMorra as a shield," Kali explained. "She must have stabbed me when she fell on top of me."

Sorcha applied a handful of cloth to Kali's wound and tried to stop the bleeding. She then realized the smell of Kali's blood was driving her crazy. She took a few deep breaths and continued to try to control the bleeding.

"I feel cold," Kali whispered.

"MOTHER!" Sorcha cried out. "Please, help me."

The room filled with a whitish fog and Celeste appeared with the other Ancients. Celeste ordered everyone to leave while she and the Ancients gathered around Kali. They laid their hands on Kali and started chanting. After a few minutes, Celeste sent for Sorcha.

"My daughter will live. She is once again whole and the poison is gone."

"Poison? She was poisoned?" Sorcha asked.

"DeMorra used a knife dipped in poison. She would do whatever it takes to get her way. That is no longer the case; DeMorra is gone, and your sister is here. Take care of her for she is weak and will need time to heal."

A slight breeze flowed through the room from the open door and the whitish fog began to diminish. As the haze disappeared, so did the Ancients. Kali opened her eyes and looked at Sorcha.

"Are you.... What happened to you?" Kali asked Sorcha.

"I'm fine," Sorcha replied.

"You look different. I sense something is wrong with you," Kali stated.

Sorcha replied, "We will take you to your house so you can get well. You have been poisoned. We will talk about me once you are better."

"Yes," said Kali. "We will talk...." Her words softened as she fell back to sleep.

Morra and Chaela looked at Sorcha,

"Sorcha! You had better rest while we figure out what to do with you."

"I am fine," replied Sorcha.

"No! You are not. Volac has bitten you. You already thirst for blood. We will stay with you, as will Kreador and his imps until we can figure this out. Kali will know what to do so we will stay with her at her house."

"I feel faint," said Sorcha. "Has the battle ended?"

"Yes," Morra replied. "With the death of DeMorra and the retreat of Volac, the creatures have scattered."

"Then you and Chaela must tend to the wounded and begin to rebuild Raven's Glenn. I ... am feeling weak."

Sorcha took a step and fell forward. Several imps who were close by caught her and gently laid her down on the floor.

Priestess Morra looked around and said, "Two high priestesses are dead, three of our houses are burnt to the ground, there are countless dead bodies lying everywhere, all of Raven's Glenn is filled with smoke, our leaders are napping, and I have to clean it up." Morra shook her head in disbelief. "So it must be. I start immediately."

After Chaela made sure that Kali and Sorcha were alive and resting in the centermost house, she went to talk to Priestesses Morra.

"Morra ... Morra!" Chaela shouted.

Morra walked out of a smoldering building, her feet, robe, and hair covered in ash. She asked,

"My dear vampire, cannot you see I am busy?"

"Yes!" Chaela replied. "I was just wondering ... is there anything Sasa and I can do to help you?"

"Speak for yourself," Priestess Sasa interrupted. "If it wasn't for you and Sorcha, we would not be in this mess."

Morra looked at the two of them and said, "Thank you, I could use the help. Chaela, could you be a dear and gather the dead? We will need to dispose of the bodies soon. See if Aleric can help you out. Sasa, you can come help me. We need to get this ruble out of this building so we can rebuild it."

Aleric spoke up, "I think Chaela and I can better serve if we take a quick run through the forest and mountainsides to make sure none of Volac's forces are still around. I would hate to see a stray arrow end another life in Raven's Glenn."

"Good idea, Aleric. Afterwards ... see to our dead," Morra replied.

After Aleric and Chaela left to search the surrounding forest, a dozen witches gathered and dug a large fire pit, large enough to hold the dead bodies of the dead witches still scattered around Raven's Glenn. After all the dead were gathered, the witches covered the bottom of the pit with dried branches, twigs, and small logs, then carefully placed the dead bodies on top of the branches. The surviving witches gathered around the fire pit and each placed another dry branch over the bodies. Several imps had made a stretcher and carried Kali to the ceremony. Weak and still under the effects of the poison, Kali stood, lit the fire, and forced herself to say goodbye to each of the fallen. After several hours, the fire burned out and a strong blast of wind emerged. The wind circled the fire pit and scattered the ashes, lifting the ashes high into the sky. Kali, now able to walk, returned to the center house where Sorcha lay ill and noticed how pale and fragile Sorcha looked.

"Sorcha ... you do not look well. Have you eaten anything lately?"

In a faint voice, Sorcha replied, "I cannot bring myself to kill something for their blood."

Kali sent for Chaela and Aleric. When they arrived, Kali told them that Sorcha now thirsts for blood, and asked Chaela and Aleric if they would go and retrieve a vial that she buried at the Sacred Grove of the Ancients. Kali explained how several years ago when Sorcha was a still a child, she rescued Sorcha when the village named Greythorn was destroyed, and brought her to Raven's Glenn.

"On the way back to Raven's Glenn," Kali explained, "I had with me a vial filled with the blood of the Ancients. The Ancients told me to hide the vial in the Sacred Grove of the Ancients. At the time, I did not understand ... now I do. It will not cure Sorcha, but it will help her. I would go myself but as you can see, I am still not well enough to travel."

Aleric popped his head up and replied, "I have never been one to just sit around, but we will have to wait until nightfall. Unlike my sister, I have problems traveling during the day. Volac's powers used to protect me from the sun ... now the sun can harm me. "

"If you promise not to abuse its power," Kali said, "I will have a pendant made for you that will protect you from the sun. It will be an advantage for you to be able to travel during the days. However, if you abuse the pendant's power, you will be destroyed. Do you agree to these terms?"

"How can a pendant know if I abuse its power?" Aleric responded. "It's just a thing."

Kali looked at Chaela and said, "Would you like to explain how the pendant's power works, or shall I?"

Chaela touched her brother on the shoulder and said, "The pendant becomes a part of you. If you start to abuse the power even without realizing it, you start to feel a tingle, and if you don't pay attention to that tingle, well, I can only imagine what will happen to you." She shuddered at the thought.

Aleric stared at his sister in horror but nodded his head in agreement.

"Good!" Kali interrupted. "It is settled, I will cast the spells needed to create the pendant. Wait here, I will return shortly."

After a few hours had passed, Kali returned with a small round pendant hanging from a black cord. The symbol of Raven's Glenn engraved on one side the other side was rough and unfinished. She took Aleric by both hands and said,

"I do not want your life ended, so please behave yourself and do not abuse its powers."

Aleric looked down at his chest while Kali hung the pendant around his neck. He felt warmth, then a chilling cold—the pendant's powers flowed through his body ... engulfing him.

"Remember, Aleric, do not abuse the pendant's power," Kali warned. "We have a special burial planned for Priestesses Alisa and Flora, then I will give you and Chaela...."

"oot em," Kreador interrupted.

"You can go with them, Kreador," Kali continued. "After the burial, I will give directions to the Sacred Grove of the Ancients.

A messenger came with word that the bodies of Priestess Alisa and Flora were placed on the altar and waiting within the Circle of Stone. Slowly, Kali headed for the Circle of Stone. Priestesses Morra and Sasa met her inside the circle. Aleric, Chaela, and Kreador helped Sorcha to the entrance but could not enter. On her own, Sorcha walked through the entrance and joined the others.

Priestess Morra handed Kali a lit torch and stood back. Kali and Sorcha approached the altar. Sorcha stumbled, and Kali caught her. Putting her arm around Sorcha's waist, Kali said aloud,

"Priestesses of Raven's Glenn, you gave your lives for us. You fought bravely, and we will never forget your sacrifice. I hope the Ancients know what you have done and reward you."

Looking upward, Sorcha shouted, "I am Sorcha! Accept these priestesses as you would accept me."

A cloud above them grew darker, and a loud crack from a lightning bolt startled everyone. Her eyes now aglow, Sorcha stood and watched as a lightning bolt flashed out of the sky and struck the altar. The bodies of Alisa and Flora ignited, the flames shot outwards and upwards and turned from a red yellow to whitish blue. Sorcha, Kali, Morra, and Sasa watched as the bodies slowly vanished; a voice from behind them interrupted their thoughts. Kali and Sorcha turned around and faced Celeste. Her image and the images of all the Ancients appeared.

"Why do you weep?" Celeste asked as she and the Ancients moved apart from each other. "Behold!" Before them appeared the images of Alisa and Flora.

"They have joined the Ancients!" laughed Sorcha.

Celeste continued, "They are not of our bloodline, but they were high priestesses of the star and their spirits shall be rewarded. Alisa and Flora have joined us; their spirits now live within the House of the Ancients."

"You must hurry and rebuild our houses," Alisa warned. "The powers of Raven's Glenn are incomplete without them. The star must be complete."

"Yes, it will be done!" responded Kali. A new sense of strength filled her body.

"You must retrieve the vial of blood for Sorcha and make her whole," added Flora.

"It will be done," said Kali,

The image of Alisa, Flora, and the Ancients faded. Sorcha and Kali returned to the center house where Chaela, Aleric, and Kreador waited.

"Chaela," Kali commanded, "it is time for all of you to leave. You will take the path through the southernmost part of the forest. From there, you will enter, pass through, exit the forest, and then turn around. Before you go back into the forest, you will summon the spirit of the forest. She will open a new path for you. Follow the white of the birch trees until you come to a clearing filled with large stones and wait for nightfall. The moon rays will shine on the clearing and disclose the Sacred Grove of the Ancients. My powers are limited right now or I would go myself ... hurry!"

Chaela, Aleric, and Kreador left at once. Outside of Raven's Glenn, Chaela and Aleric transformed into wolves and with Kreador riding Chaela, they headed for the Sacred Grove of the Ancients. Without the fear of Volac's forces, they arrived by the end of the day. Having passed through the southern part of the forest, they turned around and called out for the spirit of the forest. The hazy image of an old woman floated out of the trees and appeared suspended in front of them.

"Who summons me?" she asked.

"We come in the name of Raven's Glenn and seek the Sacred Grove of the Ancients," Chaela replied as she tried to pull a shaking Kreador out from under her.

The image floated towards them.

"Follow the path, the white of the birch tree will lead you," the old woman said as she floated through them, circled around, and vanished back into the forest.

"Kreador! Get up, get up now, it will soon be nightfall, we must hurry," yelled Chaela.

"Follow the white of the birch trees," commented Aleric.

They entered the forest and several paths appeared before them. Guided by the white of the birch tree, they took the correct path and soon came across a clearing filled with large stones.

"This is it! This must be the place," said Chaela.

They looked around and saw a larger pile of stones in the center of the clearing.

"We must rest and wait for nightfall," said Aleric

Darkness in the forest always came early, but what they did not expect was the familiar voice coming from the growing shadows.

"We meet again!"

"Volac!" shouted Aleric as he jumped up.

"You will not escape me this time!" yelled Volac.

Kreador screamed and began to dig a hole in which to hide. Surprise and fear overcame Chaela and Aleric. Searching the shadows with their eyes, they could not find where Volac was hiding. A slight breeze entered the clearing and another familiar voice filled the area.

Standing in the middle of the clearing was Kali. She raised her arms, and the sky appeared to open. Moonlight filled the clearing. As the glow of moonlight increased, the forest awakened as if daylight had arrived. The yellow glow of moonlight revealed the true circle of stone and the altar appeared. Kali placed her hands on the altar and chanted,

"From life is death, from death is life, bring forth the blood we seek tonight."

A large stone in front of the altar began to move and Volac, engulfed in the increasing light, began to burn.

"I will kill all of you yet!" Volac screamed as he ran off into the darkness of the forest. Kali called out to Kreador,

"Kreador, come here and retrieve the vial from under the stone. I cannot touch it a second time, nor can Chaela or Aleric touch it. You must bring it back to Raven's Glenn, Sorcha needs it, so hurry!"

Slowly, the intense light began to fade and the clearing returned to how it was. Kali lowered her head and whispered, "Hurry!" then she vanished.

"We must hurry! Protect the vial, Kreador, and do not drop it," said Chaela.

"Let's go before Volac comes back!" shouted Aleric.

It was daylight when the three arrived back at Raven's Glenn. Aleric stopped at the trees' edge.

"What is wrong?" Chaela asked. "We must deliver this vial to Sorcha."

"The sun, I cannot ... it is so bright here," said Aleric.

Chaela laughed, "Come on, the sun will not hurt you."

They entered Raven's Glenn and headed straight to Kali's house, the centermost house. On the way, they noticed the amount of rebuilding that had already begun. They arrived at Kali's and Kreador entered with the vial of blood in his hand. Aleric hesitated before entering, and someone shoved him through the door from behind.

"Hey! Was that necessary?" Aleric commented.

Sasa looked at him with a scolding look and said, "Yes, it was. There is too much light coming in right now, Sorcha cannot be in it. She has changed greatly in the two days you have been gone, now let me have that vial."

Aleric stumbled backward as he was trying to get out of Priestess Sasa's way and said,

"I don't have it. I cannot touch it. KREADOR! Give this witch that darn thing."

Kreador stepped out from behind Chaela and handed Sasa the vial.

"Thank you, Kreador," said Sasa. "I like you much better when you are not wrecking my house."

Kreador shrunk back and said, "yrros!"

Aleric asked, "What is this vial filled with blood supposed to do for Sorcha? She has already been bitten; the only way to change that is to kill Volac, and well ... we have already tried that."

Chaela replied, "I think the vial of blood will help her with her feeding issue. She is probably dying right now because she will not kill an animal for its blood."

"Well, did anyone ever tell her not to drink that much out of one animal?" Aleric replied. "She can still feed without killing."

Chaela glared at Aleric and said, "There hasn't been enough time to explain anything to Sorcha. We will just have to see what happens when they are done in there."

"Sorcha, you must drink this or you will die," said Kali.

"Then let me die. I will not drink it," Sorcha replied.

"Enough of this ... Sorcha," said Kali, and signaled for Morra to help hold her while Sasa opened the vial.

Morra stood with her hands on her hips and said, "We can stand here and fight with her all day, or we can do this the easy way. Personally, I vote for the easy way."

They all just nodded their heads and chuckled. Morra forced open Sorcha's mouth and Sasa carefully put a couple drops of blood into Sorcha's mouth. Once the drops fell on Sorcha's tongue, Morra quickly closed Sorcha's mouth and blew in Sorcha's face, making her swallow.

"That girl is too strong for her own good," mumbled Morra.

"I hope we don't have to do that again. I will have to bring Chaela or Aleric in if we do," Sasa replied.

"There will be no need for that," replied Sorcha. She drank more of the blood and dropped the half-full vial as she fell asleep.

After a couple hours, Sorcha woke up hungry and thirsty. The blood from the vial had worked and Sorcha appeared normal. Kali disappeared and reappeared in a few minutes with food and water. After Sorcha ate and drank her fill, Kali called out for Aleric, Chaela, and Kreador to enter.

"What are we going to do about Volac?" Aleric asked.

"Is he hunting us or are we just lucky to run into him all the time?" Chaela asked.

"em tae lliw eh dias eh!" Kreador squeaked.

"Calm down you three. I will hunt him down and kill him," Sorcha replied.

Kali shook her head, pointed at all of them, and said, "Volac is still powerful and can kill any of you. You must all be very careful and yes, you will have to hunt Volac down and rid our world of him. Sorcha, you have trained most your life for this and now the time has come for you to put that training into practice and go after Volac. The prophecy that you will rule over light and dark depends on it. You must kill Volac and the evil that rules him. You are almost well enough and when you are well enough, you will do this. Remember you are part vampire right now and the only way to change that is to kill Volac. The vile of blood has cured your thirst for blood and after you kill Volac, there is another evil you must deal with."

Priestess Morra interrupted, "Kali, there is a witch among us who you should meet. She said she is a high priestess from a land several hundred miles to the north."

"Who? What...?" Kali replied.

"She fought with us when we were attacked, and she fought very well," Morra said. "She has knowledge of things and powers I have never seen."

"Why have I not met her? Where is she?" Kali asked.

"She is instructing the others on how to build a house," Morra replied. "Where she is from, they use more stone and rock; their houses are better built than ours. They have almost completed Priestess Alisa's house and she has made a secret room in the house under the floor."

Kali thought for a moment then said, "You say she fought well?"

Morra responded, "She can best any of us with sword and bow, and her magic is strange but appears equal to yours, Kali."

"Bring her to me. Wait! What is her name?"

"She calls herself Brietta, but I heard a witch she brought with her call her Queen Brietta.

"Is it possible? No, it can't be," Kali replied.

Kali approached Alisa's house and stared in amazement. The house stood finished and built out of stone and rock. The house was round with four windows and the walls were twice as thick as before. Kali walked inside and the room was full of light; the sun's rays entered through a window in the roof. In the middle of the room stood a tall woman covered in a long hooded brown robe, she spoke in a calm, peaceful, yet stern voice.

"You pull the rope to close the window in the roof and you pull it like this to open it," said the strange woman.

Could this be the same Brietta? Kali thought to herself.

"Brietta?" Kali called out.

Brietta turned around, pulled her hood back, and let it fall over her shoulders, her long reddish brown hair falling across her face. She pushed her hair back over her ears and smiled. Her bright green eyes then focused on Kali. Brietta and Kali stared at each other for a few moments and then Brietta spoke,

"It has been a long time since we played together as children. You look well, Kali."

"Welcome home," Kali replied.

"Don't tell me I have another sister," Sorcha whispered to Morra.

"No!" replied Priestess Morra. "If this is the same Brietta, she was a childhood friend of Kali's. Brietta's mother was a great and powerful witch who once lived in Raven's Glenn. When Celeste became ruler, Brietta's mother left for the northern mountains to start her own coven. Brietta's mother and Celeste did not see eye to eye on a few important matters and since they were such good friends, she left so as not to cause trouble for Celeste. I say she would make a perfect replacement for Priestess Alisa."

Sorcha looked towards Brietta and they both locked eyes for a moment.

"I think I like her," commented Sorcha.

Kali saw Sorcha in the doorway and called out to her,

"I would like you to meet an old friend of mine. This is Brietta—a stranger to Raven's Glenn she is not."

"Sorcha ... the chosen one," spoke Brietta. "I have been raised on the ways of the Ancients and know of you."

"I know nothing of you," replied Sorcha.

"You will! And she can help you," commented Kali.

"Sorcha, you have the stink of a vampire about you," said Brietta.

"Sorcha was bit by Volac and is recovering. Do you have any knowledge of such things?" Kali asked Brietta.

"Yes! Come with me, I will make her a broth that will cure some of her ills."

Kreador pulled on Sorcha's robe and Sorcha swatted his hand away. Kreador pulled again and Sorcha told him,

"Not now, Kreador, I must go with Brietta. She said she can help me."

"emoh og ot tnaw spmi ym," explained Kreador.

"I will ask Kali and if we do not need them anymore, I will send them home."

"doog! doog!" Kreador replied.

"Come, Sorcha, sit and wait, I will be right back—and Kali, do you have any roots from the white ash tree?" Brietta asked. "I need some roots from the white ash tree, the oak tree, and some dried mint flower. I already have a pouch of horehound. We can make the broth as soon as I have all the ingredients."

"This will help me?" asked Sorcha.

"Yes!" Brietta responded.

"What are Chaela, Aleric, and Stomper doing? Kali asked.

Sorcha looked around and said, "I don't know. They did not come with us. Kreador, have you seen Chaela?"

Kreador shook his head.

Kali interrupted, "I need Kreador, Chaela, and Aleric to go and get the remaining ingredients for Brietta. Kreador, go and find Stomper, he can also help. Do you think you can do that?"

"sey,"

"Kali, not that it is any of my business," asked Brietta, "why do you have imps running around Raven's Glenn?"

Kali gave a little chuckle and said, "Well ... Brietta, Sorcha decided one day to try and help by creating an army that no one would realize belonged to us, and the imps are the result of that. However, I sent them all back, but one had escaped. Kreador managed to stay behind that first time and caused quite a ruckus, but Sorcha managed to get him to behave and here he stays. As for the other imps, we brought them over when Kreador made it known that he still had his powers when the rest of us did not."

"Speaking of the other imps," said Sorcha, "Kreador said his imps would like to go home now. Do you think we can send them back?"

Kali thought for a moment and replied, "Yes, I think they can go home, they are no longer needed. See if they need anything and thank them for their help."

"I will do that as soon as Kreador and the others return," replied Sorcha.

"Who are Stomper, Aleric, and Chaela?" Brietta asked

Kali looked at Brietta and said, "They are friends of Sorcha's. She made some interesting friends growing up.

Stomper is the centaur that you see galloping around. Chaela and Aleric are brother and sister—and vampires."

"Vampires!" Brietta questioned, "Why on earth would you allow vampires into Raven's Glenn?"

Kali responded, "I did not want to. I talked with the Ancients and they told me that they are part of Sorcha's future."

"But they walk around in the sunlight ... how?" asked Brietta.

"Yes, they do," replied Kali. "We gave them a pendant that was created special for each of them. It allows them to walk in the sunlight, and allows them to use some of their powers. Since they are vampires, we also added in a few safety precautions. They cannot harm us; if they do, they will burst into flames and die. If they take the pendants off while in Raven's Glenn, they will burst into flames and die. Believe me, they will not try to harm us. Chaela was Volac's betrothed before he turned her. She has spent over 200 years trying to get rid of him. Aleric has recently learned how treacherous Volac can be, and almost lost his life when Volac turned against him. Do not worry, Brietta, they will all be leaving once Sorcha is fully recovered. They will search for, find, and destroy Volac."

Kreador found Aleric and Chaela and told them about the roots Brietta needed to make a special healing broth for Sorcha.

"We cannot go with you," said Chaela. "The white ash can kill Aleric and me. Aleric's hands are still burnt from when he tried to kill Volac with a branch from the white ash tree."

Kali and Brietta arrived. Overhearing the conversation, Kali interrupted,

"I already have the dried mint from a previous trip, Brietta has the horehound, all we need are the roots from the oak and white ash. I see we cannot send Aleric or Chaela, the white ash will likely kill them. It surprises me that Aleric still has his hands. It is up to you, Stomper. You and Kreador will find what we need. Brietta needs those items for a broth that will help Sorcha counteract the results of Volac's bite.

"I tried to reach Sorcha when I saw her enter that house," explained Brietta. "I saw Volac enter also. There was too much going on that night. Volac's creatures were everywhere, keeping me away from the house. Then I saw someone thrown out of the house and dash back in with a branch of white ash. You arrived so I figured I would not be needed and continued fighting."

Kali could not believe what she was hearing. "You tried to save Sorcha?" Kali asked. "I did not even know you knew who she was."

"When I first arrived here in Raven's Glenn, I made sure I knew who everyone was. I came to help, for I knew Raven's Glenn could not fall. The destruction of Raven's Glenn would mean the downfall of so many secrets and worlds. Raven's Glenn is the key and protector of us all."

"I wish you had made yourself known earlier," said Kali. "Thank you for coming to our aid. Would you please consider taking Priestess Alisa's place here in Raven's Glenn?"

"The power of Raven's Glenn is made whole by the powers of the five houses of the star, the pentagram. I understand that two high priestesses have died and left two points of the star without guidance, but I am the high priestess of my own coven. How can I be both? My own coven needs me."

Kali pointed towards the north and replied, "You are here now. Who leads and protects while you are away? Raven's Glenn calls to you for this is your real home. If it needs to be, you can always return in times of trouble and have the powers of Raven's Glenn with you, or your coven can join Raven's Glenn and serve as our eyes to the north."

Priestess Brietta rubbed her chin and stared at the ground. A few minutes passed before she answered,

"If allowed to do both, I will accept your offer as guardian of the air and take my place on the point of the star. Once the damaged houses are restored, I will be ready, when all is as it should be."

Kali smiled. "Welcome back to Raven's Glenn, Brietta. We must find a replacement for Priestess Flora by the next full moon and under the moon's light, the Circle of Stone will once again play to the rituals that will join our houses and restore the powers of Raven's Glenn."

"So it will be," replied Brietta.

Stomper and Kreador returned from the forest and approach Kali and Brietta.

"stoor eht evah ew," squeaked Kreador.

Brietta smiled, "Well, then, take them to my house.... Hurry! I will meet you there shortly."

Kreador asked, "esuoh tahw?"

"Kreador, my poor Kreador," Kali said, "Brietta will take the place of Alisa and now lives where Alisa once did."

"sehctiw bmud!" replied Kreador as he and Stomper headed for Brietta's house.

Having lit the kettle of water, Brietta added just the right amount of herbs and roots. Not too much, not too little; she hummed an Ancient tune as she watched the kettle boil. *The color must be just right*, Brietta thought to herself, then stirred and watched, stirred and watched. Brietta waited as the brew slowly transformed. The clear water first turned a murky brown, and then swirls of different colors—blue, red, green, and yellow covered the surface. Finally, the brew settled, and under the hot steam, a dark, even-colored broth waited for Sorcha to drink.

"There! The brew is ready," Brietta said aloud, "but Raven's Glenn is not."

Morra and Sasa found Kali at the centermost house checking on Sorcha.

"How is Sorcha doing?" asked Sasa.

Kali replied, "She is doing better. With the blood of the Ancients and the broth that Brietta is making, she should be up and around in no time."

"During the battle," said Morra, "there was a witch from one of the mountain covens that stood out. She was attacked by many but fought well; even after being cut by a spear and nicked with an arrow, she kept fighting."

"Another one.... Who is this witch?" asked Kali.

"They call her Priestess Vevila," replied Morra. "She, too, is a priestess of her coven."

"I know of her. I once asked her to join Raven's Glenn," responded Kali.

"She just might reconsider that offer since all the witches of her coven were killed in the battle," replied Morra.

"I will go and talk with Priestess Vevila. Stay here and watch over Sorcha until I return."

"Vevila is recovering at Sasa's house," answered Morra.

Kali approached Sasa's house and heard a disturbance coming from inside. Peeking in the window, she saw several imps crawling and pulling on Vevila as Vevila tried to swat them away.

I forgot about them, Kali thought to herself as she entered through the doorway. "Priestess Vevila, how...."

"Do something with these pests!" Vevila shouted. Kali pointed at the imps and ordered them out of the house.

Kali approached Vevila and asked, "How are your wounds?"

"I will be fine. They are only flesh wounds."

"I heard your coven was destroyed in the battle. Would you consider a house on the star of Raven's Glenn as your new home?"

"I see Raven's Glenn was not destroyed, neither was all my coven at Hazel Grove. For whom do I replace?"

"You will replace Priestess Flora, guardian of the water, and take over her house."

"I would be honored to serve Raven's Glenn," replied Vevila.

"Good!" said Kali. "Your house will be restored soon and with it the powers of Raven's Glenn. With the next full moon, you and Brietta will take your places on the points of the star."

Kali summoned all the priestess to meet her at the northernmost house. Once they all arrived, she walked among them and said,

"Priestesses, the points of the star are complete again and, with the arrival of a new moon, Raven's Glenn will be restored. We must finish rebuilding Priestess Vevila's house. Brietta will oversee the construction for she has great knowledge of such things. Once all is ready, we will meet in the Circle of Stone and reconnect with the Ancients so the powers of Alisa's and Flora's house can transfer to Brietta and Vevila. Afterward, we will have Sorcha drink the broth that Brietta has made and eat the sacred bread that will be soaked in the blood of the Ancients. Sorcha will be as she was before, yet she will be different. Her powers will be as before and yet different since now she will become immortal, similar to a vampire, and have the strength of many. The blood of the Ancients and the broth from Brietta will cure her thirst for blood and rob Volac of his power over her. This was foretold by the Ancients and shall be ... blessed be the Ancients."

"Blessed be!" they all responded.

Kali left the northern house. Thinking to herself, she commented aloud, "All is almost complete. Sorcha will recover and hunt down Volac, the points of the pentagram are complete, and—oh! I almost forgot those pesky imps.

"Kreador! Kreador! Where are you?" Kali called out.

While Kali was walking around searching for Kreador, she found Stomper.

"Have you seen Kreador?" Kali asked.

"Yes, he is at your house with Sorcha," Stomper replied.

As Kali walked away, she realized something did not appear right. Kali stopped, looked around, and searched with eyes and mind. She could sense something was not right. *Umm*, she thought, *I must ask and see if anyone else can sense something wrong*. She went back to her house where she saw Sorcha and Chaela sitting in the middle of the room.

"Sorcha, where is Kreador?" Kali asked.

Sorcha looked up and said, "He is in the other room—asleep, I think."

"Is everything okay?" Sorcha asked.

"Yes," Kali replied, and as Kali walked towards the other room, she stopped and said, "Do you sense anything different today?"

Sorcha and Chaela looked at each other and Sorcha replied, "We were just talking about that. Something does not seem right, but we cannot figure out where it is coming from."

"Keep your eyes open and mind clear," Kali replied, "I have something I must do."

Kali found Kreador curled up in the corner, and she gently shook Kreador awake.

Kali whispered, "Kreador, it is time to send your people home, go and gather them up and then meet me in the northern house."

"sey," said Kreador. He jumped up and ran out the door.

Meanwhile, Kali still sensed that something was wrong. She headed out the door and started walking the round and searching the houses to make sure everyone was present or accounted for. As she was walking along, Priestess Morra ran up to her.

Gasping for air, Morra said, "Two of our witches have vanished."

"What? When did this happen?" asked Kali.

"From my understanding," Morra replied, "sometime yesterday. They were in the forest gathering roots and herbs and have not been seen since."

"Find them," said Kali. "I must go and send Kreador's imps home."

Kali arrived at the northern house. Inside, she found Kreador and the other imps waiting.

"Thank you, Kreador; this will only take a minute." Kali raised her arms and chanted three times:

"From within and without, from there to here, open the door and reappear!"

A small spinning black hole appeared before them and started to grow larger. The room filled with the twirling winds of a major storm. The imps one by one entered the black hole. After the last one entered, Kali chanted the spell backwards and closed the black hole. Kali lowered her arms and turned around, and there stood Kreador.

Surprised, Kali looked at Kreador and said, "Kreador, why did you not go with your people?"

"yats I ereh," said Kreador.

Kali laughed and shook her head. "If that is what you want."

Kali headed back to her house where she knew she would find Sorcha and Chaela.

"Sorcha, Chaela, I have found out that two of our witches are missing. We must find them," said Kali.

Before Sorcha collapsed, she looked up, and, in a trancelike state, said, "Off the path and deep in the forest you will find the remains of those you look for."

"Sorcha! Are you okay?" asked Chaela.

"This is worse than I feared," Kali interrupted. "We must reunite the points of the star ... soon. Chaela, stay with Sorcha and do not let her out of your sight. I will be back in a few minutes. I must go talk with Brietta."

Stomper in the meantime was walking in the forest when he heard Sorcha's voice in his head. *Stomper, please hear my plea. Our friends are missing and the message I am receiving from within does not make sense.... Off the path and deep in the forest, you will find those you look for. Please help.*

Stomper looked around and somehow knew exactly where in the forest to search. Deeper into the forest he went, when, all of a sudden, he heard moans and screams. He stopped and listened, and heard it again. He made a sharp right and galloped through the forest and into a small clearing, where he came upon two black shadows hovering over a birdman. The shadows appeared to be holding a witch as the birdman tore at her flesh. Another witch cowered on the ground in fear.

The birdman looked at Stomper and said, "This is what the Lord of Darkness will do to you when next you cross his path."

With sword in hand, Stomper charged at the birdman and yelled, "And this is what happens when my enemies cross my path!" With one quick sweeping strike from his sword, the birdman's head went rolling across the ground and the shadows disappeared.

Stomper walked up to the witch on the ground and asked, "What is your name?"

"A ... Aidenn," she responded.

"Aidenn, I am Stomper, friend of Sorcha. Come with me, we must get you back to Raven's Glenn."

Slowly she rose up, and said, "Faye, we must take her back with us."

Stomper looked around and realized he had no safe way of getting her friend back. He rubbed his chin and said, "One moment, I must concentrate."

Stomper lowered his head and whispered, "Kali, I know you can hear me. I have found those you look for. Sense me, hear my thoughts, and bring help."

Kali meanwhile was in the middle of talking with Brietta about the message Sorcha received before Sorcha collapsed. Stomper's thoughts arrived and interrupted hers.

"Kali? Kali, what is happening?" asked Brietta.

"Come, Brietta, hold on, we must go," responded Kali.

Brietta grabbed Kali's arm and they vanished. The forest blazed before their eyes as they appeared to flow through the branches and trees. Soon, they landed in a small clearing deep within the forest where they found a terrified sobbing witch and a nervous Stomper.

"Kali, Sorcha sent me a message. I have found whom you seek," said Stomper as he nodded in the direction of Aidenn.

Kali looked at Aidenn, and then she saw Faye's lifeless, bloody body. "Stomper, what happened?"

After Stomper explained, Kali nodded and turned to face Brietta. "Brietta, the houses must be finished by tonight, we need the points of the star reconnected immediately, and then Sorcha needs that broth. There is no more time to waste. Stomper, take Aidenn back to Raven's Glenn, Brietta and I will be there shortly."

Kali reached down and touched Faye's still warm body. "The Summerlands await you," Kali whispered, and with the snap of her fingers, Faye's body ignited.

Brietta approached Kali with concern, "Kali, I have received word that a pack of vampires have been spotted in Hazel Grove and from the description of their leader, I think I know where Volac is. Except for minor things, the houses are complete and I should go home to help my coven."

Kali replied, "Tonight is a full moon. We will restore Raven's Glenn and with it Sorcha. Sorcha will go to Hazel Grove. You will be a high priestess of the star and here you must stay. The Ancients have told us that it will be Sorcha's quest to find and destroy Volac, so it must be!"

Brietta lowered her head and responded, "So it must be."

As night approached, Kali summoned the high priestesses of Raven's Glenn. When all the priestesses arrived, Kali spoke,

"Prepare the Circle of Stone and rest; when the moon is directly above us, we will meet within the circle and make Raven's Glenn whole again. Morra, you will bring Sorcha and tell Chaela she must stay away. She cannot even look into the circle, for if she enters she will burn and I will not be able to help her."

Quickly, the passing shades of night's darkness fell to the approaching light of a new full moon. Night had arrived and silence swept over Raven's Glenn. The bell would soon ring, letting all know that the Circle of Stone awaited them.

Kali at Sorcha's side whispered, "Soon, Sister ... soon."

The bell rung and Kali gently touched Sorcha's face and said, "We must go to the Circle of Stone."

Within the Circle of Stone, a large pentagram covered the ground, etched into the soil by the high priestesses of Raven's Glenn. Kali stood at the entrance to the circle of stone. She raised her arms upwards, towards the moon-filled sky, and called for the witches of Raven's Glenn to enter and take their places on the round, the circle that connected the points of the star. Walking to the altar, she turned and called for the guardians of the star to enter and take their place on the points of the star. When all was in place, the moonlight increased and filled the circle. Kali removed her *athame* from the altar's secret place and traced a circle in the air around and above the conveners and then she knelt at the altar and chanted,

"Hail and come forth the power and sprits of the north, east, south and west. I call upon the spirits of earth, air, fire, and water and the spirits of the Ancients to open and enter the circle."

Raising her *athame* to the sky and then lowering it to the earth, Kali stood and turned to face the witches. "Blessed be the powers that be, and blessed be the Ancients!"

"Blessed be!" all responded.

Sorcha entered the circle and all eyes followed her approach to the altar. Kali sharply turned and stared at Priestess Morra, who smiled and pointed at Sorcha. Side by side, Kali and Sorcha faced the coven of witches; a thick whitish fog slowly formed and filled the area. As the fog slightly cleared, Brietta and Vevilla left their points on the star and approached the altar. Taking Brietta's hand, Kali led Brietta back to the upper left point of the star, where they stopped. Standing on the point waited Priestess Alisa.

Kali approached Alisa with Brietta and said,

"There are two of you, and now there is one of you. You are the power of the air, and your energy is great, here and now you two are connected."

Tears formed in Kali's eyes as she looked at Alisa and said,

"Good bye, dear friend, it is as it must be."

Alisa responded, "My spirit is with you and Raven's Glenn. Do not be sad for it must be. I stand aside and welcome Brietta, for now we are connected on the point as it must be."

As Alisa faded, Brietta took her place on the point and Kali returned to the altar. Taking Vevilla's hand, she led her to the upper right hand point of the star. Waiting there with a smile and open arms stood Priestess Flora.

Kali approached and said, 'There are two of you, and now there is one of you. You are the power of water and your energy is great. Here and now you are connected."

Priestess Flora reached out and cupped Kali's face and said,

"My dear friend, it is as it must be. Weep with happiness for I join the Ancients and will be with you always."

Flora faded and Vevilla took her place on the point. Kali turned around and returned to the altar and Sorcha.

Reaching for the vile of blood and the sacred bread, Kali dripped the blood over the bread and raised her arms to the sky and shouted,

"I call upon the Ancients to bless this sacred bread, that which is soaked in your own blood."

Kali took the bread and handed it to Sorcha,

"Kneel, Sorcha, and eat. The bread will make you whole."

Kali next handed Sorcha the broth that Brietta made,

"Drink and wash away what was, for your energy is great and you have returned to us."

Sorcha ate and drank and, as she stood, a strange feeling came over her. Stronger, alive and with a glow in her eye, she shouted,

"Hail to the Ancients, blessed be!"

All responded, "Blessed be!"

Kali faced the witches and called out, "Hail to the points of the star, hail to the power of Raven's Glenn, hail to the Ancients, for we are now connected as one again ... blessed be."

All responded, "Blessed be!"

Kali raised her hands for silence. "Fellow sisters, our powers, and those of Raven's Glenn have been restored. We must celebrate."

Raising her *athame*, Kali drew a circle in the sky and shouted,

"The circle is closed, and the points on the star reunited. Let us celebrate! Start the fires and drink our wine, for with the sunrise a new day arrives."

The moon's light spread outward and dimmed within the Circle of Stone, covering all of Raven's Glenn within its glow. Laughter and joy spread from building to building, witch to witch. Raven's Glenn was complete again, her powers restored.

Sorcha sought out Chaela. "Where is Aleric?" Sorcha asked.

"He and Kreador went to Hazel Grove to see if Volac was really there," responded Chaela.

"Then we must prepare to leave," commented Sorcha.

"NO!" shouted Kali. "You must first know of your new powers and how to use them. Volac can wait a few more days."

"Kali, I must go, you keep telling me that this is what I was born for. It is now time for you to let me go."

Kali looked into Sorcha's eyes with a seriousness that made Sorcha take notice, step back, and smile. "You know little of the prophecy and even less of who you will be," shouted Kali.

Sorcha was about to respond when images filled her mind, images of burning houses and vampires. Kreador was sending flashes of what was going on in Hazel Grove.

"Sorcha—what is it? What do you see?" asked Kali.

"Kali, Chaela and I must go, we will be back shortly. Chaela, hold on to me tight."

Chaela grabbed a hold of Sorcha, and in the next instant, they were gone. They reappeared right next to Aleric and Kreador.

"About time you two decided to join us," said Aleric

"Aleric, where is Volac?" asked Sorcha.

"I haven't seen him, but I know he is here," said Aleric.

"Aleric, you Chaela and Kreador wait here, Volac is mine," said Sorcha.

Before anyone could respond, Sorcha was gone. Sorcha reappeared outside one of the main houses in the village. She could sense Volac was near; she just had to find him.

Taking a deep breath, she closed her eyes and mentally searched the village. In a house in the center of Hazel Grove she found him.

"I have had enough of this. It is time to end this once and for all!" Sorcha said aloud.

Slowly, Sorcha approached the house.... Volac was inside. She looked through one of the windows to see where he was. When she looked inside, she saw a woman whose hands were tied together behind her back, lying on the floor. Volac was on top of her, using his weight to hold her down. Sorcha closed her eyes and appeared right behind Volac. In a blur, Volac turned around and grabbed Sorcha; he then threw her across the room.

"I knew you would come!" laughed Volac. "Sorcha, did you really think you could sneak up on me?"

Sorcha, still lying on the floor, slowly sat up and shook her head to clear it. Slowly, she stood up and a little shaken from hitting the wall, stared at Volac. Her eyes darkened and then appeared to glow red in color. A little startled, Volac backed away and looked around the room before he dived straight out an open window. Sorcha heard Volac laugh aloud and then everything went quite except for the moans coming from the women lying on the floor. Sorcha untied the women and noticed several blisters and burns on her arms. The door opened and Aleric entered.

"Volac is gone, isn't he?" said Aleric.

"Yes," replied Sorcha. "I need to heal the burns on ... what is your name?" Sorcha asked the witch in front of her.

"Natal ... I am the town's witch and paid to protect Hazel Grove from men like that."

"Aleric, you and the others make sure everyone else is okay. I will heal Natal and will join you when I am done," said Sorcha.

Aleric nodded and left. Sorcha looked at Natal and said, "Let me heal those burns."

Sorcha placed her hands on Natal's arm and closed her eyes while she silently chanted. The arm glowed as it slowly healed.

"Your arm is healed," said Sorcha. "What are we going to do about the condition of your village?"

"We will rebuild and add protection spells," said Natal.

Sorcha looked at her and asked, "You did not have any protection spells around your village?"

"It was not needed," replied Natal.

"I must return to Raven's Glenn. Wait here, I will be right back."

Back in Raven's Glenn, Sorcha found Brietta and Kali. The three returned to Hazel Grove.

Brietta looked around. "This was a trap for you, Sorcha. Your new powers must have confused Volac so he escaped."

"He wanted me out of Raven's Glenn," said Sorcha. "He wants me dead and will not stop trying until I am. See why I need to leave. I will figure out my powers and strengths as I go. We must go back to Raven's Glenn so I can prepare. It is time to find and destroy Volac."

Days passed and Sorcha grew restless. Her senses seemed more alive than ever as she prepared to leave Raven's Glenn. An evil darkness from somewhere within Sorcha was growing ... waiting to surface. Volac's bite delivered the evil within her; now Sorcha would have to learn how to control it.

Priestess Vevila approached Sorcha. "You will need to take your weapons with you when you leave. Almost everything else you will be able to acquire along the way. Come with me, Sorcha, I need to show you something."

Vevila entered her house with Sorcha behind her. As Sorcha entered the room, a cage made of white ash fell over her. From the shadows of the room, Kali and the other high priestesses appeared and quickly cast a spell over the cage. Sorcha's eyes turned red as she found herself trapped in two worlds ... that of a witch and a vampire. Kali walked up to the cage and pointed her finger at Sorcha.

"You think you are so powerful, but your mind is not clear. Have you forgotten your training so soon? Can you control what vampire is in you? The blood of the Ancients still brews within you ... you are not ready to leave. When your thoughts are right, you will be able to escape from this cage and then you will be ready to hunt down Volac."

Chapter Seven

$\mathcal{T}$wo days passed. Becoming more vampire than witch, Sorcha's anger increased as she tried to escape. Her powers from both worlds appeared useless as she shouted out in rage ... cursing the powers of Raven's Glenn. Priestess Morra entered the room and approached Sorcha.

"You dishonor your training and you dishonor Alisa and Flora. You are not worthy of my time ... just look at you! Have you not learned what is within you? Do you not even remember your training in the cave?"

Sorcha's eyes glowed with anger as she stared at Priestess Morra.

"Showing more anger is not the way," continued Morra, "and it will increase the power of the spells we put on the cage. You are a witch, Sorcha, a powerful witch trained to think from within. Could the Ancients be wrong about you? I think so!"

Morra turned her back to Sorcha and shook her head in disgust.

"What a waste of my time," Morra mumbled as she left the room.

Maybe it was the lecture from Morra or the years of training but a voice from within awakened Sorcha. Standing in the cage and looking around, Sorcha smiled as she lowered her head and connected with her inner spirit, bringing forward the witch that was her.

"Kreador! Kreador," Sorcha whispered. A thought flowed through the air, reaching the ears of Kreador.

Kreador soon arrived and was stunned to find Sorcha locked in a cage.

"Open the cage, Kreador," Sorcha asked.

Kreador easily unlocked the door. Stepping out of the cage, Sorcha found herself back in the cage. Again, she tried to leave the cage and again she found herself back in the cage. Lowering her head, Sorcha concentrated on the powers within her. Darkness and light flickered within her thoughts. Her head was spinning, and she felt dizzy. A bright light emerged from within her and overpowered the dark that flowed within her mind. Her powers had surfaced. Sorcha waved her hand and the cage disappeared. Sorcha picked up Kreador and kissed him on the forehead.

"I am back," said Sorcha.

"uoy erew erehw," replied Kreador.

Once outside, the high priestesses surrounded Sorcha. Looking at Priestess Morra, Sorcha laughed and said,

"Careful, Morra, I do see a toad in your future."

All the witches laughed aloud as Kali approached Sorcha and handed her a quiver full of arrows.

"These arrows were made by me and the other high priestesses and carry the magick of Raven's Glenn ... use them wisely. You are now ready to hunt Volac and fulfill the prophecy of the Ancients. Vevilla will go with you to Hazel Grove and return to Raven's Glenn once you have found the scent of Volac and begin the hunt."

Kali looked Sorcha in the eye as she touched her cheek with the palm of her hand and, with great sadness, whispered,

"It is possible we will never meet again. Blessed be, Sister, your fate awaits you."

Kali turned and walked away while Sorcha stood there for a few minutes watching her. Her eyes misty, Sorcha turned and looked at Kreador, Chaela, Stomper, and Aleric.

"Let's go kill a vampire!" shouted Sorcha.

"Follow me!" shouted Vevilla, and she vanished, arriving first at Hazel Grove, the home she gave up to be a high priestess on the star at Raven's Glenn.

Sorcha held her arms outward, and as the wind twirled at her feet, she lowered her arms and Hazel Grove appeared before them. Looking back towards Raven's Glenn, Sorcha said aloud,

"It's not your time ... Kali, we will meet again, I promise."

Sorcha spotted Vevilla by one of the damaged buildings having a conversation with Natal. Natal was explaining to Vevilla what happened.

"We heard there was a vampire in Hazel Grove and went searching for him," explained Natal.

"About the fires…," interrupted Vevilla.

"We started them," said Natal.

"You what?" asked Vevilla.

"Well, we were searching the village when we saw this large vampire attack old witch Celyn's daughter. As he carried her limp body into the house, we surrounded the house so he could not escape, and since Celyn's daughter was dead, we set fire to the house. We had to! Otherwise her daughter would have turned into a vampire."

"And the other houses?" asked Vevilla.

"There was more than one vampire," explained Natal.

Natal turned and pointed at one of the houses, "I watched the large vampire escape that burning house and run into that house over there so I followed him inside and tried to attack him. When I awakened, he was above me asking where you were. I told him I did not know but he kept burning my arms. I was just about done for when I opened my eyes and saw a woman flying across the room and he vanished out the window."

"Do you know where he went?" asked Sorcha.

Natal replied, "We think he went to Stone Hearth, the next village beyond the Dream Fields."

"Dream Fields?" asked Sorcha.

"Yes, they protect us from the outside world, the world of men. That is why we do not use protection spells."

"Oh!" replied Sorcha.

Vevilla looked at Sorcha and asked, "You do know of the outside world, don't you?"

"I have traded with the traders that pass through Raven's Glenn, and, as a little girl, I was raised in the world of men," Sorcha replied.

Vevilla interrupted, "Remember, Sorcha, in their world, they hate witches. They kill what they do not understand. They have different gods and no powers. If they ever see you and Kreador ... you will be hanging from the trees for sure. We live here, enclosed ... surrounded by the Dream Fields, for they keep us safe from men. No mortal man can pass through the Dream Fields without falling asleep. We try to toss their bodies back to their side, but sometimes the birds get to them first." Vevila shrugged her shoulders as she continued, "We feel little for their deaths since men have a habit of killing what they do not understand."

"Sorcha!" Chaela cried out, "Aleric and I have tracked Volac to a village they call Stone Hearth."

"I thought so!" responded Natal.

Sorcha touched Chaela's arm and said, "Find Stomper and Kreador, we leave for Stone Hearth."

"Be careful, Sorcha," warned Vevila.

"Vevila!" replied Sorcha, "you need to return to Raven's Glenn, these witches can clean up their own mess. Tell Kali I go to Stone Hearth."

After a long walk and just before nightfall, Sorcha and her party of four arrived at the outskirts of Stone Hearth. Off to the side of the road, Sorcha spotted a broken down cart with two-rear wheels removed and the back side of the cart buried partially in the ground. She smiled.

"I have a plan!" Sorcha said aloud. "Stomper, can you and Aleric fix this cart?"

Kreador jumped up and down, "nac I," he squeaked.

"Then the three of you fix the cart and hurry, we will enter Stone Hearth when it is dark."

Sorcha watched the narrow road that led into Stone Hearth. With the arrival of darkness, few people appeared to leave the buildings or travel the road. *This is good*, Sorcha thought to herself. Soon, darkness embraced the village and Sorcha watched the villagers light the torches. House after house lit up and cast strange-shaped shadows over the street.

"Our entrance will be of little notice," Sorcha whispered.

Stomper announced the cart was ready to go. They found the other two wheels close by and pulled the cart out of the ground—the reins were still attached and in good condition. After Stomper and Aleric attached the wheels, the cart moved freely. The cart had a wood seat up front and a short bed with low wood sides; the seat, made for two, fitted Sorcha perfectly.

Sorcha looked at Stomper and said, "You will be the ox that pulls the cart," and then she cast a believing spell over him so anyone who saw him would believe he was an ox. "Chaela, you and Aleric will transform and be my pet wolf pups."

"em dna," asked Kreador.

"Kreador ... Kreador, you will be my pet bird."

Sorcha picked up Kreador and tossed him into the air. Wings spread, he landed on the seat of the cart. Climbing up next to Kreador, Sorcha grabbed the reins and gave Stomper a little twitch on the rear end with a long, thin, hickory stick. Stomper turned and gave a smiling Sorcha a dare-not-do-that-again look, then Sorcha said,

"Let's go! We have a vampire to kill."

The dark narrow road through Stone Hearth, barely lit by the light coming from the windows, cast even darker shadows that concealed their approach as they entered Stone Hearth. Slowly, the cart passed each building while Chaela and Aleric smelled the air. Sorcha first heard a growl, then a whine from the pups. She felt it, too ... Volac was close.

Jumping from the cart, Sorcha approached a well-lit building. The laughter and words of men and women filled the air as she entered the building. Standing in the doorway, her eyes searched from person to person. A large man stood and pointed at her.

"Come in! Come in! Look, friends, more flesh to touch!"

Removing her black hood and exposing her long black hair and dark eyes, Sorcha smiled as she watched him approach.

"My! You are a pretty one," he said as he reached out to touch her.

No one really saw what happened. He quickly jerked his hand back and, with fear in his eyes, ran from the building, leaving his friends laughing and pointing at Sorcha.

In a corner of the room, hidden within the shadows, Sorcha saw a tall man with two women and started to walk towards them. A man stumbled in her path. Holding a vessel of wine in one hand, he reached out with the other and tried to hug Sorcha. With the strength of ten men and a glow in her eyes, she tossed him to the floor. As he stumbled to stand, he pointed at her and shouted,

"WECHEE!"

Immediately, the tall man in the shadows turned and faced Sorcha.

"We meet again, Sorcha," he sneered, and then tossed the two women to the side as he moved towards Sorcha with fangs out and a look of hate in his eyes.

From somewhere in the room, a voice shouted,

"Vampire! No ... Witch! No ... VAMPIRE! RUN!"

As the people screamed and ran from the building, Volac escaped; the villagers regrouped outside and circled Sorcha. Sorcha vanished and reappeared in the cart, leaping into the seat.

"Run, Stomper! Run!" Sorcha cried out.

Pulling the cart, Stomper galloped out of Stone Hearth. Soon with the lights of the village far behind them, they came across a less traveled path that led to a safe hiding place behind a large hill covered with bushes.

"That was close," commented Sorcha as she stepped down from the cart.

"Aleric, go track Volac," Sorcha commanded. "We must know where he goes."

As Sorcha searched the night, her eyes saw a faint image.

"Kali!"

The image of someone laughing quickly faded and Sorcha commented aloud,

"My eyes are playing tricks on me."

Kreador started squawking and Sorcha turned around to face him.

"What is it, Kreador?" asked Sorcha.

Kreador pointed at two glowing eyes bouncing in the darkness as they approached.

"Aleric returns," said Chaela.

As Aleric approached, he transformed back into a vampire.

"Volac," said Aleric, "is heading for a village west of Stone Hearth, a place called Willow Creek."

"We should go now while the night is with us!" Sorcha replied.

"There is a small village between here and Willow Creek," commented Aleric. "We should stop there and gather some supplies. It will be daylight before we can reach Willow Creek. However, if we gather supplies and then head out, we will be there just before nightfall; maybe then we can trap and destroy Volac."

"I do not know of any village between here and Willow Creek," replied Sorcha.

Aleric laughed, "Most people do not know of this village, they have only heard stories. The village is called Hollow's End."

"Hollow's End?" said Sorcha. "You are right ... there are only stories about that place. Chaela, do you know of this place?"

Chaela looked at Aleric and then Sorcha before she said, "Yes, I know of this place. It was destroyed many years ago. Why do you want to go to a place that no longer exists?"

"It was rebuilt, and they have what we will need to aid us in our search for Volac," replied Aleric.

"I do not understand," said Sorcha.

"Follow me and I will show you," replied Aleric.

"Show us the way," Sorcha replied. "Let's go and see this village of old."

When they reached the outer edge of Hollow's End, Sorcha could not believe what she was seeing. *How can this be...?* she thought to herself. Hollow's End appeared alive and well. As they stared at the village of tales and legends, they noticed someone was walking up a winding path towards them.

"Aleric, it has been a long time. What brings you back?"

"Zane, it is good to see you again. I have come for a brief visit and supplies."

Zane stared at Aleric, "What have you told your friends about us?"

Aleric laughed, "I have told them that you have supplies that will be needed in our journey. It is up to you if you would like them to know more."

"Come ... follow me," replied Zane, "I will take you to see Ashe."

They followed Zane down the winding path and soon stood before a wall of trees. Zane raised his arms and hands upwards, as if reaching for the sky, and quietly chanted. Zane then lowered his arms and the trees parted, revealing a different village.

"Come, Ashe is waiting."

"Wait" shouted Sorcha. "What village did we just go through if this is Hollow's End?"

Zane laughed and said," An illusion, dear one, an illusion. Visitors are not usually welcome."

Sorcha moved closer to Aleric and whispered, "What have you gotten us into?"

Aleric replied, "Just wait.... Ashe owes me, and you can say I'm calling in a favor."

Sorcha and Chaela shrugged their shoulders and followed Aleric and Zane. As they walked further into the village, Sorcha noticed how the people stared at them.

Chaela looked over at Aleric and said, "Why do I feel like we are about to meet our death?"

"Do not worry so much," replied Aleric, "Ashe would not dare hurt my sister or anyone with me."

Zane guided them up a small hill to an area covered with large thick bushes; behind the bushes hid the entrance to a large moss-covered cave. As they entered, Sorcha could smell the moist dirt. The dampness sent a chill up her spine. From deep within the cave, piercing the darkness, a voice addressed Aleric.

"Aleric, how good of you to stop by—and look, you brought guests!"

"They are not to be touched, Ashe. You know better than to even try," said Aleric.

"Do I now?"

Quickly, before anyone could move, Sorcha had Ashe pinned against the far wall. With her other hand, she formed a ball of light. As the light filled the room, Sorcha asked Aleric,

"Why have you brought us here, and who is this ... really?"

Ashe interrupted, "I was not expecting a witch to be with you, Aleric. That was a nice touch on your part and you are safe for now."

Sorcha stared at Ashe and replied, "I am Sorcha of Raven's Glenn, and if you try to harm any of us ... you will pay with your life."

Aleric laughed, "This is Sorcha, you might have heard of her."

Ashe replied, "How is it that a mere female, a witch, can attack me from across the room without even seeing me?"

"I am not a mere witch; I also have the speed and strength of a vampire, courtesy of Volac. Aleric, we will wait for you outside. Get what you need, we leave within the hour."

After they left the moss-covered cave, Chaela informed Sorcha about Ashe.

"I know who that was. He is not a vampire though," said Cheala. "At least not any longer. Aleric used to talk about someone whom he helped throughout the years. Ashe used to hunt and kill our kind, yet they are friends. How or why, I do not understand."

"Yes ... well, I do not like or trust him," responded Sorcha.

"Neither do I," said Stomper.

"I ron," squeaked Kreador.

A few minutes later, Aleric walked out of the moss-covered cave.

"Let's leave," said Aleric. "I have what I need."

"What did you need?" asked Sorcha.

"It does not concern you right now, so please do not ask again. When the time is right, I will let you know. If you want to arrive at Willow Creek by nightfall, we must go."

They followed Aleric down the path and out of the village. Back in the cart, they headed for Willow Creek. Soon, Hollow's End vanished behind them, and as they approached Willow Creek, Chaela spotted an old run-down building partially hidden behind a grove filled with trees. Sorcha thought it would be best to rest and enter Willow Creek under the cover of darkness. The road they would take into Willow Creek would be easy to follow under the light of the moon, and the old run-down building appeared safe and not far from the main road.

"Chaela," said Sorcha," go see if we can rest at that old run-down house up ahead."

No sooner had Chaela jumped from the cart when Aleric spotted a slight haze of smoke flow over the house.

"I smell something cooking," said Aleric.

"We will wait for Chaela to return before we bother whoever is inside," replied Sorcha.

Watching the tall grasses sway and fall, Sorcha could see the tip of a wolf's tail glide through the tall grasses as Chaela made her way back to the cart.

"An old lady lives in the house. She appears to be alone," said Chaela.

Sorcha looked up at the house then back at her friends and said, "Wait here, I will ask her if we can rest here for a while. Come when I call you."

Sorcha approached the door; a raspy old female voice from inside challenged her.

"Who dares to approach my house? Go away before I harm thee."

"I wish to speak with you," replied Sorcha.

The door slammed open, and a hunched over old woman with white hair and sunken eyes, wearing a tattered, worn black robe, appeared.

"I warned you!" shouted the old woman and she pointed a small crooked stick at Sorcha.

The first fireball was a surprise, but Sorcha just slapped it away. The second fireball made Sorcha angry and, with a wave of her hand, she tossed it back at the old woman. Stunned, the old woman ran back into the house and slammed the door shut behind her.

"Who are you?" the old woman yelled out. "And what do you want with me?"

"We need a place to feed and rest until nightfall," replied Sorcha.

"Who are you?" demanded the old woman.

"I come from Raven's Glenn. We mean you no harm."

The door slowly opened and the old woman stuck her head out.

"Raven's Glenn," replied the old woman. "I have not heard that name in many years ... the witches of Raven's Glenn, the stories I have heard. Oh! And I suppose you are a witch of some sort?"

Sorcha laughed as she turned around and waved for Stomper and the others to come.

"What do you see before you?" Sorcha asked the old woman.

"I see an ox, two wolves, a bird, a poor excuse for a cart, and you," said the old woman.

"Watch!" Sorcha replied.

Sorcha turned around and, with the wave of her hand, Stomper, Kreador, Chaela, and Aleric transformed back into their normal forms. With her eyes blinking and a look of shock on her face, the old woman stared at Sorcha and asked again,

"Who are you?"

"I am Sorcha of Raven's Glenn, high priestess, and next in line to be ruler of Raven's Glenn."

"I have heard of your coven and that of the Ancients. Your powers must be great," replied the old woman, "I am the last of my coven. The others have died of old age, or killed by the men from the villages. I am the last one ... I will die here alone.

"May we rest here?" asked Sorcha.

"Oh, yes! Please come in, and what is that little green thing you have with you?" she asked, pointing at Kreador.

"A pest from another world," mumbled Sorcha.

"TAHW!" squeaked Kreador.

"A friend of sorts," replied a smiling Sorcha. Kreador jumped up and down with a huge smile on his face.

"Come in, I have stew in the pot." The old woman waved for them to enter. She then turned around and walked back inside.

Chaela filled two bowls with stew and took them outside for Stomper and Kreador. Sorcha sat at a table across from the old woman and watched as she fumbled with a small stone box.

"I used to know how to open this dang thing. You twist here and pull here, and it should open," said the old woman.

"Can I try?" asked Sorcha.

"Here! I can't remember; maybe you can figure it out," replied the old woman.

No sooner had Sorcha touched the box than the old woman grasped her hand. With both of her feeble hands covering Sorcha's hands and the box, she leaned closer to Sorcha and whispered,

"It is you...."

A glimmer of youth appeared in the old woman's eyes as she stared at Sorcha.

"Look! The box opens," the old woman said, and she pointed at the box.

Sorcha looked down at the box; it appeared to come alive, changing slightly in color and size. Sliding the top off, Sorcha reached inside.

"Where did you get this?" Sorcha asked the old woman.

The old woman replied, "When I was young and my coven flourished, a strange but powerful witch visited us. Back then, the men of the village respected us and would often visit and ask our advice or pay for spells that could help them. One day, a powerful vampire arrived and killed several women in the village. They soon turned into vampires and began attacking other villagers. Out of fear, the men of the village turned on us and started killing witches. That was when the powerful witch appeared and saved us. When she left, she handed me this box and told me that someday before I die, another witch would visit, and she promised me that I would not die until I delivered this box to her. She said I would know and the box would know when the time was right. I am old and tired and wish to die soon, so I am happy that you have finally arrived. I am tired and wish to rest. Consider my house yours until you leave."

Sorcha nodded her head in agreement; the old woman struggled to stand, and then walked to the corner of the room where a large sac filled with straw covered the floor. She slowly reached down and fell on the sac of straw. Sorcha's eyes, fixed on the pentagram and leather cord she retrieved from the box, and now in her hand, did not see the old witch as she lay herself down to sleep.

"This is exactly like the one Kali wears," Sorcha said aloud and then placed it over her head and around her neck.

The room grew dark ... then light. Images from the past and future filled Sorcha's mind. Other worlds, strange worlds, worlds filled with things Sorcha had never seen before, appeared and faded, and a clutter of voices echoed throughout the room.

"Sorcha!" said Chaela, "Sorcha, wake up."

Chaela stood over Sorcha ... shaking her, but Sorcha fell deeper and deeper into a trance. Kreador came running into the room and grabbed Sorcha's head with both hands,

"kcab emoc!" Kreador yelled,

Kreador focused his thoughts; using skills only he had, his mind linked with Sorcha's and he was able to pull her back. Sorcha's eyes opened and she smiled.

"I know, I know," Sorcha repeated.

"You know what?" asked Chaela.

"I know!" replied Sorcha as she stood and pushed herself away from the table. "Where is the old woman? I need to ask her something."

Chaela looked around and answered, "She sleeps in the corner."

Sorcha walked over to the old woman and touched her; the old woman did not move.

"She is dead," said Sorcha.

Reaching down, Sorcha closed her eyelids and said, "Thank you, you served Raven's Glenn well."

Aleric walked into the room and said, "The night will soon be with us, it is time we go to Willow Creek."

Seeing the old witch on the floor, Aleric commented, "Should we bury her?"

"No!" Sorcha replied.

Sorcha took a few steps back from the old woman, and, with both hands, created a fireball and tossed it at her. The fire spread quickly and soon the whole house became engulfed in fire.

"We go to Willow Creek," said Sorcha, and then she climbed up on the cart and seated herself next to Kreador.

"What happened in the house?" Aleric asked Chaela.

"I think Sorcha just became Sorcha," Chaela replied.

"What?" asked Aleric.

"She knows," Chaela replied.

"Knows what?" asked Aleric.

"Everything!" replied Chaela.

The road into Willows Creek was busy and, unlike Stone Hearth, these villagers did not fear the dark. Dusk had arrived and it would be dark soon.

"We must be careful and find Volac quickly," Sorcha said aloud.

"How?" replied Aleric "He can be anyplace."

"I will ask around and see if any strangers have arrived within the past few days," Sorcha replied. "Volac likes the women. We start with them."

"LOOK!" shouted Chaela.

A large gathering of villagers appeared up ahead.

"Wait here!" Sorcha whispered.

Sorcha climbed down from the cart and walked over to the villagers. A young girl lay in the street with her throat ripped open. The villagers surrounded the young girl's body and then they noticed the lack of blood.

"Vampires!" someone said aloud.

The word soon passed from one to another that a vampire was among them and the village became alive with panic. Sorcha headed back to the cart.

"Volac is close. Wait here, I will find him," Sorcha told the others.

They waited and waited and after what seemed forever, Chaela faced the others and said,

"I'm going after her. We can't let her do this on her own."

Chaela hopped down off the cart and wondered off. As she disappeared between the houses, she turned herself into a wolf cub. Darting between buildings and trees, she kept a look out for anything unusual. Silently, she made her way to the center of the village, where she found several groups of people had gathered. *I wonder what is going on*, Chaela thought, then she sneaked closer so she could hear what was being said.

"Vampires I tell you, they killed old man Cob and took over his house," said a man in the group.

Another asked, "Why would they want his house?"

"I don't know," said another.

"We should burn the place down while we have a chance," said another in the group.

"Let's burn them out!" they all shouted and headed off in the direction of old man Cob's house. Chaela, against her better judgment ... followed.

They reached the house only to find it in shambles.

"Wha ... wha ... what do you think happened here?" asked one of the group.

"Vampires ... that is what happened," said another.

"Wait, look!" shouted a man, and pointed towards a cluster of trees.

Chaela looked where the man had pointed and saw several vampires hung from the tree branches—their clothing and skin appeared to be melting off their bodies.

"It looks like the trees are holding them in place," laughed another.

Chaela transformed back to herself and laughed aloud, then whispered ... "Sorcha."

Sorcha appeared at the outskirts of trees and saw the group of people standing there ... watching her.

"Behold, I am Sorcha of Raven's Glenn, fear these vampires no more."

Quietly and without notice, Sorcha snapped her fingers, and the vampires burst into flames. Sorcha saw Chaela standing behind the villagers and walked towards her while the group was busy watching the vampires burn.

"Come, Chaela," said Sorcha, "let's get out of here."

After one last glance at the villagers, Chaela joined Sorcha. They reached the cart and Chaela hopped in. Kreador took his seat in the front and patiently waited for Sorcha to join him. As they left the village, they heard the villager's question how the vampires they found hung from the trees had burst into flames. Other villagers argued about there being another person there that caused the fires.

"I had better be more careful next time ... I guess," Sorcha commented.

"So where are we going now?" asked Stomper.

"The people of Willow Creek were no help, and there was no sign of Volac," replied Chaela.

"What do you mean no sign?" asked Aleric.

"I mean just what I said," responded Chaela. "Volac sent those vampires here to throw us off. Now we need to find him again. I think we need to split up."

Sorcha agreed and said, "Aleric, you and Chaela go to the northern village of Red Grove. Kreador, Stomper, and I will continue down this road to Hell's Canyon. We will search out both places and meet at Hell's Canyon. One day's time is all you have."

Chaela and Aleric nodded in approval and turned themselves into wolf form before they headed off in the direction of Red Grove.

Sorcha sighed and said, "Well, are you ready for the village of hell?"

Stomper replied, "You mean Hell's Canyon?"

Sorcha stared at the road in front of them and did not answer. The countryside passed slowly and the road narrowed as they approached Hell's Canyon. The cart moved slowly through the narrow canyon road, its wheels just inches from the edge of the road; a steep drop off and certain death awaited those who rode too close to the edge.

"Easy, Stomper, take it slow," Sorcha warned as they approached the village.

Twice they almost slipped off the road and cheated death. The canyon was deep and littered with the carts of those who passed too fast and lost control. Half way through the canyon pass, the canyon widened and Hell's Canyon came into view. The buildings in the village appeared to hang on the side of the canyon walls and the road curved through the village, winding its way around the houses. Almost all the houses in the village were made of rock, stone, and wood, and located right on the main narrow road. Sorcha slowly guided the cart to a water-filled gully and a bridge that gave entrance to the small village. A short, fat man with a red face and large eyes, his clothes baggy, worn, and tattered, greeted them at the bridge.

"You have business in Hell's Canyon, or just passing through?" he asked Sorcha.

"I am looking for a tall man with dark hair and black eyes. He would have passed this way within the last day or so," responded Sorcha.

"I have seen no such stranger. Regardless, you must pay to cross my bridge."

"PAY!"

Sorcha stepped down from the cart and removed her hood. Her long black hair covered her shoulders and fluttered in the slight breeze. She approached the man. Taken back by her beauty and piercing eyes, the man fumbled as he tried to stand taller. *This beauty is a fine one*, he thought to himself as he tried to figure out a way to touch her flesh and have his way with her. He had done it before; why should she be different?

"Maybe we can make a deal," he asked Sorcha.

"What kind of deal?" replied Sorcha.

"It has been a while since a woman has entertained me," replied the short, fat man, and then he reached out and touched Sorcha's arm.

Stomper and Kreador turned just in time to see the fat, little man fly through the air, and the splash he made when he landed in the gully of water made them laugh.

"I can't swim!" he shouted. Sorcha clapped her hands and bowed.

"I am quite entertained, thank you, and enjoy your bath," replied Sorcha, and then she guided the cart across the bridge.

Close to Red Grove, Chaela and Aleric changed back into human form. Appearing as any other villager, they decided to walk the rest of the way and maybe ask a question or two of the villagers. After passing a sharp curve in the road, the village came into view, and at the same time, the sound of an approaching horse from behind them grabbed their attention. Stepping aside just in time, a large man—fully armed and riding a reddish colored horse—passed them, stopped, and turned around.

"I come from Willows Creek!" he shouted.

"I search for a tall man with dark hair and black eyes. He would have passed this way within the last day or so."

Chaela and Aleric looked at each other.

"What business do you have with this man?" Aleric asked the rider.

"I believe he is a vampire and he killed my daughter. I will not rest until I have taken his head with my sword."

"We must be careful of this man," whispered Chaela

Aleric shouted back, "I have seen no such man."

The rider nodded and galloped off towards Red Grove. Aleric commented, "I agree he may cause us problems, but then he may also lead us to Volac. We should follow him."

"How long must I stay in this form and pretend I am an ox?" asked Stomper.

Sorcha gave Stomper a little tap with the hickory stick and replied, "We are in the world of men. Remember men kill what they do not understand, so have patience, Stomper. When we find Volac, I will change you back. Now be quiet, we enter Hell's Canyon."

The men of the village appeared as any others. They walked from building to building, talked with each other, and boasted of doings that never happened.

Where are the women of the village? Sorcha thought to herself. The cart rounded a turn and Sorcha saw a gathering of men in the road. The cart came to a stop. Sorcha, Stomper, and Kreador watched as the men dispersed. There in the road, tied to a large pole, hung the limp body of a partially naked woman.

"What evil is this?" Sorcha whispered as she drove the cart closer to the woman.

"Stop, Stomper!" Sorcha yelled.

Sorcha pulled up her hood and jumped from the cart. As Sorcha approached the woman, she could see the bleeding wounds across her back. The woman's skin was pale white, with trails of blood flowing down her backside and legs. Sorcha touched her face and moved the sweat-drenched blonde hair from her eyes. Slowly, the woman opened her eyes and stared at Sorcha.

"What are they doing to you?" Sorcha asked as the woman tried to talk.

"I ... I... did noth...."

"WHO ARE YOU?" shouted a man.

Sorcha quickly turned around. Several men had gathered and demanded to know what business she had for interfering.

"Why do you do this?" asked Sorcha.

"It is no concern of yours, stranger! Now move on or you will be next!"

"I will ask you again: Why do you do this?" Sorcha replied.

"We do not have to explain anything to a woman, but since you're a stranger, I will tell you. This woman is the property of farmer Hade and was caught with another man."

"I ... did ... noth...," whispered the woman.

Sorcha looked at the woman and then the men.

"Do not believe her!" shouted the man. "She was caught talking with another man and you know what that leads to ... she must be punished! What business do you have in Hell's Canyon?"

"I search for a tall man with dark hair and black eyes," replied Sorcha. "He would have arrived in the past day."

The man replied, "You are the only stranger to arrive, and I warn you ... LEAVE, or we will tie you to the other side of the pole and you will suffer the same fate."

Sorcha pulled back her hood and placed her hands on the woman's back. A slight yellowish glow emerged from her hands as the wounds closed and life returned to her limp body.

"od ot tahw swonk ahcros, yats repmots," whispered Kreador and then took flight above the men.

"WITCH!" screamed one of the men as he aimed his bow at Sorcha and released an arrow.

Sorcha turned in time and swatted the arrow away. Eyes now glowing, she pointed at Kreador in the sky above the archer and waved her hand. Kreador transformed and landed on the man with knife in hand. One easy swipe across his neck and the man fell to the ground. Sorcha pointed at the man who threatened her and, with the wave of her hand, turned him into a fat smelly pig ready for the slaughter and the dinner table. Fear came over the group of men as they backed away from Sorcha, shock and fear appeared in their eyes.

"SPARE US!" they cried out.

"You will never do this again!" Sorcha warned as she pointed at the men and then released the woman from the pole.

"Leave this horrid place," Sorcha told the woman.

Facing the men, Sorcha warned them, "I will return someday and if I find that you still torture the women in this village, I will turn you all into goats and pigs and sell you as meat at the traders market."

After the men scattered, Sorcha looked at her cart and saw Kreador cleaning his little knife.

"Time to go, Volac must be in Red Grove," commented Sorcha. "We must hurry and join Chaela and Aleric. Kreador, it's time to turn you back into a bird."

"Tahw!" replied Kreador as he looked up and put his knife under the cart seat.

After turning Kreador back into a bird, they left the village as they entered by crossing the bridge. Stomper halted the cart while he and Sorcha watched the little fat man run and hide behind a tree.

"It's okay, Stomper," laughed Sorcha, "he will not bother us. Let's go, we must hurry."

Upon entering Red Grove, Aleric grabbed Chaela's arm and pulled her to the side of the first building. "I saw his horse. He should be close by."

"Whose horse?" replied Chaela.

"The rider from the road.... Look, there he is talking with those men.

Aleric and Chaela peeked around the side of the building and watched as one of the men pointed towards a building down the road. The rider removed his sword that hung from the saddle and proceeded to walk towards the building.

Aleric looked at Chaela, "Go! Circle around the back of the building, I will follow the rider and enter the building after he goes inside. Do not enter until I call out for you. We must try and take Volac by surprise."

After the rider entered the building, Aleric snuck up under the open widow and peeked inside. The rider had approached a tall man with dark hair and black eyes. As the man turned around to face the rider, his face glowed in the sunlight from the open window.

"It's not Volac!" Aleric mumbled to himself as he ducked below the open window.

The rider's voice was loud and stern, and Aleric soon learned that another man with the same description had recently left with a young attractive woman from the village. Walking to the rear of the building, Aleric found Chaela hiding behind a cluster of bushes.

"Volac was not inside. He just left with a village woman."

"Then we must follow the rider. He does know where Volac went ... doesn't he?" responded Chaela.

"I'm not sure, but we can follow the rider just in case, or we can find out who this woman is and where she lives."

Chaela looked at Aleric, "I will find out about the woman. You need to follow the rider."

"Agreed!" replied Aleric.

The sky was blue and cloudy and the sun's heat was just beginning to affect Stomper. The road to Red Grove was long and Stomper was tired. Off in the distance, they spotted the village of Red Grove. Sorcha guided the cart around a sharp curve in the road, and, up ahead, she could see the villagers enter and leave Red Grove. Finding a side road, Sorcha gave Stomper a little friendly smack with the hickory stick.

"Turn here," said Sorcha. "We will find a place to hide this cart and you can rest. I will walk into Red Grove by myself. You two will wait with the cart until I call for you. Look! Over there behind that large hut is an old run-down stable, we can hide the cart there."

Chaela entered the building where Volac was last seen. In the corner of the room sat two women arguing over something, and as Chaela approached the two women, she overheard some of their conversation.

"She left with that tall stranger," said the one woman.

"That's not like her. Are you sure?" replied the other woman

"She was a child in his hands. I have never seen her act that way. I tell you, it was as if that man possessed her. What are we to do now? She was supposed to bring the cooking pots so we could feed the men after they work the fields today."

"Where does she live?" Chaela interrupted.

"Who are you and what concern is this of yours?" replied one of the women.

"I know of this man and your friend is in great danger, so please, if you know where she went, tell me. My friends and I may still be able to save her."

The two women stood and headed for the door.

Looking at Chaela, one woman said, "Come outside with us, and I will show you where she lives."

Chaela followed the women outside, where they walked to the center of the road. As the woman pointed down the road, she explained,

"Before you enter Red Grove, there is a sharp curve in the road. Just past the curve, there is a side road. Follow the side road until you come to a large hut made of logs and stone ... she lives there."

Chaela thanked the woman and began looking for Aleric.

"Kreador," said Sorcha, "fly over Red Grove and see if you can find Aleric and Chaela. I need to change out of this heavy robe ... the day is too hot."

Replacing the black-hooded robe with a light, loose-fitting linen white top and trousers made of goat leather, Sorcha selected a green cape and bull hide sandals. Feeling much cooler, she attached her sword to her leather belt and concealed it within the green cape

"Ahh ... just about ready to visit Red Grove," commented Sorcha when Kreador returned.

"aleahc dna cirela was I," Kreador informed Sorcha.

"Well, good! Then I should have no problem finding them ... stay alert," Sorcha replied, "I will return soon, and if I do not return by nightfall ... find me!"

The road through Red Grove was crowded with villagers as they talked and traded among themselves. Few noticed Sorcha while she walked among them. A man or two glanced Sorcha's way, and were soon discouraged by the cold look in her eyes. Searching from one end of the village to the other, Sorcha did not find Aleric or Chaela. Passing two women on the road, Sorcha overheard their conversation.

"She was so pale looking," said the one woman, "I don't think she was well."

"I hope she finds our friend," said the other woman. "What if that large man decided to have his way with her?"

Sorcha stepped in front of the two women. "The pale woman you just described, I think she is my friend. Do you know where she went?"

Aleric and Chaela found each other at the same time.

"I know where Volac is," Chaela informed Aleric. "A woman from the village told me of a large man that took her to her hut."

"A farmer told me the same thing and the farmer showed me a path that will lead us to the rear of her hut," replied Aleric. "We need to take wolf form and find her hut."

The path started at the edge of the village and circled around a small valley before entering the woods. It was not a direct route, but no one would see you approaching. In wolf form, they covered the distance in what appeared to be a few minutes.

Once Chaela and Aleric arrived at the hut, they transformed back and Aleric decided to peek inside and see if the woman and Volac were inside. Peeking through the rear window, Aleric spotted Volac and the young woman sitting on a large goatskin-covered mat. Turning around, Aleric signaled for Chaela to come.

"Stay here, Chaela. After I enter through the front, you enter through the rear window ... we will take Volac by surprise and finish this."

"We should wait for Sorcha," replied Chaela.

"Who knows where Sorcha is and we have Volac before us. No! We must attack Volac now before it is too late and he vanishes again.

"You are such a pretty young thing," Volac told the woman as she smiled and looked into his eyes.

The fear that flowed through her body came too late. Volac ripped her blouse from her chest and sank his fangs into her neck. At that moment, the door flew open, and just as Volac turned, Aleric was on him. Grabbing Aleric by his clothes, Volac tossed him on the floor.

"You ... again!" Volac shouted. "Why do you insist on trying to kill me?"

"You left me at the mercy of DeMorra's witches!" Aleric replied.

"It was you that broke their laws, not I. I tire of you, Aleric. Your heart will look good on my dinner table."

Within the blink of an eye, Volac was on top of Aleric. Volac grabbed Aleric by the neck and prepared to rip out his heart when a wolf leapt through the window and landed on his back, sinking its teeth into the back of his neck. All three started rolling on the floor. Volac grabbed the wolf and tossed her at the door, just missing a tall man with a sword in his hand. Now holding Aleric by the neck and shaking him like a doll, Volac tossed him to the side as he stared at the man in the doorway.

"Who are you?" demanded Volac.

"You killed my daughter!" yelled the man and he charged at Volac.

Sorcha stood on the road looking at the two women and again asked, "Do you know where she went?"

"Yes, she went to find and maybe save our friend. I gave her directions and maybe she went there."

"Where is this place?' asked Sorcha.

"Before you come to Red Grove, there is a sharp curve in the road; just past the curve, there is a side road. Follow the side road until you come to a large hut, that's where she lives."

Sorcha was stunned. She had just hid their cart by a run-down building behind the same large hut. Hands open and outward, Sorcha lowered her head and vanished.

"Did you see that...?" said the one woman. "She vanished!"

"Quiet! We saw nothing," said the other woman. "Do you want the men to hang us from the trees? This never happened I tell you ... never happened."

The rider was brave but foolish. Volac snapped his wrist like a twig, taking his sword with one hand and then twisting his head with the other hand. The crack of his neck bone echoed in the room while Chaela and Aleric tried to stand. Approaching Aleric with the rider's sword raised, Volac shouted ...

"YOUR HEAD IS MINE!"

As the sword sliced through the air, a dark shadow appeared in the doorway and the sword became water, splashing at Volac's feet. Volac looked towards the doorway and a tall woman approached.

"SORCHA!" Volac screamed.

The rays of light from Sorcha's hands slammed Volac into the far wall. Grabbing Chaela, Volac moved towards the window. In an attempt to stop Volac, Aleric jumped to his feet and attacked. Tossing Chaela at Aleric gave Volac the split second he needed to escape—he leapt out the window and vanished.

"I have told you before. You are no match for Volac. Your foolishness almost got you killed ... what am I to do with you two?" scolded Sorcha

Aleric responded, "We thought the two of us could surprise him. We did not know where you were. If the rider did not get in the way...."

"Stop!" shouted Sorcha. "If that man did not get in the way, you would both be dead right now. Because of your foolishness, Volac has escaped again. Now we must hurry before his trail becomes cold. Hurry and pull yourselves together, Stomper and Kreador are close by."

After the three left the hut, Sorcha set fire to it and said, "See! Two are dead and it was too close to being four. Next time, wait for me, do you understand?"

"YES" they both replied.

"Where is the next village?" asked Sorcha. No one answered.

Chaela transformed herself into wolf form and started scratching and sniffing the ground, hoping to pick up Volac's scent.

Chaela turned back to human form and said, "I'm not sure which path Volac took, his scent is all around us."

"Kreador!" interrupted Sorcha, "I am going to transform you back into a bird. Fly up ahead and see if you can locate Volac. He can't be that far ahead of us."

Kreador nodded and, with a flick of Sorcha's wrist, Kreador was once again a bird. Sorcha watched as he took flight and disappeared in the sky. Aleric touched Sorcha's shoulder,

"I need to go and do something," commented Aleric. "It should not take more than a couple of days."

"Now?" Sorcha responded. "What about Volac?"

Aleric laughed and said, "If you haven't noticed, we have had little luck in catching him, but I have an idea, and I have to do it alone."

"What are you up to, Aleric?" asked Chaela.

"You will find out soon enough," replied Aleric. "I need to go now if my idea has a chance of working."

Sorcha looked at Aleric and said, "I will let you go, but two days is all you have. You can use the power of your pendant to find us again."

"If my idea works," said Aleric, "we will be seeing each other soon."

Aleric vanished. When Sorcha looked to see where he went, she saw the tip of a wolf's tail disappear into the woods.

"Is Aleric accustomed to doing only what he wants to do?" asked Sorcha.

"I have no idea," Chaela replied. "If I remember correctly, that is the first time he has asked for permission to leave."

"Humm ... maybe so," sighed Sorcha. "Keep an eye on the sky, Kreador should return soon."

"Zane!" Aleric called out.

"Ashe has been waiting for you," Zane replied. "You took longer to come back than he anticipated. As you know, Ashe is not a patient ... man."

Aleric chuckled. Under his breath, he said, "If that is what you want to call him."

"Careful, Aleric, you know he hears everything," Zane replied.

When they arrived at the building where Ashe was waiting, Zane said, "Go on in, and don't keep Ashe waiting any longer than you already have."

Zane walked off and left Aleric standing outside the door.

"Are you planning on standing out there all day or are we going to get this over with?" shouted Ashe from inside the building.

Aleric sighed, opened the door, and entered. He was surprised when he saw that Ashe was well and looking young again.

"Well, you seem to be feeling better than the last time I saw you," commented Aleric.

Ashe laughed and said, "If it wasn't for your witch friend, I would still be wasting away for eternity. Her powers gave me strength."

Aleric snickered and replied, "You would not have allowed that to happen. The reason for my visit—should I tell you, or do you already know?"

Ashe looked at Aleric and said, "I do know you are looking for Volac, and that he has killed many people, the most recent in the village of Red Grove—thanks to you and your sister, and that you almost did not make it out of Red Grove. What a pity that you did, I could have finally rested ... knowing I would never have to see you again."

Aleric moved quicker than Ashe could and grabbed him around the neck.

"Remember, Ashe, if it were not for me, you would be a pile of bones right now rotting in that filthy moss-covered pit ... forgotten. You begged me to help you, and so I did. Now it is time for you to help me and we will call it even."

"Very well," Ashe replied, "I will help you, and then I never want to see you again ... understood? Now let go of me and tell me what you want me to do."

Sorcha was waiting for Kreador to return. Looking towards the sky, she finally spotted him.

"Look, Chaela, Kreador returns!"

Kreador landed on the side of the cart and, with a flick of Sorcha's wrist, was back in his natural form.

"Kreador, where is Volac?" asked Sorcha.

"dne srevir," Kreador answered.

"I will be back soon, wait here," Sorcha replied.

Aleric and Ashe had already found out where Volac was hiding and arrived at River's End.

"It looks like it is time to set the trap," said Aleric.

Ashe looked at Aleric and asked, "How do I know you will set me free?"

"You will have to trust me," replied Aleric

A soft breeze filled the area and there stood Sorcha.

Sorcha smiled and said, "It is about time you two showed up."

Aleric looked at Sorcha and said, "How did you know I would be here?"

Sorcha replied, "I am Sorcha—my sources stretch the imagination ... dear one."

"Sorcha!" gasped Ashe.

"Yes, Ashe, it is I," Sorcha replied. "It took me awhile to figure out who you were, but with a little help from my mother...."

"And...," replied Ashe.

"You should have been dead years ago," interrupted a voice. "I see my punishment is still in place."

Startled, Ashe turned around to see who spoke. Sorcha recognized the voice and said,

"I believe you know my mother."

"Celeste, but ... how?" Ashe mumbled.

"I am an Ancient now and have been for many years," Celeste replied. "If you were not such a coward, you would have known that."

Ashe puffed up his chest and said, "I am no coward. I was stuck in a pit and forced to beg and plead for help from this vampire just to get out of there. If it wasn't for you, I would still have my powers, and I could have summoned myself out, but now I am in debt to a wretched vampire!"

Celeste laughed and said, "Not all your powers were taken, Ashe, otherwise you would be dead. I made sure though that you would have to suffer for eternity for the damage you did. You see, for as long as you have just a small amount of your powers, you can never die."

"WHAT!" Ashe roared, "How did you learn such a thing?"

"A trick my grandmother taught me," replied Celeste.

"That batty old woman, she couldn't perform any magick. I would have sensed it," replied Ashe.

"You knew nothing of what my grandmother could do," said Celeste. "She had many secrets."

Ashe looked at Celeste and asked, "Did you come here just to argue with me, or is there a reason you showed up?"

"I wanted to see for myself if it was really you," laughed Celeste. "It is you."

Celeste reminded Sorcha, "Remember what I have told you; Ashe is not to be trusted, no matter how little of his powers he has left." With that said, Celeste disappeared.

"I wish you witches would stop doing that," Aleric shouted. "Now where are the others?"

"They are around, and will reveal themselves when the time is right," Sorcha replied. "For now they stay hidden, and why are you using Ashe as bait?"

"Volac has been after Ashe for many years," Aleric replied. "You could say Ashe outsmarted him and got away. I found Ashe trapped in a large pit and made a deal with him. Between your mother and Volac, he is lucky to be alive."

"Ashe, what did Volac want with you?" asked Sorcha.

"I was once a very powerful wizard," replied Ashe. "Many years ago, Volac thought we could make a deal, and with my help he could destroy Raven's Glenn and in return I would become like him ... immortal. At first, I thought it would be worth it, so I cloaked him and tried to sneak him into Raven's Glenn. Celeste caught me and took my powers. Volac thought I betrayed him, and then one day I slipped and fell into that pit. I'm sure Celeste was behind that. After a few days, Aleric came by and found me. He was supposed to take me back to Volac; however, we struck a deal, and he set me free. Now I am paying back my debt and will soon be free of him. That is if Volac does not kill me first."

"When we were at Hollow's End, what did you need from Ashe?" Sorcha asked Aleric.

"Simple ... his blood," replied Aleric.

Sorcha shook her head and said, "So what is your plan?"

"Well, I am going to set a trap using Ashe and his blood. Volac knows the smell of Ashe's blood, and I believe he will come after Ashe and seek revenge."

"Do you really think Volac will not see right through that?" Sorcha asked. "Knowing we are after him, you think he will just follow the scent of Ashe's blood?"

Before Sorcha could say another word, they heard ...

"ASHE, I thought you were dead!"

"Volac!" Aleric whispered.

"Where is Ashe?" asked Sorcha.

"He was right here a second ago," responded Aleric. "I think Volac and Ashe have vanished together."

"I hope Ashe cannot regain his powers," said Sorcha. "Kreador, take flight and see if you can spot them."

Kreador did not reply; he looked at Sorcha and walked away.

"Kreador, come back here!" Sorcha called out.

Aleric tried to interrupt, Sorcha signaled for Aleric to be quiet.

"Now that Ashe and Volac are together," Sorcha whispered, "we will rest here until tomorrow and make plans on what to do then."

Kreador returned and together they built a fire. Sorcha snuggled close to the fire and looked around at her companions. Stomper lay asleep on his side snoring. Kreador was by Sorcha's side, rolled up in a green ball. Chaela and Aleric left minutes ago to feed in the wilds. The sound of the fire called out to Sorcha. The crackle from the burning wood and the flicker of the fire's flame was so mesmerizing that Sorcha became lost in the fire's dance. Sorcha stared at the flames and Raven's Glenn appeared. Sorcha looked deeper into the fire, and Kali appeared; it was night and Kali was entering her house. Sorcha raised her arms, palms facing towards the sky, and with her hands slightly open, she lowered her head and vanished.

Kali turned to close the door when a soft breeze filled the doorway.

"Sorcha ... welcome home."

The two briefly embraced and Sorcha began telling Kali about Ashe. Kali sat and listened, raising an eyebrow when Sorcha mentioned Celeste's name.

"I was a little girl when all this happened," Kali interrupted. "I remember mother's fight with Ashe ... the wizard, and if I remember correctly, it took the powers of the Ancients to defeat that wizard. This all happened so long ago and I often wondered what happened to him.

"I know nothing of wizards, why is that?" asked Sorcha.

"We make fun of them and call them the men witches," laughed Kali. "They are like us but men. Wizards can be powerful, like Ashe. Some wizards have no powers and hide behind Ancient spells. We really have no use for them, and besides, they think as men do. Why would we bore you when you had so much to learn?"

"Now I have to deal with one and know nothing," replied Sorcha.

"Yet here you are asking what you already know. Your powers are greater than that of the greatest of wizards. Fear them not, but still you must be careful around them. Remember they are men and think as men do."

"Why," Sorcha asked, "would Volac want anything to do with Ashe? Ashe's powers are pretty much useless, and he isn't much to feed on."

Kali interrupted, "If Ashe's powers return, and Volac can control him by turning him into a vampire, you would have to face an immortal wizard with the skills of a vampire, and, dear Sorcha, you do not want to battle that kind of creature. You really do need to kill Ashe, and the sooner the better."

Kali looked Sorcha in the eye, "Remember ... it is best if you kill Ashe."

"I must go," Sorcha responded, "Chaela and Aleric will return soon, and soon it will be daylight. With the morning sun, we will begin our search for Volac and Ashe."

"Follow the road that leads to Craven's Bend," Kali suggested. "It is a village suitable for the likes of Volac, but be careful. Now that Volac has Ashe with him, they could try to trap you."

Stomper opened his eyes after a slight breeze caused sparks to shoot from the fire. Chaela and Aleric stood just outside the fire's heat talking while Kreador slowly stood and stretched his green little body, making some awful noises as his bones shifted within. Sorcha turned her back to the fire and faced the new sun as it appeared over the treetops.

Sorcha spoke aloud, "Today we head for Craven's Bend, I have reason to believe Volac and Ashe will go there. Aleric, do you believe it is possible that Volac and Ashe would work together again?"

"Maybe," responded Aleric. "They really do hate each other. Possible ... yes, it is possible."

"Do you believe it is possible Ashe could regain his powers by some quirk or another?"

"I do not know," Aleric replied. "I have heard that wizards have an endless bag of tricks, so, maybe it is possible."

"Then Aleric you do understand why I must kill him."

Aleric sighed and said, "I know you must kill him, but first we have to find him."

After a day's journey, they arrived within view of Craven's Bend. Sorcha told her companions to hide and wait for her while she explored the village. After a chilly night, Sorcha had changed back to wearing her black hooded robe and now pulled her hood over her head. She then left her companions behind and walked towards Craven's Bend. As soon as Sorcha left, the others started discussing Volac and Ashe.

Stomper asked, "What about Volac?"

"Right now, Ashe is more of a threat than Volac," responded Chaela. "We will wait here for Sorcha to return."

Sorcha returned from the village and told Stomper and Kreador,

"I need you to stay here. Aleric and Chaela, come with me."

Aleric and Chaela followed Sorcha to the edge of the village. Sorcha looked at them and said,

"I really hate to do this, but I need you two to distract Volac while I go in and get Ashe."

"Where is Volac hiding?" asked Chaela.

Sorcha replied, "He is in a building next to the village pub located in the center of the village. It is the only building with a wood roof ... you cannot miss it.

Aleric and Chaela disappeared into the village while Sorcha waited for a few minutes. After several minutes had passed, Sorcha pulled her hood back over her head and went back into the village. Soon she was close to the building where Volac was hiding and saw Aleric and Chaela approach the rear of the building. Sorcha stopped to watch and see what they would do. As she waited, she heard a disturbance off to her left. Sorcha cautiously looked to her left and saw Kreador kicking up a fuss as Stomper pulled the cart up the road. *I thought I told them to wait for me outside of the village*, Sorcha thought to herself. Not amused by their actions, Sorcha quickly glanced back towards Aleric and Chaela. Aleric had moved to the front of the building and Chaela had transformed into a wolf and waited outside a rear open window. Aleric saw Sorcha and realized he needed to hurry. In a blur, Aleric entered through the front door; at the same time, Chaela jumped through the open rear window.

"About time!" Sorcha said aloud.

Aleric came running out of the house with Volac close behind him and a wolf not far behind Volac. Aleric stopped running as soon as he reached the tree line. Stomper and Kreador were there waiting. With Volac out of the way, Sorcha entered the house and found Ashe tied to a chair.

"Well, well," Sorcha said.

Ashe slowly looked up and said "Sorcha, please help me."

Sorcha looked at Ashe and said, "I am afraid I cannot. I am also afraid I cannot leave you here with Volac either."

Sorcha focused on Ashe and chanted:

"The power within will no longer be, make this wizard a mortal so he can be free."

271

Ashe felt a warm wet pain in his neck, a pain he had not experienced in many years and gurgled, "Why?"

Sorcha wiped Ashe's blood off the blade of a dagger and placed her hand on Ashes's shoulder. Volac appeared in the doorway and shouted,

"What have you done?"

In an instant, Sorcha and Ashe disappeared. Sorcha found the others and asked what happened with Volac. Aleric told her, "Once Volac realized you were after Ashe, he vanished."

"I must deliver Ashe's body to Raven's Glenn," said Sorcha. "The Ancients must dispose of his body."

"But he's dead," said Chaela.

"Maybe," Sorcha replied. "Hide until I return."

Sorcha placed a hand on Ashe's body and as she raised her other hand, all motion around her froze in place. Stomper and Kreador quit moving and talking, Chaela and Aleric appeared frozen in mid-stride as they walked away; even the air around her seemed to take on a haze of solitude and stillness. Sorcha looked at her hands and arms and everything appeared as it should be. *What is this?* Sorcha thought to herself when an elderly voice from behind her interrupted her thoughts.

"We have come for the body of the wizard Ashe."

Sorcha immediately turned around and faced three elderly men each with long snow-white beards that reached the ground and wearing white and gold robes. All three carried large staffs that glowed slightly and towered over them. Their eyes were soft in color yet radiated a power Sorcha has never experienced.

"Who are you?" Sorcha asked.

"We come for the body of Ashe."

Sorcha took a step backwards as her powers from within awakened, stirring that special area of her soul. Her eyes glowing, she asked again.

"Who are you?"

"Stop ... Wait! Sorcha, we mean you no harm. We are the Elders from Azelwood. We cannot allow you to take the body of Ashe to Raven's Glenn. Ashe's body belongs to us. He was one of us—good, or evil ... he was one of us, and only we can dispose of his body ... his soul still lives."

Sorcha replied, "I cannot allow Ashe to live again. He was a threat to Raven's Glenn and tried to destroy us. Why should I trust you? I know nothing of you Elders."

"You have your Ancients. From the land where Ashe is from, you can say we are the Ancients. Each wizard selects his own path—we have no control over that. Some walk the path of good ... others evil; regardless, when they die, only we can put their souls to rest. If we do not do this, then Ashe will never be truly dead and there is always the possibility he can take human form and live again."

"How do I know what you say is true?" Sorcha asked.

"We know of your Ancients and your mother Celeste. We have common goals and have worked together in the past. You will someday be queen of Raven's Glenn and, as queen, you will make decisions that will affect all those around you. Today you must make one of those decisions and think as a queen would. We know of your powers and do not wish to find out which of us is greater, but we will do what we must in order to still the soul of Ashe. It is time for you to decide—if it's a battle you want ... we are ready for you."

"Wait! Take his body and do as you wish," Sorcha answered. "If you deceived me, you will not only battle me but the Ancients and all of Raven's Glenn will rise against you."

"You have made a wise decision, one worthy of a queen."

The three wizards lowered their heads and in the blink of an eye, they were gone and so was Ashe. The haze of stillness evaporated and Sorcha looked towards her companions.

"That was fast; back so soon?" said Chaela. Sorcha turned and faced her friend.

"Volac is still here in Craven's Bend. He thinks we left with the body of Ashe, so we should be able to surprise him if we can find him. Look for signs; he seems to leave a clear trail no matter where he goes. Take Kreador with you as your pet bird, and Chaela, be careful. If you find Volac, stay with him and send Kreador back to me. That vacant building over there, the one you see with most of the roof missing—we will rest and wait for you there."

There was no door and the walls barely supported what was left of the roof but Sorcha felt tired and needed to rest. *Anywhere will do*, she thought to herself as she closed her eyes and slowly drifted into darkness.

Chaela asked Kreador if he would fly above the rooftops and search. The villagers found it too amusing for such a large bird on her shoulder and she was attracting too much attention. She continued to search each building, peeking in windows and sometimes talking with the women of the village. Having searched the last building in the village, she turned around and noticed several men had gathered in the road. *What is this?* Chaela thought to herself as she decided to walk past the group and maybe overhear what they were discussing. A tall man from the center of the group was speaking.

"He warned us, I tell you ... there is an evil witch among us. She is tall with dark hair."

"I saw her walking down the road not long ago," another villager added.

"Volac," Chaela whispered. "He has turned the villagers against Sorcha. I must warn her."

Signaling for Kreador to come, Chaela hurried her pace and headed back towards the run-down building where Sorcha was resting.

"Sorcha, Sorcha!" Chaela yelled as she ran through the doorway.

"The villagers come for you, wake up!"

"What?" Sorcha responded as she slowly stood gathering her thoughts. "What did you say?"

"The villagers think you are an evil witch! Volac has turned them against you—they gather now and soon will head this way."

Sorcha dashed for the doorway. Peering down the road, she saw a large gathering of men heading her way. Her eyes widened as she noticed the tall man with black hair and evil eyes leading them.

"Volac!" Sorcha sneered. "Stay calm."

A nervous Kreador started squeaking out sounds and jumped up and down in panic. Chaela slapped him across the back of the head.

"Calm yourself, Kreador," Chaela yelled.

Stomper kicked out the back wall. Sorcha raised her arms and smiled.

"We are surrounded!" Aleric shouted. "They have torches."

Volac was the first to toss his torch on the roof of the old shamble of a building. Others followed and soon the place was in flames. Sorcha walked calmly to the center of the room. Hands facing outward and arms slightly raised, she chanted,

Fire above, fire below, I dance within your flames that I control, seek out those who gave you birth and under their feet scorch the earth.

The fire turned on the villagers as the ground around them ignited.

The old wood of the building fell as Stomper's hoofs destroyed what was left of the wall. As they exited the burning building, Sorcha turned and saw Volac standing in the doorway. Sorcha smiled and waved as the screams of the villagers masked his response.

Once they gathered outside of the village, Chaela asked, "What now?"

"We hide and wait," responded Sorcha. "Volac has outlived his welcome and will soon leave Craven's Bend, if he hasn't already."

"I doubt there will be a Craven's Bend by the end of the day," said Aleric as he pointed at the village. "Look!"

Under the spell of an uncontrollable fire, the village burned. Sorcha turned to watch and smiled as the flames reached the top of the trees. Her smile soon faded when her thoughts were interrupted by a voice.

"He heads for *Tir Na Marbh*, Land of the Dead."

"Kali!" Sorcha responded.

"I have come to warn you," said Kali. "Volac seeks the protection of his master, the Lord of Darkness. You must return to Raven's Glenn and prepare before you journey into his world."

"I am not afraid of Volac or the Lord of Darkness," replied Sorcha. "I will follow him to the ends of all worlds if need be."

"Sorcha, listen to me. In our world, his powers are limited. In his world, your powers are limited; remember, he sent the forces that killed your mother. You will not be able to use all your powers when you enter the Land of the Dead. You must return to Raven's Glenn and prepare or you may fail—and do not use your magic, you must travel on foot so he cannot detect where you are. Leave the cart here; bring everyone with you. Raven's Glenn prepares and waits for you—now hurry."

"I did not know this," replied Sorcha. "We leave for Raven's Glenn immediately."

Chapter Eight

After several days' journey, Sorcha finally reached Raven's Glenn. Stomper, weary and travel worn, asked Sorcha,

"Why did we have to walk all the way back here? Why couldn't you just do your disappearing thing to bring us back here?"

Sorcha replied, "I did not want to be detected, and it takes too much energy to go back and forth with others."

Before entering Raven's Glenn, Chaela looked at the others and said, "Aleric and I are going hunting, we need to feed."

"Be careful," Sorcha warned them, and entered Raven's Glenn.

Kali and the other priestesses were waiting for Sorcha at Kali's house, the centermost house, located in the center of the star. The five houses located on the five points of the star stood erect, freshly rebuilt, or repaired, and with their powers restored, Raven's Glenn again flourished. Sorcha walked into Kali's house where everyone was waiting for her.

"Sorcha, I'm so glad you made it back safely," said Kali. "Where are the others?"

"Stomper went to rest, as did Kreador. Chaela and Aleric went hunting."

"Good, you can let them know what I have to say later," Sasa interrupted.

Sorcha turned around and said, "It's good to see you again, Sasa."

Sasa looked at Sorcha and said, "You do not seem worried about the information that Kali gave you. We thought you would be home days ago."

"I did not want to be detected, so we took the more traditional way—we walked."

"Okay, okay," responded Kali. "The important thing is everyone is back safely; however, now we need to let you know about The Lord of Darkness."

Sorcha looked at Kali and asked, "Why do the others need to be here when you tell me?"

Kali took a deep breath and said, "Because I do not know what will happen to me, so our priestesses are here ready to cast any spell needed."

Sorcha looked at Kali with worry on her face and said, "I think we should wait for the others. I want all to be here."

Kali replied, "Sorcha, your friends are not witches and their powers are limited. They may or may not be able to help you. We have the power to help you and you will need our help and all of Raven's Glenn powers when the time comes. You can inform your friends later, we must begin." Sorcha nodded in agreement.

Brietta, Vevila, Morra, and Sasa sat while Kali stood and addressed Sorcha and the high priestesses.

"I have summoned all of you here so we can plan a trap for Volac and the Lord of Darkness."

"Lord of Darkness?" questioned Brietta. "I thought he was immortal, ruler over the underworld, as well as the land of the dead. His powers are great."

"Yes," Kali replied, "but he can be destroyed. This has been the plan of the Ancients from the beginning, and the reason Sorcha was born. Raven's Glenn was developed to protect us from his evil, and the powers of Raven Glenn have increased with the passing of each ruler. Celeste, my mother, was the last to pass and we now believe we are strong enough to rid our world of the evil the Lord of Darkness has bestowed on us. If not, my passing will surely be enough to destroy him. The prophecy states that Sorcha will someday rule over all that is good and evil in our world. In order for this to happen, the Lord of Darkness, must die. "

The priestesses were stunned at what they had heard. All eyes widened, and their mouths dropped open, the look of shock covered their faces as they stared at Kali ... speechless. Brietta was the first to regain focus.

"You mean you must die in order for the Lord of Darkness to be defeated?" Brietta asked.

"No," replied Kali. "The Ancients have planned for this day. Sorcha is the chosen one, only she will be able to deliver the final blow. The Ancients have brought us all together for this day. But Sorcha, the chosen one, is the only one who has the powers within to be able to channel all our powers. She alone must face this evil, we may or may not survive, for even the Ancients are unsure of the outcome ... we may all die."

"I now understand why you did not want the others to hear this," commented Sorcha as she lowered her head. "I wonder if I am ready for such a large task. Is this is why I was born, why my mother left Raven's Glenn, why you saved me and brought me here to learn the ways? Did the Ancients know I would be bitten?"

"Yes," replied Kali. "We had the power all along to cure the lust and cravings that would take over you."

"Why?" asked Sorcha, "Why allow Volac to do that to me?"

"Volac is a pawn in this battle between us and the evil that is taking over. You need to be immortal for the final battle. Remember the great darkness that appeared and took your father from you. The Lord of Darkness missed ... he was coming for you. His powers are limited outside of his world and we were able to save you. He knows who and what you are and that you can destroy him. He has always known this."

"So, if Volac has been bidding his master's wishes, why did he not kill me when he had the chance?"

"Dear Sorcha, Volac is still a man filled with ego, and he lusts for power. He had hoped to convert you or take your powers, thus making himself more powerful. I am sure the Lord of Darkness is not pleased with him and, just maybe, this will give you the advantage you will need to defeat both of them."

"I wish to discuss this with my friends," replied Sorcha. "They may sacrifice their lives before this is over. They need to understand why and of their own free will, decide if they are willing to take the risk and join me in my final battle."

"I understand," Kali responded, and she searched the eyes of all those present. "We will gather at the northernmost house, the house of the Ancients, at sunrise tomorrow. Go, speak with your friends."

Sorcha left to go find Stomper and Kreador, and to see if Aleric and Chaela had returned. She walked out of Kali's house and saw a commotion across the way, by the outskirts of the woods, and went to see what was going on. She found Aleric and Chaela fighting as wolves. Sorcha looked at both of them and asked,

"What are you two doing?"

They both looked at her and transformed back into their human forms.

Chaela responded, "We were just taking out some aggressions, why?"

"Save those aggressions, you may need them later. Come ... we need to go find Stomper and Kreador."

Aleric and Chaela shrugged their shoulders and followed Sorcha. They found Stomper and Kreador by the well, sleeping.

"Wake up! We need to talk," Sorcha said. "Please follow me."

Sorcha headed into the woods and kept walking until she reached an opening and stood in the middle of a field filled with flowers. Sorcha wanted her friends to be at ease with clear heads when she talked to them. Within this field of flowers, the air was clean, and the smells from the plants and flowers relaxing.

Chaela asked, "What is going on, Sorcha?"

Sorcha took a deep breath and explained, "We have been through so much together, who would have guessed that an imp from another world, a centaur, and two vampires would end up being my closest friends. I ask you now to listen and think about what I am about to tell you. If you decide to join me for what might be our final battle, meet at the northernmost house tomorrow at sunrise."

Chaela looked at Sorcha and said, "Okay, we need to think about what you are about to tell us, so tell us already ... please."

"I have to destroy the Lord of Darkness and Volac with him."

Stomper started stomping the ground in irritation and said, "WHAT! That is impossible, no one can kill the Lord of Darkness—he is immortal and cannot be killed."

Sorcha looked at Stomper and said, "Even immortals can be killed."

Kreador looked down and said, "eman sih swonk ohw?"

Sorcha, a little startled, just looked at Kreador and replied, "Kali."

Kreador jumped up and said, "ton tsum ehs! ON"

"Kali feels she has no other choice; this is the reason she still lives. She has to make this sacrifice for the good of everyone," responded Sorcha.

"Umm ... excuse us, but do you mind letting the rest of us in on what is going on?" asked Aleric.

"eman sih yas ot sdeen ehs skniht ilak," said Kreador.

After Kreador spoke, he headed back to Raven's Glenn. They all watched him go and Sorcha said,

"In order to kill the Lord of Darkness, I must know his name, but those who speak his name aloud die. It is my destiny to defeat the Lord of Darkness. I also had to become what I am to be able to do this. If I succeed, our world will be peaceful once more. I now leave it up to you to decide if you will join me. You will not be able to destroy the Lord of Darkness, but you will be able to destroy all who get in our way. I do not know if Kreador will join us or not, think about it. If you decide to join me, remember you may not return. I will wait at the northernmost house at sunrise. If you decide to join me, meet me there."

Asleep, the wind felt fresh, the coolness of the wind tingled the skin on Sorcha's face as her hair fluttered behind her in the breeze. Lower than higher, faster than slower, Sorcha soared through the sky as the ground beneath her took shapes and colors only seen from the skies above. In an instant, Sorcha awakened and jumped out of bed; her bed cooled as a soft breeze entered through the window and swept across her bed.

"I fly as the bird and see through the bird's eyes ... I am the bird!" Sorcha said aloud with a smile.

The first rays of sunshine floated through her open window, highlighting the floor in front of her. Walking into the light, Sorcha looked outside and saw Stomper heading for the House of the Ancients. A warm feeling came over her as she thought to herself, *My brave, brave Stomper, what will become of you?* Putting on her sandals, Sorcha stepped outside and, for a second, she saw a little girl running down the path that led to the home of Kali.

"Talia," Sorcha said aloud. The girl turned and smiled at her. Sorcha blinked and the little girl was gone.

On her way to the House of the Ancients, Sorcha stopped and looked around. Raven's Glenn was quiet, peaceful in her sleep, and yet, there was a strange feeling in the air, a feeling of hope and despair. Soon, Sorcha arrived at the House of the Ancients. Stomper alone was there to greet her.

"The priestesses are inside waiting for you," Stomper whispered.

"And the others?" asked Sorcha.

"I have not seen Kreador since yesterday, and I do not know where Chaela and Aleric are," Stomper replied.

"I understand," said Sorcha. "Please wait here."

All the priestesses stood and bowed when Sorcha entered. Kali was the first to speak.

"We know what you must do in order to defeat the Lord of Darkness. Somehow, you need to trick him into leaving the Land of the Dead. Once he steps outside of his realm, you will have the power to kill him and he will not have the power to stop you."

"How do I kill him?" asked Sorcha

"With our help!" replied Kali.

"How?"

"We will wait here in the House of the Ancients where our powers are at their greatest. Once you have the Lord of Darkness outside his realm, call for us and I will reveal his name to you, then we will channel all of our powers into you. We must wait until the last second or he will know what is about to happen and our trap will not work. You already have the sword of the Ancients. With our spells and your sword, you will need to strike at the moment his name is spoken."

"And Volac?"

"Hopefully you will have killed him by then. If not, he will perish when his master is dead."

"Not much of a plan," replied Sorcha. "And how do I trick the Lord of Darkness?"

"Find what he cherishes more than life and use it against him."

"Any ideas?" Sorcha asked.

"We do not even know what he looks like. Until you call for us, you are on your own—and, by the Ancients, I hope we trained you well enough."

"I guess I will know soon enough," replied Sorcha. She smiled and headed for the door.

As Sorcha walked towards the door, she turned around and searched the eyes of the priestesses.

"I shall return," Sorcha assured them. "Blessed be ... Sisters."

"Blessed be!" they all replied.

Once outside, Sorcha hugged Stomper and smiled when she saw Chaela and Aleric walking towards her. Feeling a slight tug on her robe, she looked down ...

"Kreador! Where have you been? I've been so worried."

"ylimaf ym ot eybdoog yas em depleh ilak" Kreador replied.

Sorcha rubbed him behind the ears and looked at her friends.

"Gather close around me," Sorcha told her friends. "We leave for what may be our last adventure together. We leave for the Land of the Dead."

A wind torrent suddenly formed around the group. Sorcha raised her arms with palms facing upwards; the wind increased snapping her garments against her skin. Her hair in her face, she lowered her head and they vanished.

"I was a little girl the last time I was here," commented Sorcha.

"Don't forget, I was with you," replied Stomper.

A voice from nowhere interrupted,

"All fine and nice, but what is your plan today?"

"Morra!" Sorcha quickly turned around.

"Yes, it is I. Appears you forgot a few things in your haste, Stomper. Care for your shield and spear. And how about your bow and arrows, Sorcha? At least you remembered your sword. Here is Kreador's dagger—and Sorcha, I have something special for you also. Here is a pouch filled with dry dirt from Raven's Glenn."

"Dirt?" Sorcha asked.

"While in the Dark Lord's realm, toss it in the face of those that come at you; the dust is Raven's Glenn—it will blind them for a few minutes."

"Thank you, Morra." Sorcha bowed slightly. "Will my training ever end?"

"After you're done with the Dark Lord, that will just about do it," replied Morra. "I must leave quickly—what is your plan?"

"I guess I will just announce myself and see what happens," Sorcha replied.

"He knows you're here already. Enter from the south; he will expect you from the north since Raven's Glenn is located to the north. Divide those that he sends at you and deeply annoy him, tease him, challenge him, build anger under his skin and stoke the fire in his heart. He must thirst for you. If you are hoping he will make a mistake, make him thirsty! Remember the pendant the old witch gave you. When the time is right, it will offer you a brief time of invisibility ... use it wisely, it will only work once."

"She's gone! No weapons for Aleric or me?" Chaela asked.

Sorcha laughed, "Morra cares little for you. You are vampires after all, not really a dinner guest at her table and you will have all your powers in that place."

"You will also have those vampire powers, Sorcha. Don't forget whose fang marks you carry," Chaela replied.

Sorcha turned to face Chaela, and Chaela continued speaking, "After Volac and his master are dead, what will become of Aleric and me? Will we even still be vampires—will we die?"

"You will not die, I promise. I do not know the rest, but remember the power of the Ancients, of Raven's Glenn—and I will be there. If not, then we are all dead and it does not matter."

Aleric interrupted, "Time to rid our world of a stain. Let's go now, Sorcha."

Sorcha turned and faced the Land of the Dead. With all her powers still intact, she raised her arms and shouted at the top of her voice ... "VOLAC!" The sound was so loud the ground shook and, for a brief moment, the dark skies opened and the sun's rays glittered across the Land of the Dead.

"That should get their attention," laughed Sorcha. "Quickly, gather close!"

They vanished and reappeared at the Lands of the Dead, southern boundary.

Volac stood there shaking as the Lord of Darkness was about to deliver the final blow.

"Please—please, forgive me!" cried out Volac, when out of nowhere the wind called his name.

"Ahh! I see Sorcha has arrived for you," hissed the Lord of Darkness. "If ... you wish to live, then go and kill her. She arrived from the north ... now go!"

Back in Raven's Glenn, Kali and the other high priestesses were discussing different ways Sorcha could destroy the Lord of Darkness. Deep in thought Kali's eyes widened and she was just about to speak when Celeste and one of the old wizards appeared in the middle of the room.

"Mother!" said Kali. "What brings you here—and who is this?"

"This is Blaine; he is one of the wizards who live beyond the rise of the two rivers. He knows of the Lord of Darkness and can help Sorcha."

Celeste turned to face Blaine and pointed at the high priestesses, "Please tell them what you told me."

Blaine faced the priestesses, his eyes narrowed. Stroking his long white beard with the fingers of his left hand, he pointed towards the Land of the Dead with his right index finger.

"The object the Lord of Darkness cherishes the most is a pendant that hangs from a chain around his neck. It is made of a dark green gem with red spots on it—known as a bloodstone. He wears the bloodstone so that he does not have to seek out humans for food. It is the source of his immortality. The gem has magical powers equal to your powers and it helps him survive. Destroy the pendant and you can destroy the Lord of Darkness."

"I suppose Sorcha will just ask and he will give her the gem," sniped Brietta.

Blaine's eyes widened as he stared at Brietta but continued, "Next thing to know is this: Few have survived seeing him. He is tall with large broad shoulders and large hands; he glides, not walks on the ground below him. He wears dark clothing and hides in the shadows. His hair is black as night and long, his eyes are as green as emeralds and sometimes glow. Stories tell that men cower in his presence, for death is certain. He mesmerizes the women and they easily fall prey to his wiles and desires. Sorcha must not let him look her in the eyes for too long. If she falls under his spell, then we are all dead."

Brietta stood and pointed her finger at the wizard, challenging his words.

"I know of you wizards and have dealt with you many times. I am new to Raven's Glenn but not to the ways of you wizards. We have crossed paths before and to say you are all but honest is a joke. Whose interests do you really serve? You wizards are not to be trusted!"

Blaine looked shocked as he stepped backwards and turned to face Celeste.

"How dare this witch talk to me in that tone of voice? You called on the Elders so they sent me to help. I have little concern for you witches, and it is true the less of you there are, the better my life would be. What reason do I have to lie to you now? If Raven's Glenn falls, we are next! I serve both our interest."

Celeste raised her hand and signaled for quiet.

"Yes, it is true witches and wizards have not always been on the same side, but now we have a common foe, one that can destroy both our ways of life. The Ancients and Elders have discussed this and decided to work together and rid our lands of this evil."

"Trust a wizard? This is madness," replied Brietta.

"I will go find Sorcha and tell her what this wizard said. He best speak the truth."

"I am done here," responded Blaine.

"Wait!" Kali called out. "Before you leave, do you have any idea how Sorcha can steal the pendant?"

"She can't—he will sense her, even while he rests. Tell Sorcha to use that little green pet of hers ... he is not of this world, and will not fall prey to his ways. The Lord of Darkness rests under the earth. You will find his chambers under the place where Volac lives."

"Volac!" replied Kali. "I knew he came from the Land of the Dead. I did not know he sleeps above the Lord of Darkness."

'Yes," responded Blaine. "Volac's place is a guise and hides the home of the Lord of Darkness ... he lives below."

"The eyes—we have the eyes to see within Volac's realm."

"No we do not," explained Priestess Sasa. "The eyes have vanished days ago."

"The Lord of Darkness has now surfaced," Blaine pointed out. "He would have sensed the eyes at once and destroyed them."

Blaine pointed at Brietta, "Someday, Brietta, I will teach you the manners you lack."

After Celeste and Blaine vanished, Kali looked at Brietta and laughed.

'I'm guessing he was an old friend of yours."

"Wizards.... Just another man, we would be better off without them. I leave to find Sorcha. If what the wizard said is true ... I must hurry."

Sorcha had just arrived at the southern boundary of the Land of the Dead when she heard her name called. Appearing in front of her was a smiling Brietta. Sorcha listened as Brietta explained what the wizard told the priestesses. Kreador overheard that he must steal the pendant and started shaking in fear. Sorcha rubbed him behind the ears as he hung on her robe. Aleric and Chaela looked at each other then stared at Sorcha.

"Aleric and I know the way to Volac's home," Chaela said with a smile. "We did not know the Lord of Darkness lived below; no one was ever allowed in the tunnels and caves except Volac."

Brietta warned Sorcha about the power the Lord of Darkness has over women, and the power of his eyes ... green eyes of ice. While Brietta was talking, Celeste appeared.

"Mother, why are you here?" asked Sorcha.

"I must speak with Kreador," Celeste replied.

Celeste whispered in Kreador's ear so none could hear. Kreador smiled and nodded his head in agreement, then Celeste turned to face Sorcha,

"Your fate awaits you, Sorcha. It is time for you to do what the Ancients have prophesied. We will be there for you when the time comes. Show no fear, and strike quickly."

Celeste and Brietta vanished. Sorcha's eyes looked forward—deep into the Land of the Dead.

"It is time," Sorcha said aloud. "Aleric ... Chaela, lead the way."

Deeper and deeper into the Land of the Dead they walked. The sky had long ago turned grey and cloudy, the air around them chilled and darkened. Sounds of agony—cries from tormented souls—increased with each step. From a faraway place, wicked laughter pierced the darkness. Aleric pointed at a hill and signaled for the others to stop and keep quiet. On the south side of the hill stood two guards heavily armed with spears and swords. Both carried shields and wore leather armor. The guards were taller than the average person, though they appeared very human as they stood in front of a large opening in the hill.

"Guards!" Sorcha whispered

"They guard one of the entrances to the caves and tunnels below the earth," said Chaela.

Sorcha looked closer and said, "Humans!"

Aleric laughed and said, "Yes, humans. Someone has to guard the entrance during the day."

"Wait here," said Sorcha.

As the guard slowly raised his hand to wipe the sweat from his forehead, he felt a cool breeze pass ... raising the hairs on his arm. As he lowered his hand, he noticed the blood and tried to scream a warning, but the gurgle sound was silent as he fell to the ground. Hearing spear and shield hit the ground, the second guard advanced quickly and died in mid- stride, falling near the first guard.

The others watched as the guards fell to the ground, and then Sorcha appeared. The pendant around her neck glowed.

"How does she do that?" asked Aleric.

Chaela replied, "I do not ask ... look! Sorcha's pendant glows; her powers have diminished and the old witch's pendant helps her. Soon she will lose all her powers ... we must hurry.

They followed Sorcha to the cave's entrance and stopped. Looking into the darkness, Sorcha told them she could not enter into the cave.

"My powers are limited here," commented Sorcha. "I need to find Volac. Chaela and Aleric, you must take Kreador with you. Find the pendant and the Lord of Darkness, I will go find Volac and kill him, hopefully before the Lord of Darkness finds me."

Aleric and Chaela nodded and motioned for Kreador to follow. They disappeared into the cave.

Sorcha turned to Stomper and asked, "Are you ready for what might be our final battle together?"

Stomper looked at her and said, "Climb on, let us kill this monster once and for all."

Sorcha smiled and climbed up on Stomper's back. Stomper took off at full gallop and, after a few minutes, they found damaged weapons littered on the ground, a sign they were closing in on Volac's forces.

Sorcha looked around and said, "We must go to the left. I can feel Volac. He hides in that direction."

Stomper headed off to the left of the path and cautiously moved forward.

"Something does not feel right," said Stomper.

"I agree," Sorcha replied.

As they approached a second hill, Sorcha whispered in Stomper's ear to stop.

"This is the place," said Sorcha. "Wait here, I will be right back."

Sorcha slid off Stomper and silently walked up to the hill. Slowly, she touched the hill, looking for an opening. She walked around the hill, all the while running her hand over the surface. She glanced down at a point where she saw some earth disturbed and bent down to take a closer look. Swatting away the dirt, sticks, and branches, Sorcha glanced back at Stomper and signaled that she had found the entrance and then she disappeared into the hill. Slowly, she walked down a narrow, dark, winding tunnel until she saw a flicker of candlelight dancing on the walls and ceiling in front of her. Peeking around the corner, she saw an opening, a doorway that led to a large room. There in the middle of the room stood Volac.

Eyes fixed on the candle's flame and deep in thought, Volac did not hear Sorcha as she snuck up behind him. From somewhere deep inside, Volac's senses awakened and he slowly turned around. Quietly and quickly, Sorcha took out her sword and gripped it with the strength of ten men; their eyes met and, with one quick swing, Volac's head fell. His head lay on the ground, eyes open, a look of shock and surprise greeting Sorcha. Sorcha reached down and grabbed his hair; lifting his head, she looked into his eyes and smiled.

"You will never cause destruction to my people again," Sorcha sneered, and then tossed his head back on the ground ... hair face-hair face, the bloody head rolled, gathering dirt before it slammed into the cave wall.

Before Sorcha left the room, she once again picked up the cold bloody mess that was once Volac's head and placed it next to his headless body. After she left the room, she turned, and, with a snap of her fingers, Volac's lifeless body ignited in a blaze of red, yellow, and black flames. Once back on the surface, she found Stomper waiting.

"It is done. Let us go back to the first cave and see if the others have found the Lord of Darkness."

"What about Chaela and Aleric?" asked Stomper. "You just killed Volac, what happens to them?"

"I do not know for sure, we must hurry back to the cave."

"What if we are too late?"

"Meet me there, Stomper!"

Sorcha vanished and reappeared at the entrance to the cave. Kreador was waiting with panic in his eyes. Jumping up and down, he pointed towards the cave.

"cirela, cirela!" he screamed in a loud squeaky voice.

Sorcha ran into the cave and down the dark tunnel. The walls were moist and the floor was damp as her clothes gathered wet dirt. She found Chaela and Aleric lying in a shallow pool of water; both lifeless bodies lay still, their reflections muddied in the water.

"No!" cried Sorcha. Her voice echoed in the cave.

Reaching down, she picked up Chaela. Her strength not even tested, she raced for the entrance. After placing Chaela on the ground, she returned and carried Aleric from the cave. Once outside, she called on Raven's Glenn.

"We are here as promised."

Sorcha looked up and smiled. Before her were the high priestesses of Raven's Glenn. Kali signaled for the others to form a circle around Chaela and Aleric.

"Finish it, Sorcha!" Kali's voice was stern, her eyes as ice. "Finish it. We will take Chaela and Aleric back to Raven's Glenn. Do not worry ... we know what we must do. Go, you know what you must do."

Sorcha looked at Kreador.

"Well, did you find where he lives?" Sorcha asked.

"sey!" Kreador replied.

"Stomper," Sorcha called out, "follow this path back to the southern border of the Land of the Dead. Once there, cross over to the side of light and wait for me. Kreador, take me to his chambers."

The tunnel was dark, cold, and narrow. Sorcha's eyes glowed, giving light as they moved closer to the Dark One's chambers.

"pots,"

Kreador held up his hand and pointed at an empty room up ahead.

"Kreador, you must sneak in there and cut the pendant from his neck.

"tahw!"

"Do it—I will wait here. Bring it to me—quickly!"

Kreador slowly moved into the room and crept towards a large bed. The Lord of Darkness laid still, eyes wide-open and glowing green, the pendant resting on his chest. Kreador reached for his dagger and slowly sliced through the leather cord, removing the pendant. Sneaking back out of the room, he found Sorcha and handed her the pendant. Sorcha grabbed the pendant and they both ran back through the tunnels. With the entrance in sight, they heard a loud roar.

"SORCHA!"

"He wakes!" screamed Sorcha. "Run!"

Sorcha tried to disappear, but her powers were now too weak. Running out of the cave, she ran into Stomper.

"I told you to meet me!"

Stomper smiled, "Get on, we must hurry."

Sorcha grabbed Kreador and jumped on Stomper's back. Running for their lives, they raced down the path. Behind them, a coldness was fast closing in, nipping at Stomper's tail.

"We can make it, Stomper—faster!" yelled Sorcha.

With only a few feet to go before they reached the Land of the Dead's border, Sorcha felt a pain in her head. Gliding within the air behind them, the Lord of Darkness had caught up with the fleeing trio and with one swipe from his powerful arms, knocked Sorcha and Kreador off Stomper. Sorcha landed on her back, staring upwards into the dark grey sky. Kreador rolled into the daylight outside the realm of darkness and jumped to his feet. Lying on the ground, Sorcha blinked and then looked up and into the eyes of the Lord of Darkness.

Reaching down, he grabbed Sorcha and tossed her in the air—laughing.

"You and I have unfinished business," he snarled. "Where is my pendant?"

"ereh!" screamed Kreador, and he tossed the pendant straight up into the sun's light that waited on the other side of the border.

In a blur, the Lord of Darkness leapt toward the pendant. As the pendant floated, a slight breeze took it deeper into the light and out of the reach of the Lord of Darkness. The Lord of Darkness reached out and clawed at the empty air, falling to the ground empty-handed and outside his realm of darkness that protected him. The Lord of Darkness slowly stood; his body glowed, encased in a bluish white haze, his piercing green eyes darkening as he tried to reenter the darkness of his world. Stomper reached for his spear and rammed his spear through the Dark Lord's midsection. Sorcha jumped on his back, grabbed a handful of hair, and pulled his head back. Using the knife Morra gave her, Sorcha quickly cut and sliced deep into the exposed neck, stopping when she felt the neck bone grab at her blade. The bluish white haze that surrounded the Lord of Darkness engulfed Sorcha, and when she felt the Lord of Darkness's warm blood flow over her fingers, her mind filled with images of the underworld, a dark place where evil flourished, voices calling out her name as they welcomed their new queen. Sorcha quickly pushed away from the Lord of Darkness, who stood alone in the sunlight, dying.

"NAIDRAJ, NAIDRAJ, NAIDRAJ," yelled Kreador. Who else but Kreador could speak the name of the Lord of Darkness and survive. Last time they met, Celeste had whispered his name to Kreador. From another world and speaking backwards, he was the perfect choice.

Outside his realm of darkness, his name now spoken, the Lord of Darkness sneered as he faced his death.

The Lord of Darkness stood ... both hands on his neck. Black and red blood oozed from between his fingers and dampened the ground under him. His eyes began to roll backwards as he tried to remove the spear. Sorcha moved in closer with sword now in hand.

"Morra would be proud of this swing," Sorcha said aloud, and she raised the sword behind her shoulder. With all her strength, the sword sliced the air and through the neck of the Dark One.

"It is finished," Sorcha sighed.

For the first time in hundreds of years, a blue speckle appeared in the sky above the Land of the Dead. White clouds appeared and the sun's rays slowly returned. Sorcha fell to her knees, smiling as she watched the body of the Lord of Darkness dissolve and fade into the soil.

"Sorcha, Sorcha," a voice echoed.

Alisa and Flora, once high priestesses of the star, now in death, Ancients, appeared and gave warning, "You have seen the underworld, and now rule over its unspeakable evil ... be cautious, it may consume you. Soon you will rule over Raven's Glenn and be master of both worlds. Your power over light and dark will be great. Use your powers wisely, or the powers of the star will destroy you. Hurry back to Raven's Glenn. Raven's Glenn awaits you still, something's never change."

Carrying Kreador, Sorcha walked over to Stomper. With tears in her eyes, she kissed Stomper's forehead and placed Kreador on Stomper's back, then she reached down and picked up the pendant.

"Let's go home."

Chapter Nine

Sorcha watched in amazement as the skies above the Land of the Dead opened and allowed light to enter, forcing the darkness to fade. Birds flew overhead while the animals of the forest slowly returned, sniffing the ground as they approached. Water from the surrounding rivers flowed again, filling the dry ravines, and bringing life back to a land that once belonged to Raven's Glenn. Sorcha smiled as she watched the transformation unfold. Pointing at a raven flying above, she noticed her arm and the color of her skin returning.

"We must hurry to Raven's Glenn, Chaela and Aleric need me." said Sorcha.

"Help us along; otherwise, it will take us awhile," replied Stomper.

Sorcha sighed, "We need to walk awhile, my powers are still weak and I need to rest."

Sorcha and Kreador climbed up on Stomper's back, and they headed north for Raven's Glenn. Within minutes, Sorcha fell asleep. After traveling a mile or so, Sorcha awakened and was startled to find herself back in Raven's Glenn, lying on her old bed. *How did I get here?* Sorcha thought to herself as she stood and headed for the door. About halfway to the door, the door flew open and Kreador came running in.

"ahcros, ahcros" shouted Kreador as he launched himself at Sorcha. Caught off guard, they both crashing to the floor.

"Kreador, get off me. What is wrong?"

"ilak ees ot deen."

Startled, Sorcha asked, "Are Aleric and Chaela okay?"

Before Kreador could respond, Sorcha was on her feet and through the doorway, knocking Priestess Brietta to the ground.

"That answers the first question," said Brietta. "You are awake."

Dusting herself off, Brietta stood and lowered her hand to help Sorcha back on her feet.

"I see you are in a rush to get someplace, what is the hurry?"

"Chaela and Aleric, are they alive?"

"Oh, yes, alive—and very human," laughed Brietta.

"Human!"

"They are as human as a villager, born of their mother's womb. They are resting at Vevila's house. Would you like to see them?"

"I know the way and will visit them shortly," replied Sorcha. "Where is Stomper?"

"He prepares to go home and is waiting to see you. Kali is trying to convince him and his kind to move into the Land of the Dead and settle there. Lamehoof is here and he will have nothing to do with it.... We are hoping you can convince them."

"Change the name of the place," replied Sorcha. "The Land of the Dead sounds—evil."

"We have given it some thought. What would you suggest, Sorcha, the Land of the Living?"

"What was the Land of the Dead called before the Lord of Darkness took it? I must see Stomper before he leaves and I will convince them to move."

"Kali will be moving also and I with her."

"What?" Sorcha replied.

"But ... but ... why?" asked Sorcha.

"It is time for you to take your place as ruler and protector of Raven's Glenn. Kali and I will travel to Hatana and undo the evil DeMorra left behind. For now, that is our future. Your future will be very different. You are now of the dark and light—immortal. You can use either of those powers as needed. In order for the prophecy to come true, you must rule both realms and insure a proper balance exist between the two. As we speak, the powers of darkness are alive and growing stronger, something evil is growing in the north. Your time to rule has arrived."

"I will have to talk to my sister and prepare for your departure," replied Sorcha. "I will miss both of you. Have you tried to talk with Lamehoof about moving and resettling?"

"No," replied Brietta. "We are waiting for you to discuss the matter with them."

"Then I must talk with them and change their minds."

Sorcha found Stomper and Lamehoof arguing near the edge of the forest.

"Lamehoof!" Sorcha called out.

"Sorcha, I am sorry but I will have nothing to do with moving to the Land of the Dead. I have a home, why would I want a new one?"

Sorcha replied, "It is no longer the Land of the Dead. We once called that area the Low Lands and renamed it so. I know what we are asking is difficult for you. You love the home you have and the land is sacred to you. Your land will always belong to you for as long as I am alive and from what I understand, that will be for a long time to come. I need you and Stomper to help me once more. Please help me and show the way so others will join you. The Land of the ... I mean the Low Lands was once rich in fertile soil and flourished. Lamehoof, I know you know the stories of how it used to be, your ancestors once lived there. You also know it was a land that flourished, so please if you could just remember how it was and help me bring it back to its glorious form."

"Sorcha is right," replied Lamehoof. "It was a glorious place once."

Lamehoof looked up towards the sky and then into the forest before responding. "Yes, we will move to the Low Lands, but only until others follow."

"Thank you, Lamehoof," Sorcha replied. "I will come and see you at your home when the time is right. For now, you must get the rest of the centaurs to join you."

Sorcha said goodbye to Lamehoof and headed to the House of the Ancients. On her way, she spotted Brietta.

"Brietta," Sorcha called out, "Lamehoof and Stomper have agreed to move."

Brietta nodded and said, "Kali will be pleased."

Sorcha went to see Priestess Vevila. As she raised her hand to knock on her door, the door opened, and there stood Vevila.

"I was wondering when you were going to come by. Aleric and Chaela are resting in the other room. If you would like, you may come in."

"Thank you," said Sorcha.

As Sorcha walked through the doorway, Kali appeared.

"Sorcha, I am glad you are here. We need to talk."

"I agree," replied Sorcha.

Kali looked at Sorcha and said, "I know Priestess Brietta talked to you about us leaving, and I know you have talked Lamehoof and Stomper into moving. Now we need to discuss what we are going to do about Chaela and Aleric."

Sorcha looked at Kali and said, "That is easy, I will teach Chaela the ways. Aleric can go with the wizards and become one of them. You never know when we might need them again. I think it is time for an alliance with the wizards."

"It sounds like you have been thinking about this," replied Kali.

"It is time for change. Why not start right here in Raven's Glenn?"

"You do understand," replied Kali, "Chaela and Aleric were close to death when we came to get them. They were without soul and nearly died when Volac died. If it was not for the pendants we gave them, we would not have been able to save them. They are human now and you say you want to make Chaela a witch ... hmmm, are you sure of this?"

Sorcha decided not to answer and explained to Kali that she would discuss the matter with Chaela during the celebrations that evening. Stomper and Lamehoof would leave in the morning and she still had Kreador to deal with. Kali nodded in agreement.

Sorcha entered the House of the Ancients and stood in the middle of the room staring at the altar. The sun's light covered the front half of the altar; the back half was dark with shadow. Sorcha approached the altar and placed her right hand on the surface—it felt warm. The sun's rays had warmed parts of the surface, while the dark shadow cooled the other half. Sorcha stepped backwards. She removed her pendant and placed it on the altar. Reaching into her robe, she found the bloodstone, the pendant that once belonged to the Lord of Darkness, and placed it on the altar next to hers. Immediately, the sky above Raven's Glenn blackened as large dark clouds gathered. The air cooled, and the wind began to swirl as it swept through Raven's Glenn, forcing everyone inside. The walls inside the House of the Ancients turned a deep red color, blood red. The floor and ceiling turned black. Fire erupted at Sorcha's feet, igniting her clothing. Surrounded by flames, Sorcha's clothes burned. Sorcha felt no pain as the flames increased. A voice sounded from within the flames.

"Sorcha, you burn within the fire, your clothes are gone, yet your skin is untouched by the flames. You feel no pain."

"Who are you?" asked Sorcha. "What is the reason for this?"

"I am the first of Raven's Glenn, for I named this place and cast her first spells. I am your blood, your ancestor, first ruler of Raven's Glenn, and the first of the Ancients."

"Mirra?"

"Yes," replied Queen Mirra. "You stand here naked bathing in the fire, quenching the evil inside you. You now have the powers of dark and light, but the bloodstone you carry can destroy you. I have come for the bloodstone. Someday you will have a need for its powers. Until then, it will be safe with the Ancients."

Mirra's voice faded, replaced with hideous sounds and wicked laughter, sounds that came from somewhere evil, a world beyond death, a place concealed within the realms of darkness.

"Be still!" commanded Sorcha, her eyes glowing.

The sounds and flames around her faded. Standing naked in the middle of the House of the Ancients, Sorcha raised her arms while spinning in circles ... laughing. A neatly folded black robe appeared on the altar. Curious, Sorcha reached out and touched the robe. The robe felt different; it was made of a material she had never touched before. The material was thick with a strange crisscross weave, very light, and had a shimmering glow to it, where her old robe was heavy, made of common wool and dyed black. She put the robe on and twirled around in circles, watching the robe while she spun faster. It started to change color. She stopped and looked down and it was once again black. *I must ask about this robe*, Sorcha thought to herself ... It feels too wonderful.

Sorcha stepped out of the House of Ancients and spotted Stomper.

"Stomper, are you staying for the night?" Sorcha shouted.

Stomper shook his head and said, "My father is in a hurry to get back home. I came to say goodbye."

Sorcha wrapped her arms around Stomper's neck and said, "We will see each other again. Tell your father thank you, and have a safe journey home."

Stomper turned and waved as he left Raven's Glenn. Misty-eyed, Sorcha waved and watched as Stomper disappeared down the path.

"eyb," yelled Kreador as he jumped up and down waving good-bye.

"Where have you been?" yelled Sorcha, grabbing Kreador's hand. "Come with me, I need to check on Chaela and Aleric."

On her way to Vevila's house, Sorcha found Priestess Vevila by the well filling a bucket with water. Vevila told Sorcha that both Chaela and Aleric were awake and asking for her.

"Thank you," replied Sorcha; then she reached down and smacked Kreador across the back of the head. "Be still, Kreador, we will be there soon."

Sorcha continued her walk to Priestess Vevila's house. When she arrived, she heard Chaela and Aleric arguing with each other. Sorcha chuckled and shook her head.

Chaela and Aleric looked up when they heard Sorcha enter.

"How far did you have to chase a witch to steal that robe?" laughed Chaela.

"How are you feeling?" asked Sorcha

"I have never felt more alive ... it has been so long since I have been able to feel the sun's warmth," replied Chaela.

"I am glad," Sorcha replied. "Now we need to discuss a few things. Chaela, I was wondering what would you think about staying with me here in Raven's Glenn and learning the ways of my people?"

"You want me to become a witch?" asked Chaela.

"Yes, Kali and Brietta are leaving. They are going to Hatana. Will you stay here in Raven's Glenn and learn our ways? I can give you a day's time to decide. I think Aleric would make a wonderful wizard. I have already talked to

Blaine, and the wizards would be delighted to have you join them. You can have one day's time also to decide. Both of you think it over, I will ask for your answer tomorrow. Kali waits for me; if you are up to it, come and join us in our celebration tonight."

"I see the Ancients dressed you today," muttered Kali as she looked away from the window and stared at Sorcha.

"Oh, the robe!" replied Sorcha. "It appeared in the House of the Ancients."

"The robe has powers," replied Kali. "It will blend with anything ... if you will it. You will learn its powers."

Kali reached out and put Sorcha's hand in hers. A slight warm breeze flowed through the window and the two vanished, appearing on a mountain ledge overlooking Raven's Glenn. It was here Kali told Sorcha her plans for Hatana and handed Sorcha her pendant.

"Your pendant is your power ... you must keep it," said Sorcha

"No, it is Raven Glenn's power. Your power, it belongs to you now. I have my own power and in many ways, I am even more powerful now than I was as ruler. I will leave in two days for Hatana and soon Hatana will become part of Raven's Glenn. A warning came on the wind last night. Something evil is growing in the north, beyond the land of the wizards. You must convince Aleric to join them and Chaela will join Raven's Glenn. I have asked that the Sacred Circle be prepared so you can make her one of us ... a witch. This will be your first ritual as leader. Do it soon. A full moon will be here in three days ... be prepared."

Kali reached into her robe and pulled out a pendant. It was similar to the one she had but different. The center house was missing on the engraved surface. She hung the black cord around her neck and tucked the pendant beneath her robe. Catching Sorcha's eye, she smiled. Sorcha reached under her robe and pulled out her pendant. Engraved on the surface was the center house. Sorcha looked up at Kali.

Kali bowed and said, "The center house is yours now, and you control the northernmost house ... the House of the Ancients. Tomorrow you will convince Aleric to do what is best for us. Tonight we celebrate our good fortune."

Kali blinked and saw a quick glitter of darkness surround Sorcha.

"I wonder how long it will take," Kali whispered. "Something is stirring in the wind ... something dark."

Sorcha and Kali returned to Raven's Glenn and entered the center house, soon to be Sorcha's house. Sorcha stood by the window and watched as the witches filled the fire pits with wood. All around Raven's Glenn witches were preparing for the celebrations that night.

There are several good reasons to celebrate tonight, Sorcha thought. The Lord of Darkness was defeated, Kali's departure, and a new ruler would soon take control of Raven's Glenn. Sorcha watched the witches of Raven's Glenn as they worked and noticed Chaela among them and decided to ask her if she was going to join Raven's Glenn. Chaela looked up and saw Sorcha walking her way.

"Sorcha!" Chaela called from the fire pit.

"Chaela, I am glad to see you have recovered and eager to help out. I was hoping you would be able to join us tonight."

"I wouldn't miss it," replied Chaela. "I know you gave Aleric and I one day's time to answer you, and we have talked about what you suggested and we accept. I will stay here with you and learn the ways of your people and Aleric will join the wizards. We would like to continue to help in any way that we can. We owe you our lives."

"Then welcome to Raven's Glenn," Sorcha replied. "I must let Kali know, she will be pleased to hear the news."

"What news?" asked Kali.

Startled, Sorcha and Chaela whirled around to see Kali standing there.

"Chaela was just telling me that she will stay here with us, and Aleric will join the wizards and learn the ways of their people."

"Are you ready to become a witch and learn the ways?" laughed Kali. "Remember, Chaela, it will be your duty to protect Raven's Glenn at all cost. Train her well, Sorcha."

As the dark of night arrived, the celebrations started. Raven's Glenn filled with the sounds of laughter and mindless chatter, all woes forgotten ... saved for another day. All the witches of Raven's Glenn had approached Kali and wished her well. Sorcha took her place as the new queen and walked among the groups of witches, visiting with each campsite. The celebration ended when the sun peeked over the tops of the eastern mountains.

The following morning, Sorcha found Kali and Brietta on a mountain ledge overlooking Raven's Glenn. With Brietta at her side, Kali bowed, and they both vanished. Sorcha felt the air where they were standing and a slight chill cooled her hand. Sorcha gazed over Raven's Glenn and noticed how the rising sun's rays mixed with the lingering night darkness and formed shadows that slowly vanished as they crept from house to house, skipping the House of the Ancients.

"I must visit with the Ancients today," Sorcha said aloud. A familiar voice interrupted her thoughts.

"You were just a child when we use to meet here in the mountains," interrupted Chaela. "The bones from my feedings lay all around us. Now you are high priestess, queen, and ruler of Raven's Glenn, and I am a normal human, at least for another day."

"I wonder if I could just bite you on the neck," laughed Sorcha. "We have so little time to train you. You, Kreador, and I will always be between the dark and light ... controlling the shades of darkness while bathing in the light. A witch you will become; however, you will need more powers to survive by my side. I will ask the Ancients for advice on how to make you stronger. As for Aleric, he is just a man and will soon learn to kill what he does not understand. Wizard training will save him from himself. I find I have no patience for mere men and their ways."

"Bite me on the neck!" replied Chaela. "I am not even a witch yet and you think of such things. There is darkness inside you, Sorcha, its scares me. I do hope you can control it."

"Our battles have just begun, Chaela. I already feel evil to the north and someday we will go there. For now, we rest and make Raven's Glenn stronger than ever. You will learn the ways, and hopefully take Brietta's place on the star and control her house. Until then, we must search for ways to increase your powers. Has Aleric left?"

"Blaine came for him at first light but was upset when he noticed the pendant still hung from Aleric's neck. Aleric refused to take it off and they argued for some time. Blaine finally gave in."

"Good!" replied Sorcha. "Aleric will stay attached to Raven's Glenn as long as he wears the pendant. He will serve us well in the future."

Sorcha left Chaela and walked to the House of the Ancients. The room was dark when she entered and she fixed her eyes on the outline of the altar. As Sorcha approached the altar, the darkness faded and the room clouded over with a whitish fog. Celeste greeted Sorcha as the spirits of the other Ancients appeared and floated around the room. The Ancients welcomed Sorcha as the new ruler and ordered her to disrobe. One by one, the Ancients passed in front of her then through her, merging spirit and soul. As the Ancients departed, Sorcha's vision changed. From inside her head, all she could see was a bright yellow color; except for the objects in front of her, they had no detail and appeared black in color. Reaching for her robe, she noticed it glowed of yellow and black. Sorcha grinned as she put on her robe. For the first time, Sorcha controlled the darkness within her and was able to see as evil sees.

"Tomorrow, Chaela becomes a witch," Sorcha commented. "Our fate and future will begin then and I think I will allow Kreador to join us in the ritual."

Celeste blocked her path as Sorcha tried to leave the House of the Ancients and warned Sorcha that Kreador could not enter the Sacred Circle. He will die, warned Celeste. Sorcha agreed and left for Morra's house.

Priestess Morra was gathering oils and incense for Chaela's cleansing bath when Sorcha arrived.

"You have grown into a fine woman, Sorcha. You will make a great ruler. How may I help you this fine day?"

"Gather the high priestesses and sit with me around my fire tonight. I wish to discuss the future of Raven's Glenn and a replacement for Priestess Brietta."

The high priestesses gathered at Sorcha's house later that night. Morra, Sasa, and Vevila joined Sorcha at the fire pit in the center house and openly discussed a replacement for Brietta. Sorcha had asked for Chaela to be considered for the position; however, the other high priestesses did not agree. Priestess Morra was the first to speak against Chaela and expressed concern for Chaela's lack of experience. Priestess Sasa mentioned that Sorcha's friendship with the past vampire had clouded Sorcha's thinking, and how could Chaela become a high priestess when she was not even a witch. Priestess Vevila wanted to know why Chaela was living in Raven's Glenn when tradition clearly forbids non-witches from living there. Sorcha responded by explaining the past deeds performed by Chaela and how she almost gave her life in the battle against darkness. All the priestesses reminded Sorcha that others also gave their lives and everyone sacrificed during those dark times. After a long discussion, they agreed that Chaela could become a witch and stay in Raven's Glenn; however, another should be selected as high priestess. Sorcha asked the high priestesses to select someone and all agreed on a descendant of a previous high priestess, the witch known as Ladia. Sorcha agreed.

Witch Ladia was a few years older than Sorcha; not a tall woman, but strong and powerful. Her shoulder length black hair and deep narrow blue eyes highlighted her high cheekbones, full-figured and just a bit chunky she was well liked by the other witches and looked just like her mother, a high priestess when Celeste ruled Raven's Glenn. She was experienced in the ways—a good choice, thought Sorcha.

While the high priestesses talked, night had passed, and the early morning sounds of a new day greeted them when they opened the door and left Sorcha's house. Sorcha reminded everyone to meet later that night at the Sacred Circle when the moon was full. The ritual would be simple, just a formality. Chaela will become a witch and Ladia the next high priestess.

Sorcha found Chaela and Kreador gathering wood for the night's fires and approached them.

"Tonight you will become one of us," Sorcha told Chaela.

Chaela smiled and replied, "Tonight I become a witch. A few days ago I was a vampire."

"A dead vampire," commented Sorcha. "Meet me at dusk and we will prepare you for tonight."

As Sorcha turned to walk away, she heard a faint howl. *Wolves are close by*, Sorcha thought to herself. Chaela looked towards the forest and asked Sorcha if she heard a howl. Sorcha replied that she did.

"What made the howl?" asked Chaela.

"A wolf," replied Sorcha.

"I often took wolf form and hunted these hills and forest. That was no wolf," replied Chaela. "I have never heard such a howl before."

Sorcha ignored Chaela's concern and reminded her to meet at dusk.

Dusk arrived and Sorcha impatiently waited for Chaela. *Where is she?* thought Sorcha. Priestess Ladia is waiting, the witches are restless. The full moon would soon be above them and Sorcha had to attend to the ritual for Witch Ladia, which was soon to start. Sorcha entered the Sacred Circle ... the witches of Raven's Glenn waited while Sorcha raised her *athame* and chanted, opening the circle, and calling on the Ancients to accept Ladia. Ladia completed the oath and Sorcha guided her to the empty place on the star.

"Blessed be," said Sorcha. "Take your place on the point, High Priestess Ladia. All hail Priestess Ladia, the star is complete once more!"

"Blessed be!" they all shouted.

Suddenly, laughter erupted from the witches; all noticed a green head peeking up over the stone and rock wall that surrounded the Sacred Circle. His hand covered his eyes and Kreador was trying to speak. Sorcha walked up behind Kreador, grabbed him by the arm, and dragged him away.

"Kreador, what is it?" asked Sorcha.

"aleahc," replied Kreador.

"What about Chaela, where is she?" asked Sorcha

"esouh rouy," replied Kreador.

Sorcha rubbed Kreador's head and thanked him for the message, then ran to her house. The door was open ... Sorcha rushed inside and found Chaela pacing back and forth.

"Where have you been? Do you know what it took for me to get the other witches to allow you to become a witch, and then you don't even show up to the ritual for Priestess Ladia."

Sorcha stopped and watched as her friend just kept pacing. Chaela did not even seem to hear her.

"What is wrong?" asked Sorcha.

Chaela looked at Sorcha and said, "I went into the forest to look around, to see if I could find what was making that noise."

"And?" asked Sorcha.

"And, nothing" said Chaela.

"I told you it was just a wolf," replied Sorcha.

"If it was just a wolf, there would be tracks, something, but I am telling you there is nothing. And around here nothing usually means something,"

Worried, Sorcha folded her arms inside her robe while she watched Chaela continue to pace, distracted.

"Okay, Chaela," Sorcha commented. "After you become one of us, we will go into the forest and see what we can find. I will seek out the creatures of the forest for help. Maybe they know what is making the howls. Until then, please, I need you to be here, you become one of us tonight."

"Something is not right, Sorcha, but I guess we can wait."

"Good. Now get ready, Chaela, everyone is waiting. Meet me at the hut next to the Sacred Circle, and hurry."

As Sorcha left, Chaela said under her breathe, "I do not believe we have that long."

Chaela arrived at the hut and, after the cleansing bath, Sorcha escorted her to the Sacred Circle. Priestess Morra challenged her entrance and Chaela responded with no fear in her answers and allowed to enter. The ritual began. The witches decided before the ritual that Chaela's name would remain the same. For two-hundred years, she was a vampire named Chaela, and they could come up with no reason to change her name now.

Standing before the altar, Sorcha cut Chaela's finger with a knife. A series of long, eerie howls echoed from the forest. Sorcha looked at Chaela and then at the other witches; uneasiness was starting to settle in.

"I must hurry with the oath," Sorcha said aloud.

The witches were starting to act nervous. Those standing within the inner circle looked over their shoulders and towards the sky. Those outside the Sacred Circle pointed at a wall of fog that was slowly approaching from the north. Another cry of howls and yelps sounded.

"Chaela," spoke Sorcha. "Chaela, are you ready to swear the oath?"

"Yes!" replied Chaela.

"Kneel, Chaela, show us the blood you offer. Repeat after me, say what I say."

"I, Chaela, do of my own free will promise to protect and defend all that is Raven's Glenn, to keep secret all that must not be revealed. This I swear on my grave and my hopes of future lives."

Chaela repeated the oath and Sorcha shouted out, "So it must be!"

"So it must be!" the coven of witches replied.

Sorcha stepped to the side and ordered Chaela to stand. The witches rushed forward and grabbed Chaela. They lifted her into the air and carried her three times around the circle, ending at the altar.

Sorcha stepped forward and spoke. "Chaela, the hands that touched you are the hands of Raven's Glenn. Thus you are brought into our world, and thus you are brought into our coven." Sorcha faced the witches and called out. "Behold, guardians of the points, behold Ancients of the past, behold witches of Raven's Glenn ... behold Chaela."

"Behold Chaela!" the witches shouted.

"It is done," whispered Sorcha. Chaela nodded, and then pointed at the dense gray fog that was almost upon them. "It is only fog," snapped Sorcha.

"What is in the fog?" asked Chaela.

Sorcha and Chaela looked up; the gray fog swept in, bringing twirling winds with it. The sounds of snarling howls and barking screeched across the sky. Ghostly images of large, doglike creatures jumped over the walls of the Sacred Circle and floated above them. The witches panicked and started to run. Sorcha stepped in front of them and shouted for all to stay within the Sacred Circle.

Out of the thick gray fog, images of large webbed paws with razor-sharp claws appeared above the Sacred Circle. The winds increased and large ghost like sharp claws swooped down and scooped up a few witches that stood outside the Sacred Circle. Shredded robes and blood rained on the witches below.

"Enough!" yelled Sorcha.

Arms raised at her side, eyes glowing, Sorcha called on the darkness within her. A spinning black hole appeared on the ground and from inside the hole came a dark mass of air, deep black in color and spinning; it approached Sorcha and gradually grew larger. Cries and moans of tortured evil demons surfaced from the holes darkness and appeared to circle Sorcha, waiting.

Spinning with arms raised, Sorcha commanded the darkness around her to attack the fog above her. The sky lit up with fire and flashing light as the two evil forces met. Horrendous sounds of howls and screams filled the sky as fire rained down.

"Watch out!" screamed Chaela. The altar started to glow and then exploded, shooting a large bright white light into the night sky. From within the altar, the spirits of the Ancients ascended. Hiding within the light, they overpowered both evil forces.

The winds began to cease, and the howls and screams faded. Sorcha stood in the center of the Sacred Circle, eyes aglow ... slowly returning from somewhere deep within the dark. Outside the circle, bodies of dead witches littered the ground. The first of the Ancients ... she who gave birth to Raven's Glenn—Mirra—appeared, and gave warning.

"Sorcha, you must find the source of the fog and destroy those who are responsible. Go north, north to Azelwood ... seek out the home of the wizards.

About the Authors

$\mathcal{S}$ teven Cardea was born in June of 1953 in Chicago Illinois. He grew up in Elmhurst Illinois with a brother and sister. Stevens first enjoyable writing experiences centered on prose and poems, later in life, he developed a desire to write stories. He enjoys nature and his hobby is his dogs.

$\mathcal{C}$ aterina Beck was born in August of 1976 in Grand Forks, North Dakota. Caterina is married and has three daughters and a son. Her hobbies are reading, drawing, painting, and writing.

Through conversation and a battle of ideas, we developed the story, 'Sorcha the Beginning,' and the place named Ravens Glenn. We began by researching myths, folklore, and life styles of witches, ancient druids, and demons. With myths and facts, armed with imagination and a creative pen, Sorcha, became alive, and seduced us into her world.